CW00481505

WHAT'S THE TIME, MR. WOLFE?

TRACIE PODGER

Copyright 2023 © Tracie Podger
All rights reserved.
This is a work of fiction. Characters, names, places and incidents,
either, are products of the author's imagination or they are used
factiously. Any reference to actual locales, or persons, living or dead,
is entirely coincidental.
No part of this book may be reproduced in any form, or by any
electronic, or mechanical means, including information storage and
retrieval systems, to include, by not exclusive to audio or visual
recordings of any description without permission from the copyright
owner.

S&P Publishing

Cover designed by Francessca Wingfield PR
Editing – Anna Bloom

CHAPTER ONE

I slammed the front door behind me, not in anger but because the stupid landlord still hadn't repaired the lock. I gave it a good shake to be sure it wouldn't open again.

My red hoodie was all I had to keep the chill from my bones, and I vowed that, when I could, I'd invest in a decent coat. In the meantime, all money had to go towards keeping me and Grandma fed and housed. For the millionth time, I cursed my father.

I'll come back for you. Don't worry, Chica, he'd said in his Spanish accent.

Except he hadn't. He'd headed to Spain to collect some items we'd left there before we moved back to England, and he'd never returned. He hadn't called, written, emailed, nothing. For a couple of years, I'd badgered the police to find him, but he'd simply disappeared, along with the money from the sale of our home. The home my mother left her half of when she'd died. *My* half of the money!

I believed my father was still alive, probably in Cuba. He wouldn't go anywhere he couldn't speak the language and it was cheap enough there for him to live the lifestyle he believed he deserved.

I growled out loud, scaring a couple taking their dog for a last toilet break before bedtime.

When I flicked up the hood to my hoodie and tucked in my dark curly hair, a throwback to my Spanish roots, I upped my pace, knowing I was likely to be late. The screen on my phone had cracked so badly, I couldn't tell the time. I was stunned it was still useable. Not that I had anyone to call, other than Grandma, of course.

As I pushed through the doors directly into the kitchen, I slipped down my hood and called out, "I'm sorry, I'll work late." Only to receive a mouthful of abuse and waving of arms in return.

I headed to my station, the sink, which was piled high, and pulled off my hoodie, replacing it with an apron. I wished I had earphones so I could drown out the restaurant kitchen noise and lose myself in the enchanting sounds of the piano. I used to play, back in the day when we could afford a piano, but hadn't played in years.

I set about to wash and restock the kitchen with crockery and pots and pans.

I worked solidly for three hours, continuing after service had finished. Then I darted into the restaurant to clean tables, mop the floor, and finally, the toilets. My hands ached and stung with all the chemicals and products I mixed. Even though I wore gloves for the worst of the jobs, the skin on my hands cracked and my nails bent with weakness. I bit them, not from habit, but simply because I couldn't find a nail clipper anywhere and it was quicker to bite off the length.

"Ruby, here," I heard and I turned to see Diego with a carrier bag in his hand. I smiled at him.

"You didn't need to do that," I said, although my stomach growled at the scent of hot food.

"Yes, I do. Now take it and get home. Tell Grandma I asked after her."

Diego my boss, was a friend of my grandma's, and I guessed that was the only reason I had my job, despite my constant lateness. His father had started the restaurant, and he'd taken over a few years prior. He was a good man, a doting husband and father, and I often envied his children, wishing I had someone like him.

I took the bag from him and headed back into the

kitchen. Without hanging around, I swapped my apron for my hoodie and left by the back door.

It was dark and drizzly. A mist hung in the air, the kind that found every tiny hole or parting of thread in the weave of material and seeped its way in. I shivered uncontrollably all the way home. While I stood on the pavement and fished in my jeans pocket for my key, a large black car sped past. Not only was it roaring along a street of residential properties way too fast, but the driver also got close enough to the kerb to cause a puddle to wash over me like a bloody wave. I turned and screamed abuse at the retreating vehicle.

Much to my amusement, the vehicle stopped, its red lights bright in the mist. Much to my dismay, the white reverse lights came on.

I stood my ground, though. The arsehole had soaked me and was going to get a piece of my mind. As the car levelled up alongside and the rear window started to lower, I gave the occupant both barrels.

"Not only are you a bloody arsehole for speeding on this road, but you've ruined my dinner and my bloody clothes. This..." I said, grabbing at the red hoody, "This is the only bloody dry thing I had to wear tomorrow!" I was aware of how many times I said, 'bloody' and I didn't think it was near enough.

My abuse came to a halt as the window lowered completely. Sitting in the passenger seat was a man with dark hair and piercing blue eyes. He smiled, his teeth a bright white.

"I'm so sorry. My driver lacked his usual concentration there," he said, and his voice was like liquid chocolate. His low tone vibrated through my stomach as his words washed over me, soothing and... tasty.

I blinked a few times, then let my usual bolshy and obnoxious self come back. "What are you going to do about this?" I said, dumping the sodden carried bag of food on his bonnet.

"I'll replace it all."

"Good, leave it at my front door."

I turned and walked up the garden path to my door, grumbling as I did.

"Oh, for Christ's sake," I said, loudly, as I tried to turn the key, getting it stuck.

"Shall I help?" I heard.

The man had left his car and was standing behind me. He'd approached so silently; I hadn't heard him. I sucked in a breath.

"Don't sneak up on people, it's rude. No, you can't help, unless you're the bloody landlord of this shitshow of a property."

"This *shitshow of a property*?" he laughed as he spoke.

I spun on my heel. "I'm not entirely sure what you find funny, and I don't appreciate you on my property.

You owe me dinner, that's all you need to do. Fetch," I said, waving my arm as if throwing a ball for a dog.

His eyes widened at my cheek and his smile slipped. For a split second a little quiver of fear slid over my skin. However, his smirk was quick to form again.

"Of course, ma'am. Your dinner is already on the way. I believe it will be here in ten minutes."

"Yeah, sure," I replied, turning back to the door and finally getting it unlocked. I kicked at it until it opened.

"As for *your property*, I own the company that owns this house. And many others in this street. I see you're having problems. I'll make sure someone attends tomorrow."

Without another word or backwards glance, he walked back down the path and slid into his car. The car pulled away from the kerb silently and carried on in the direction it had originally taken. I stood, open-mouthed, and stared after him, until, once he'd turned the corner, I raised two fingers to him.

"Is that you, Ruby?"

"It is, Grandma. I got splashed by a puddle, so I'll just change quick. Diego sends his regards." I raced up the stairs and into my cold bedroom. I did everything in a rush, not because I wanted to be back down in a hurry, but because the heating didn't work, and it was bloody freezing. It was a drill now; clothes off, new ones on, with as little body exposed as possible.

As I walked back down the stairs, there was a knock on the door. I opened it, puzzled. A restaurant courier stood holding a brown paper bag.

"Deliver For You," he said, either announcing his courier company name or missing the 'y' off the word 'deliver.'

I reached out and took the bag. "Where is this from?" I asked, looking inside to see silver tubs of diving smelling food.

"Yantze. Didn't you order it? This is the right address," he asked, showing me his delivery note.

Girl in the red hoodie, 78 Queen Anne Cottages and then the rest of the address was printed. I laughed.

"Yeah, thanks."

I kicked the door shut. So, he *had* ordered me food, and from a rather nice Chinese that I could never have afforded myself.

"Are you hungry, Grandma? I have food."

CHAPTER TWO

The following morning, as I made Grandma her breakfast and sipped a cup of tea, I pondered on the stranger. There was something compelling about him, but also scary. I shivered as I thought of him and wondered about the authenticity of his statement, unable to decide if I should write a list of faults in the property, just in case he owned it and was going to send someone. He had made good on replacing my food, so...

After I'd settled Grandma back in her bed in the living room, I sat at the kitchen table and wrote all the things wrong with the property. The leaking guttering that meant Grandma couldn't use her bedroom upstairs because it was damp and mouldy. The heating and hot water not working full time, how the lock on the front door was sticking and that it didn't shut without slamming and causing the surrounding plaster to crack. I gave good reasons why these things should be repaired. I'd never missed a rent payment in the two years Grandma and I had lived there. I nodded to myself once I'd finished. If a repairman didn't turn up, I'd be calling at his offices, for sure.

I was about to head to college when there was a knock at the door. For the second time, I was stunned. Standing on the step was a maintenance man wearing a t-shirt with the landlord's logo on it.

"You have problems?" he asked.

"Lots, I hope you're here for the day," I replied, stepping aside, and letting him in, knowing I wouldn't make college.

While I made him a cup of tea, he read all the faults I wanted looking at.

"Okay, I was told to fix everything needed, regardless. But I'll have to call a plumber for the boiler." He looked around. "I can't believe you've been living like this. You have complained, haven't you?"

"Many times and have been ignored many times. I was going to withhold my rent this month if I didn't get a response."

I'd already spoken to the housing advice officer at my college and although they advised against withholding rent, they had said I could deduct any costs if I felt the landlord wasn't repairing what they were legally obliged to. Of course, they had also said I'd need to get an agreement for that, but I was pig-headed. I had planned to find a repairman, pay him, but then send the bill to the landlord for effect.

I sat with Grandma sipping tea and listening to her stories of the past, stories I'd heard thousands of times but ones that kept her alive as far as I was concerned, while the repairman did this thing. A couple of hours later, a boiler engineer joined him, along with someone in a suit.

"Ruby, this is James. He's our surveyor. I'm not happy about the mould. It's black mould, and that's dangerous," he said to us both.

"It would have to be tested to be verified," James replied.

"Bollocks to that, you know damn well I know what I'm talking about," the maintenance guy said.

It seemed a row was about to happen between them.

"If it's black mould, I want rehousing. My Grandma has dementia, she's not well. I don't want her exposed to anything dangerous. I'm at college and I work three jobs to pay for this place," I said, folding my arms across my chest.

I'd heard of black mould. It was no wonder Grandma constantly had lung and chest infections.

"If you don't sort this, you can tell your boss I'll be going to the press."

James smiled at me, a false pacifying smile, and I raised my eyebrows at him.

"Don't worry, I'll tell him," he said, but I highly doubted he would. "Let's get sorted what we can, and I'll report back," he added, turning his attention back to the repairman.

With a nod to me, James left.

"He will, you know. The boss has told us to do whatever it is you want."

"The boss?"

"Mr. Wolfe. Sebastian Wolfe is his name. Never met him myself, though. He doesn't speak to us lowly operatives. How do you know him?"

"I don't... not really." I hesitated with my answer. I didn't want the repairman to think I didn't know Mr. Wolfe in case he decided not to take the instruction to do 'whatever was needed' seriously. Equally, I didn't want him to think we were best friends, either.

"No one really knows him, from what I understand," the repairman said.

I wasn't particularly interested in talking about Mr. Wolfe, and I certainly wasn't interested in having a conversation with the man meant to be working. I'd offered him tea and biscuits and now I wanted him to get on with fixing the door. He'd already done the *scratching under his chin and sighing* thing I'd expected, talking about how we needed new windows as if he was a salesman and I'd be paying for them.

"Well, one of us has work to do. So, I'll leave you to it," I said, heading into the living room and Grandma. I had books I could go through to keep up with my college work.

I could hear him chuckle, and I was sure he called me *spunky*! I screwed my nose at the thought.

I sat with Grandma while she watched her game shows and clapped along when she knew the correct answer. I knew there would come a time when I'd need help and the daily carer, Monica, who came to us already wouldn't be enough. Monica and I had talked about care homes, but I wasn't ready, and Grandma sure wasn't, either. We were managing, even if I was exhausted all the damn time.

I picked up a college book. I'd flunked out of school, scraping through basic Maths and English. I'd had too many other issues to deal with; a missing father and money for one, plus a sick relative to care for. It was only when a sympathetic teacher discovered my situation one day that I got a place in college. I wanted to be an architect. I loved buildings and structure, but I needed some serious studying and resitting of exams before I could get into university.

As I read and wrote, Grandma answered the most random questions on a quiz show.

Some time later, the repairman announced he'd done all he could. The boilerman followed shortly after, telling me that although he'd got the heating and hot water to work, I needed a new boiler. I asked him to inform the owner of the property since I wouldn't be replacing it myself.

With the men gone and a mess left in their wake, I set about to make some dinner. Well, I reheated the last of the Chinese we hadn't eaten the previous evening.

As I sat at the table and ate, I thought about Mr. Wolfe. His piercing blue eyes and skin tone suggested Nordic roots, but his dark wavy hair didn't fit. I chuckled as I remembered I thought his teeth were so perfectly straight and white. Why I noticed them, I wasn't sure. I raised my spoon before taking the last mouthful in salute of him. A silent thank you for a delicious meal that I'd never have been able to afford without him.

———

I had settled Grandma in bed. She'd pulled her blankets up to her chin and smiled with teary eyes.

"I need to go in a home," she said, and for the first time in a long while, her voice had clarity. It stopped me in my tracks.

"Sorry, Grandma?" I asked, wanting her to repeat her sentence.

"You look just like my granddaughter, Ruby," she replied, and I smiled at her.

"You've said."

"She's lovely, is my granddaughter."

With that, I left her bedroom and sniffed back tears that threatened to fall. There were days when she knew me, but in the evenings, when her brain was tired, she'd forget. It was called 'Sundowning' and is common with dementia. As the days came to a close, the *victim* tired and their memory clouded further.

Victim. Monica, who the dementia charity had sent, used to chastise me for using that word, but it was exactly what I thought of Grandma. Dementia was a terrible illness, and she *was* a victim. She hadn't wanted it, hadn't sought it out, it had chosen her. But every now and again, like half a minute before, the cloud in her brain would clear briefly and the old Grandma would reappear.

I angrily wiped at my tears knowing my eyes would be red rimmed. I was an ugly crier, for sure. I'd always longed to be the Disney Princess type, one that could just dab a delicate piece of material to the corner of their eyes. No, me? I'd have a red nose, snot, and blotchy cheeks. And if I really got going, puffy lips and eyelids to boot.

As I sat at the kitchen table, I slid one of my college books towards me. I wasn't in the mood but knew I had to catch up on a day missed. I had an assignment to hand in. Instead, I moved to my drawing pad and flipped it open.

All the drawings were of buildings. All different types from my dream cottage in the woods, a residential home (the one I'd buy with my lottery win so my grandma and others like her could live in luxury), to the skyscraper in the city.

I turned to my dream cottage in the woods.

Solitude should have been my middle name, and I wondered if my fondness for all things dark and quiet were because my childhood was so loud. My parents argued like the proverbial cat and dog. There were always parties and drunkenness. They often left drugs just in reach of childish hands, and houses, not homes, were a constant mess. It was no wonder my mother eventually died. Why I hankered after a father that facilitated her drug and alcohol abuse was beyond me.

My cottage in the woods was peaceful, surrounded by nature and the protection of trees—the lungs of the earth, I called them, and ones that cleansed. It was the cleansing that I needed for a long time.

At my birth, drugs and alcohol had flooded my system, not that I remember, of course. As a child, I had ingested cocaine and was rushed to the hospital. Social

Services was non-existent back then, or they certainly were in my case. It was only when my grandmother intervened, I started to live a normal life. I'll forever be grateful to her. If she hadn't, I'd be dead, too.

As I sat with my drawing pad, I drew internal rooms. I wanted a large kitchen to be the heart of the home. I planned Grandma's room and her ensuite bathroom knowing she'd never use it. And unless I got my money, I'd never build it, either.

I was so engrossed in my fantasy home that I when I heard a knock on the door, it startled me. I picked up my phone automatically, knowing the shattered screen wouldn't show me the clock clearly enough. I frowned.

I crept to the front door and listened. A second knock came, more forceful than the first. I pulled the front door open fast.

"What?" I demanded before I clocked who was standing there.

"And a good evening to you," he answered.

"Huh?"

"Good evening," he repeated.

Standing on my doorstep with a brown paper bag smelling of hot food was Mr. Wolfe.

"What's the time, Mr. Wolfe?" I demanded.

"What's the time?" His brow furrowed in confusion.

"A simple question." I placed my hands on my hips to show I wasn't messing around.

Mr. Wolfe looked at his watch. "Just gone ten."

"Do you think that's an appropriate time to knock on my door? I could be in my pyjama's, or in bed."

I grew frustrated at the smirk that grew across his face and once again, noticed his perfect teeth.

"I hadn't realised the time. Please, accept my apologies." He placed his hand over his heart. "I was working and hungry and wondered if you might like to join me for dinner."

"It's too late for me to leave the house," I said, and as much as I didn't want to, I looked over my shoulder.

"Your grandmother is sick, I hear?"

"Well, I don't know who you heard that from and I'd ask you to tell them to keep their nose out of my business, although I assume it's your *staff* reporting back. Why?"

"Because I asked them to. Now, this is getting cold, would you like to join me in eating it? I'm happy to sit on your doorstep, if you'd prefer."

Although I had already eaten, whatever was in the bag was calling to me and I wasn't wealthy enough to turn down a free meal. I stepped aside and let Mr. Wolfe enter.

Squeezing past him, I led the way to the kitchen. He placed the bag onto the kitchen table and picked up my drawing book before I could get to it myself.

"This is really good," he said, his voice rising slightly, as if in surprise.

I held out my hand to take the book back. "A silly dream," I said.

Mr. Wolfe stepped back, taking the book with him. He flicked through the pages. "This is *really* good. You have a talent for architectural drawing, Ruby."

I didn't recall giving him my name the night before, but I doubted it would be hard to find. I was on the rental agreement. Something stirred inside me, a flutter in my stomach, and I wasn't sure I liked it. I wasn't used to being praised other than by my technical drawing lecturer, who also believed I had a talent.

"Is that what you want to do?" He finally closed the book and handed it back to me.

"I'd like to be an architect, eventually. That's providing I don't lose my jobs, or my landlord puts my rent up and I can't afford to go to uni."

I made an effort to smile slightly. I didn't want him to think I was a total cow. Smiling wasn't something I did often. Grandma used to remind me.

He laughed, and the sound startled me. It was a gravelly laugh, and one that hit me at my very core.

"Let's hope that horrid landlord of yours remembers that. Now, shall we eat? I'm hungry," he said, flashing his teeth.

He set about to empty the bag, putting delicious smelling tin foil dishes on the table. I grabbed a couple of plates and forks. When he has done, he indicated to a chair.

"What?" I asked, already sitting and opening lids.

"May I?"

His level of politeness startled me. It was a complete contrast to his looks. He had that alpha-arsehole vibe going on. I waved to the chair as I took a mouthful of food.

"This is gorgeous," I said, remembering to at least cover my mouth as I spoke with it full of food.

"Japanese. One of my favourites."

For a moment, while we continued to help ourselves, we were silent, and I could study him. He was a very attractive man, older than me, obviously, and... I couldn't put my finger on what it was about him. Power. Money. Good looks. Maybe not that, but something else. Something predatory that had me intrigued, although the fluttering wasn't masking the red flags waving beside them.

"This is odd, don't you think?" I said.

"What is?"

"Us. Sitting here eating when we don't know each other at all. In fact, if you intend to kill me, at least I'm thankful, I'll go with a belly full of nice food. Just don't piss off and leave my grandma on her own, yeah?"

He chuckled, a deep throaty sound. "I promise to call the authorities and take care of Grandma."

"But not promise not to kill me?" I laughed, but then stopped abruptly. I didn't know the man sitting in my house and for a moment, nerves for the better of me.

"I promise not to kill you. Is that better?" He laid his fork down and smiled at me.

"You must have a great dentist," I blurted out.

He frowned. "A...?"

"Sorry, that was a dumb comment. You have great teeth," I said, shrugging nonchalantly but knowing my cheeks were flaming with embarrassment.

He stared at me. "All the better to eat..." He tailed off, not finishing his sentence, and I swallowed hard.

I coughed, clearing my throat. "Well, that was lovely, but I think I need to... you know? Catch up with college and... whatever."

He nodded and smiled but it didn't quite meet his eyes. "Thank you for your company and joining me for dinner."

I wanted to stay in the kitchen, but I also didn't want to be rude. I rose and followed him to the front door. "I appreciated the meal. Thank you."

He nodded once more, and I pulled open the front door. It was cold and drizzling out. A low-lying mist had formed. He slipped on his overcoat and flipped up the collar, tucking his chin inside.

"You're welcome."

He didn't look back as he walked down the path and out into the street. I stood for a moment, watching as he disappeared into the fog, and then closed the door. I leaned against it.

"Jesus fucking Christ," I said.

The words... *All the better to eat...* ran through my mind as I cleared up, causing my core to pulse with want and need. I hoped the missing part of his sentence was *you with.*

Mr. Wolfe, I thought, *a man who would most certainly live up to his name.*

CHAPTER THREE

The following day, I settled Grandma after breakfast, waited for Monica to arrive, and then rushed off to the first of my jobs. I cleaned a bar, a shady, shitty establishment, that often had me worried if I needed regular Tetanus injections. Once I'd done that, I headed to college for an afternoon lecture. All my tutors were aware of my situation and most gave me some space and leeway, most. One didn't, and it was that one I had to sit in front of that afternoon. Mr. Jenkins and I had a mutual dislike of each other that was immediate. I don't know why, but anyone who targeted me, who humiliated me, wasn't getting a shred of my respect. On my first day, I happened to move my watch on my arm. He made me stand in front of the entire class, remove it, while asking me if I was bored and clock watching. I had a fucking itch, that was all!

When he, or the school, then lost my watch, I got mad, and that hadn't helped my cause. Since then, I snarled, and he bullied.

"Nice of you to join us, Ms. Montando." He knew my name wasn't pronounced as he said it, but he didn't try and get it right. His three syllables were another slur, in my opinion.

"Trust me, I didn't want to," I replied, sliding into my seat. I wasn't late. Two other pupils had followed me in, and neither received his snark.

He ignored me for the rest of the lesson, which wasn't ideal as I hadn't understood the lecture. I sighed, switching off, knowing I'd have to find my own way of learning the crap science I wouldn't need once I sat my final exams. All I needed were the right grades to get me into university. I should have done better at school. I could have, but life had other plans for me. Now I was catching up; I was two years older than most in the college, but I was determined. Maybe it was time for me to reach out to my counsellor again. I could do with an advocate on my side. Tears pricked at my eyes, making me angrier. I hated my *weakness* as I saw it. I hated having no one, but I didn't want anyone, either. I didn't trust, and that made me difficult, I was sure.

Before I was aware of the time, the class had

finished. I gathered by unopened science book and placed it back in my bag. As I stood to leave, Mr. Jenkins asked me to wait. I rolled my eyes, not helping matters.

"I'm concerned about you, Ruby. You're falling behind a lot." He licked his lips, and I squirmed, keeping my distance from him.

"Yeah, well, I have plenty on my plate, and your constant criticism of me doesn't make me want to participate," I replied, ballsy.

His eyes opened wide. "No one is forcing you to retake this class."

"I am, Mr. Jenkins. I'm forcing myself because it would be super easy just to quit. I know I'm falling behind. I don't understand and I don't want to ask you for help. I'll catch up." I hitched my bag higher on my shoulder.

"If you need... additional help..." his gaze travelled over me and made my skin crawl.

It was my turn to widen my eyes. "I'll manage on my own, thank you. But I will let the head of college know about your kind offer."

I left the room fuming, and also knowing I couldn't report him. He hadn't *technically* done anything wrong other than make me feel very uncomfortable.

Thankfully, my last lecture was my favourite. Technical drawing.

"Ruby, one day you're going to design a house for

me," I heard. I looked up and into the face of a smiling Mr. Trent. "Super, well done."

"I think I can do better," I replied.

"I'm sure you can. We can always do better, but sometimes we have to stop fiddling and find satisfaction. Put your pencil down. Close your eyes and walk through this building. What do you see? What do you feel? If it all adds up, then that's the best you can do on this project."

I did as he asked and imagined myself walking home from work. I pictured arriving at a gateway in a lane that led me onto a pathway that wove its way through trees. I could hear the birdsong, smell the fallen autumn leaves. I felt a chill as if someone had walked over my grave and I shuddered, not understanding why. I breathed in deep, inhaling the scent of earth and foliage. And then I glimpsed, in my mind of course, a figure shadowing me. I sped up, running through the woods, trying to look over my shoulder as I did, gasping for air and holding onto my bag as if it contained precious possessions.

I woke with a start and gasp. The classroom was empty. Mr. Trent looked up from his desk and smiled at me.

"What the...?"

"You fell asleep. I guess your imaging was so lovely that you wanted to dream it as well," he said, chuckling.

I didn't tell him it wasn't a dream, but a nightmare. I was so embarrassed at nodding off, however.

"I can't believe I did that." I knew I'd be mocked by my fellow students the next time I saw them. "And now I'm late."

I rushed from my desk.

"Ruby, wait," Mr. Trent called out. "It's okay. You were tired. I imagine life is a little hectic right now. I'd rather a half hour of quality time with you than an hour and a half of you tired."

That was why I loved Mr. Trent as a teacher. He was one of a kind and if I could have hugged him, I would have. I smiled my thanks and left. I was late for my shift at Diego's, as usual.

———

"I am buying you a watch, Ruby!" Diego shouted from the stove.

"I fell asleep in class."

He turned to look at me and gave me a small smile and a nod. I was on the till that day. I covered any job going, grateful to have one. I whipped off my hoodie and pulled a restaurant polo shirt over my t-shirt. I tied my hair neatly in a bun and headed out front.

"Thanks, hun," I heard, and Cathy gave a kiss to my cheek as she rushed off.

She was another one of Diego's charity cases, as we called ourselves. I smiled and waved. She was a single mum of two and, like me, did all the jobs she could to pay the bills.

I started to layout the order details in time they came in, knowing those would be the people likely to pay first and I wouldn't have to flick around the paperwork finding the right diner.

The evening seemed to fly by. I loved being busy. It gave me less time to think about all the things that weighed heavily on me. My Grandma's ever-increasing needs were getting beyond my capability and Monica, and I needed to sit down and have a chat about it.

"Excuse me, Miss, this is the wrong amount," I heard in a not too pleasant tone.

Dragged back from my thoughts, I looked up. A woman stood by my side and held out a bill.

"Have you checked with your waiter?" I asked.

"Do I need to? Isn't that your job?" she replied, snarkily.

"I don't know what you ordered, only what has been written down. That's the amount owed for what was written down." I took the bill from her hand.

"You have a terrible attitude," she said. I smiled; she wasn't wrong.

Before I could respond, Harry intervened. He took the bill from my hand and headed out back. While we waited in silence, she smirked at me. I shrugged my shoulders in a 'and?' kind of way.

"Just pay the bill, Amelia." I didn't need to look to see who had spoken.

"It's not correct, Sir."

Mr. Wolfe stepped into my line of sight. "Are you stalking me?" I asked.

"No, I wasn't aware that you worked here." He reached into his pocket and retrieved his wallet. He pulled out a credit card and placed it on the desk beside me, not once diverting his gaze from mine.

"I wouldn't have thought this kind of food was your thing," I said, taking his card and inserting it. I handed him the machine so he could input his security number. He handed the machine to Miss Wide-Eyed-And-Annoyed. I smiled at her as she took it. "Would you like to add a tip?" I asked.

She huffed and keyed in his security number. I wondered why she would know it. She didn't look his type, but then, I didn't know him to know what his type would be. And she'd called him *sir*.

Mr. Wolfe exchanged a twenty-pound note for his card just as Harry returned. "It's correct, I'm afraid. You ordered the..."

"It's sorted," I said, cutting him off.

The woman looked down at her feet. "Would you like me to get the door for you?" I asked her, pushing my luck really, but I was pissed off that Mr. Wolfe was in my place of work, and I wasn't sure why it should annoy me. He was allowed to eat wherever he wanted.

She walked out. Mr. Wolfe chuckled and, again, that sound travelled through my stomach. "You are extremely feisty, Ruby. I like that. I might have an opportunity to discuss with you. I'll be in touch."

Before I could reply, he, too, left.

"Who the fuck is that?" Harry asked, licking his lips. I slapped his chest. "He's super... alpha and yummy. Please tell me he's your boyfriend."

"I don't do *boyfriends* and he's too old. He's actually my landlord."

"No way? Oh, he's whatshisface." Harry waved his hand in the air as if the answer would magically appear. "He owns, like, everything, around here. Bit of a gangster, so I hear."

I sighed and shook my head. If every successful man was a gangster, as Harry thought, there would be no legitimate business owners left in London. Mind you...

I cashed up and helped clean as soon as the restaurant closed. As was becoming the norm, we divided the leftover food among us. I took my bag and headed home. Monica would have been that evening and put Grandma to bed. I knew I'd pop my head into the living room and she'd be snuggled with the blanket pulled up to her chin. She'd knitted the blanket years ago, and it needed a wash. But like a child, or a dog, she wasn't giving it up just yet. I'd have to sneak it into the wash while she was asleep.

I set off on my journey home, flicking my hood up and knowing it was getting closer and closer to needing that winter coat. I shivered and shoved my hands into my pockets. I had arrears on utility bills that needed to be a priority. I didn't have enough left over each month to even pick up a decent coat in a charity shop.

———

I heard nothing from Mr. Wolfe for a few days, although the boiler man had returned to install a new heating system. That was a bloody nightmare, and I was at the point of either pulling my hair out or contacting him myself. The house was cold, and Grandma was getting affected by the noise and activity. At no time in their training had any of the plumbers learned to shut a bloody front door, either!

"Close the frigging door!" I shouted. "There is a poorly elderly woman in this house."

Apologies were abundant and the door would be closed until the next time someone needed something from their van.

A day and half later, we had heating and hot water. And both at the same time! New windows would be next, then a repaint of both the inside and out. Apparently, the entire street was getting a make-over. It was about time. It looked like a slum most days. If people took pride in their homes, it might help and I hoped that a fresh coat of paint, that might encourage them.

Later that evening, I dug out my lease agreement. Mr. Wolfe had said that he owned the company that owned the street. His name wasn't listed anywhere, but I didn't expect that. I circled the email address, making a mental note to write with some form of thank you.

Years ago, I used to love writing letters. My grandma would encourage me to write a thank you for any birthday and Christmas presents I received, and I used to enjoy doing it. I guessed, as life got harder, those things, and most that gave me joy, went out the window. I sighed. Nostalgia wasn't worth the effort or the upset. My focus was simply on the here and now and paying the next bill.

Despite my thoughts, I emailed, and the following day received a response from Mr. Wolfe thanking me for thanking him! I wasn't sure his response was necessary and once again wondered why he'd received my communication, and not an employee at a lower level.

I was contemplating a reply when my mobile rang. I stared at it and the unknown number for a while before I picked it up. I wasn't even sure it would answer, the screen was so damaged.

"Hello?" I asked, tentatively.

"Ruby. I wanted to see if you had received my email."

He didn't announce himself; he didn't need to.

"You just this minute sent it and this is creepy."

He chuckled. "You do like to insult me, don't you?"

"Not intentionally, but you often deserve it."

I found it strange that I wasn't mad. I settled back in my chair with a smile on my face. If I was honest, I liked the banter. There was something about Mr. Wolfe that I enjoyed, and his voice was nectar for my broken soul.

"I'm sure I do. You offered your mobile number up when you signed your contract. I think, if you read the small print, it says we may need to contact you by telephone."

"Mmm. Is it normal to call someone to check they received an email?"

"In my world, yeah. How is the heating?" he asked, changing the subject.

"Warm, on constant, for once." I still couldn't help with a jibe. "What a shame it took you drowning me for that to happen."

His laugh rolled over me, stopping at my core.

"You amuse me, Ruby." His laugh had stopped, and his voice dropped a notch.

"I'm glad I do."

For a moment, there was silence.

"Sleep well, Ms Montando." He pronounced my surname perfectly.

"I will now," I replied, then switched off my phone.

I sat for an age, thinking about him. I had no idea how old he was, where he lived, what he did for fun, nothing. But there was something compelling, for sure. Perhaps I just needed to get laid, not that there were many offers on that front. I sighed. A couple of guys had shown an interest in me at college, but I was too tired, too moody to take up any offers of dates. All that would have to wait, I'd decided.

I went to bed that evening frustrated, and much to my annoyance, had wild dreams about him ravishing me. I woke annoyed and more frustrated.

CHAPTER FOUR

Grandma didn't cope well with the window replacements and since it was soon to be December, neither did I. Monica and I decided it might be better for Grandma to go into respite for a few days. I'd never given her up and the guilt wracked my body when I took her to a local home. She was confused and upset, tearful, and angry with me. She soon settled with a cup of tea and a biscuit handed to her by a chap she'd named Louis and who she thought was her son. I'd never known her to have children, other than my father, and Louis wasn't a particularly Spanish name.

Grandma had reverted to speaking mostly in Spanish as she got older. More so when her dementia took hold. It was as if she'd forgotten to speak English. She'd been in England for years and years, but never lost her accent. I was grateful that Louis had a basic command of the language and he soon had Grandma settled.

I, however, bawled all the way home.

Monica led me back into the house and all works stopped while the window fitters looked to see if I was okay. No one snickered or looked embarrassed. In fact, the work supervisor, Derek, came and wrapped an arm around me.

"Horrible, love, aint it?" he said, his gruff London accent comforting me. I nodded and snotted into his t-shirt. "You did the right thing, and when she comes home and it's all nice and snug, she'll love it."

I doubted she would even know the windows had been changed, but I appreciated his comfort. I untangled myself from his arms and headed into the kitchen. I made two pots of tea and handed out mugs to the window fitters before settling down and cupping a mug in my own hands.

"I heard you were crying."

I spat my tea across the table and stood. "What?"

"I heard you were crying. I wanted to see if you were okay," Mr. Wolfe said.

He'd approached so silently I hadn't heard him.

"Why are you sneaking up on me?"

"The front door was open, and I wasn't sneaking, but next time I'll be sure to stomp. I wanted to see if you were okay. As I said, I heard you had been crying."

I narrowed my eyes at him.

"You have big ears if you heard me crying from your office," I said, challenging him.

"I have exceptional hearing and I was outside letting you have some time to settle before I made an appearance, seeing as I rile you so much."

"Do you check up on all your tenants?"

"No, I have a management team for that."

"Why me, then?" I asked.

"Because I want to, Ruby." He gazed intently at me, and I could feel those butterflies in my stomach flap their wings erratically.

"Tea?" I asked, holding my mug aloft. I didn't want to offer him tea, I wanted him to leave, but it was the first word that left my lips.

"Coffee would be nice. There is a nice café locally if you'd like to escape the noise."

I placed my mug down and grabbed my red hoodie to pull on. I was aware my t-shirt rose slightly as I struggled into it. I just hoped he wasn't.

"Lead the way," I said, and then promptly walked past him. I heard the deep chuckle that had filtered through in my dreams. I smiled, thankful I had my back to him.

As I left the house and turned out of the gate, he

grabbed my arm and pulled me to the kerb and to the side of his car. A large black car with darkened windows. I had no idea of the make, but it was super shiny and way out of place on my London street. I imagined curtain twitchers were desperate to know the occupant of the car.

"People will talk," I said, as he opened the rear door and ushered me in.

"Let them."

He slid in beside me and I shuffled to the furthest corner. The car was so plush and large that my feet didn't reach the carpet. I sat, giggling, and swinging my legs. That was until I saw him smile at me, then swipe his red tongue over those perfect teeth.

All the better to eat you with, shot straight to my mind. I coloured; my cheeks burned at the memory. He frowned. "Did you say something?"

"Nothing. Now, why don't we fuck the environment up further by driving this gas guzzler the short distance I assume it will take to reach the café?"

"It's electric," he replied, then sat back in his seat and laughed. He made eye contact with the driver, and the driver simply nodded. I wondered how he knew where to take us since no instruction had been given.

The car made no noise. I hadn't noticed when he'd drowned me with the puddle. But the silence was unnerving.

"Don't know that I like this. Can people on bikes or horses hear you coming?" I asked the driver.

"Yes, ma'am. The car emits a sound to alert our presence."

Oh, very formally answered. I nodded in approval.

"What's with the black windows?" I asked.

"So no one can see in," Mr. Wolfe replied.

"You like anonymity in your car, but happily strut into a stranger's house?" I teased, smirking at him.

"I don't think I've *strutted* since my teens."

"Stalk then, you stalk or... what's the word... skulk?"

"Skulk? Interesting choice of words, Ruby." He didn't expand on why he thought it was interesting. "How's college?"

"When I can get there, great. I have to do my uni applications soon, and worried about that—" I shut up, not wanting to divulge any personal information to him.

"Why are you worried?" He tilted his head and furrowed his brow in confusion. "Your drawings are amazing, so I assume your grades will be as well."

Too late, I guessed. I would now have to answer. I shrugged my shoulders. "Lack of confidence, I guess."

His eyes widened and his grin spread. "You... lack of confidence?"

I turned in my seat to face him. If I could have put my hands on my hips, I would have. "Yeah, and?" I asked, sassily.

He laughed. "A lack of confidence isn't something I get from you."

"I have a lot riding on this. It's all right for people like you, Mr. Wolfe. People like me don't get places without a lot of hard work and knockbacks. That's eroding."

Before he could answer, we pulled over. He opened the door and slid out, holding the door open for me to join him.

"My name is Sebastian. My employees call me Mr. Wolfe, as they should. I was an orphan, placed in a children's home, abused and beaten, until I *escaped* with only one idea. That was to never be beholden to anyone. So, as for *people like me*, don't be so quick to judge the cover. Shall we?"

He held out his arm, pointing towards a café. He slammed the car door shut and took the couple of steps up to the shop. He opened the door and stood to the side, allowing me to haul my rather embarrassed arse through and into the warmth of a lovely café.

"I'm sorry," I mumbled.

"Accepted. Would you like to take a seat there?"

Without waiting for an answer, he strode over to a table by the window. He waved to a man behind the counter. I assumed they knew each other. I also noticed two female servers elbow each other in their haste to get to us... him.

Without asking me, he placed an order for two coffees, one black and one latte. I hoped I was getting the latte; he certainly seemed the black coffee type of man.

"I'm sorry I made an assumption earlier," I repeated, pulling my big girl pants up.

"No need to apologise twice," he replied.

"Sometimes my mouth runs away from me," I said, laughing but still embarrassed. More so when he stared at my mouth and licked his lips again.

"I like that it does. You have spirit, Ruby. You're challenging and bolshy, and I have no doubt you'll go far. I'd like to help with that."

"Yeah, well, I don't do sex in return for a favour," I blurted out rather loudly, and exactly as two coffees were placed on the table.

I covered my mouth with my hand. It was a joke, but poorly executed and badly timed. I think even my eyelids turned red.

Mr. Wolfe looked at the hovering server with such a glare, she practically shrivelled.

"Jesus, Ruby! You need something large in that runaway mouth to shut it up sometimes."

I coloured further, the fluttering in my stomach turned into a Tsunami, and my hands shook. "And I'm not offering a favour... Although I do require something in return." He raised his eyebrows in challenge.

"Oh God, I'm so sorry. It was meant to be funny... except it wasn't." I blurted out, not fully processing his last sentence.

"No, it wasn't. Comedic timing isn't your strong point, is it? Now, shall we back up a couple of minutes?"

"Yes, please. Oh, God, I can't believe I said that."

I picked up my coffee and wanted to laugh purely from embarrassment.

He closed his eyes and shook his head as my shoulders lifted and tears filled my eyes. I was desperately trying to hold back the laughter.

"Laugh. Get it out of your system so we can get back down to business."

Having got permission, I placed my mug back on the table, lowered my head to my arms I'd folded beside the mug and laughed, biting my hoodie so as not to make too much noise. When I was done, I wiped my eyes dry with my sleeve and sat back upright. I picked up my mug.

"Now, where were we?" I asked.

"You were probably insulting me, yet again, while I was about to make you an offer I think you'd like."

"Ah, yes. Okay, go on."

"I have an opening for an assistant to my architect...." He held up his hand as I opened my mouth to speak and before I could get the words out, he'd stuffed a napkin in.

I spat the napkin onto the table and glared at him.

"This isn't a secretarial role, before you complain. It's a genuine assistant's role. I have spoken to my team, and they agreed a trainee would be the best solution. You work three days and attend uni for two."

"I wasn't going to complain," I said, lying.

"Really? Then you need a far better poker face."

He picked up his coffee and took a sip. His eyes bore into mine without blinking, and I swear they darkened. I wanted to shiver, or at least place my hands on my thighs to stop them twitching.

"Okay, I'm interested," I replied. And I was. Who wouldn't be? Working while studying would be an ideal situation, although I knew I'd be studying for way longer.

"Good. I'll collect you tomorrow and you can come into the office to meet your *boss*."

I smiled, and it was a genuine smile, and probably the only genuine smile I'd offered to anyone for a long time.

"I don't have anything to wear for an interview," I blurted out.

"Come as you are. I prefer my staff to be comfortable and I rather like you in that red, dirty hoodie."

He picked up his cup and sipped, all the while staring at me over the rim.

"It's not..." I picked at a splodge of mud from my sleeve. "I wonder if I can get to the launderette in time."

"You don't have a machine?" he asked.

"No, haven't been able—"

"I'll have one sent this afternoon," he said, picking up his mobile. He typed a message as I protested.

"Mr. Wolfe... Sebastian, please stop. Why are you doing this?" I asked.

He placed his mobile back on the table. For a moment, he didn't speak. "Something tells me to," he said, quietly.

"Something...?" I wasn't sure what else to say.

"I want to. Have you finished?"

I hadn't, but I picked up my mug and drowned the rest of my hot coffee. "Yes."

"I'll take you home."

I could have walked, but I wanted to spend a little more time with him. I wanted to know what the *something* was. I wasn't responsible for his conscience, and I didn't want the *only* reason he helped me to be because he felt he had to. I didn't want help, yet I knew I needed it.

We drove back in silence, him looking out one side of the car and me the other. It was with a pang of disappointment that I left his car and watched it drive away. I sighed. He was a problem I didn't need.

As promised, a couple of hours later, a van arrived

with not just a washing machine, but also a tumble dryer. I had no idea how he'd arranged for their delivery so quickly, and just assumed he held stock. Maybe his *posher* properties came fully furnished. The van driver told me he was to install the appliances as well, and I was grateful that the old outside toilet had electricity and plumbing. It made for a perfect utility room.

When he had gone and the window fitters had finished, I stood in the empty house. It was a mess but warm, and, more importantly, so very quiet. No road noise, not that it was a busy road. No kids from next door screaming in the garden. No dogs barking from the often reported puppy farm behind me. I sat on the floor and closed my eyes and just... be.

———

It took an hour to straighten the house and clean it. By then, I had the *cleaning bug* and rushed to the local store. I bought washing powder and softener, desperate to have fresh smelling bed linens. As much as I was fastidious about clean bed linen, especially for Grandma who spent so much time in bed, the laundrette didn't provide nice smelling products. I stripped both beds and got such silly enjoyment out of using the new machine, I actually clapped when it started.

I opened my phone and sent an email.

Thank you. I'm washing sheets! And other stuff, and I'll wash some clothes so I look smart.

I pressed send before I read it back and only after realised how juvenile it sounded.

"Jesus, Ruby," I muttered and then cursed that there wasn't a way to retract and delete emails before they were seen.

I could pretend that, because of the shattered screen, I couldn't actually see what I was typing, I guessed. Although, I doubted he'd fall for that.

Clean sheets are a favourite of mine ;)

He winked in his reply! I wasn't sure Mr. Wolfe had the capability of a wink; his humour was so dry. I laughed, not entirely sure what he meant.

After remaking the beds and making sure that Grandma's bedroom was perfect for her return, I stood in front of my wardrobe. I had clothes, I even had a dress I'd forgotten about. I tended to wear jeans and t-shirts, because they were easy, and jeans didn't need to be washed after every wear. I had shoes. Well, I had one, and I was sure I could find the other. I pulled everything out and laid it on my bed. Some items made me smile, while some made me cry. I hated that memories were attached to some, but there they were, no matter how silly. The dress that no longer fitted me, I remembered wearing, as my mother and I ran across the beach when we first moved to Spain as we splashed into the sea fully clothed. I picked it up and held it to my nose, wishing it still smelled of her or the sea. It didn't, of course.

My mother was English. She'd fallen in love with my father the minute she saw him, so she'd tell me. She had no parents, no one that she talked about, and I never questioned that. She laughed a lot. She smiled a lot more. Until the drugs and the drink ravished her, destroyed her soul, leaving nothing but a shell of a woman desperate for her release.

I knew exactly how she died but never said. Others said it was an accidental overdose, that she would never leave me intentionally. I didn't blame her, though. She did the right thing for her. She hated her life, and she knew she'd ruin mine if she continued. Her only way of ensuring I'd be safe was to take herself completely out of the picture. To me, that was a brave thing to do. I loved her, then and now, and I would continue to thank her for what she did. Although my life was tough, I knew that wouldn't last forever. I could have an amazing life because of her. I was tenacious enough to go for it.

I shuddered to rid myself of the thoughts. I didn't want happy or sad. I wanted angry because that's what drove me so hard. Anger at my father, anger at the illness that was slowly taking my grandmother, and anger at... I wasn't sure what else, but I knew I'd be angry at it, whatever it was. I chuckled. My brain was fucked up sometimes.

By the end of the day, I had a sparkling house, clean clothes laid out for my *interview* the following day, but it was too quiet. I walked into the living room and turned on the television. I was just in time for one of Grandma's favourite quiz shows. I found myself answering questions and turning to an empty chair to chat to Grandma. I missed her desperately, but there was a tiny part, deep inside, that I wanted to suffocate, that liked the peace, the solitude, and the knowledge that I might get a full night's sleep.

CHAPTER FIVE

I was a bag of nerves the following day. For two reasons. I had my appointment with my new boss—although I wasn't sure when I would start work since I hadn't finished college—and Monica was collecting Grandma and bringing her home.

As I dressed, my mind was in a whirl. How would I manage a full-time job and care for Grandma at the same time? The local council gave me an *allowance* to pay for Monica, but it would never be enough to have full-time care.

By the time Sebastian's car arrived outside, minus Sebastian, I was pleased to note, I was in a state. I wanted to cry. This was an amazing opportunity and in my head, I knew I might have to turn it down. My dream of becoming an architect might just have to stay that way... a dream.

Although the driver greeted me, we continued the journey in silence. I was thankful for that. I was sure that my nerves would show, and my voice would crack with the conflicting emotion. I was excited; I was nervous, terrified, and upset. Mixed together, that manifested itself as my usual gobby self. I would have to learn to bite down hard on my tongue.

We pulled up alongside an impressive building, all glass and stainless steel, and it puzzled me to see arrowhead designs everywhere. At least, I thought that was what they were. A smartly dress woman stood up from behind a desk to greet me by name.

"Ms. Montando, welcome to P.I.F. Would you like to follow me?"

She smiled and displayed, like Sebastian, the whitest of teeth. Perhaps they all got a dentistry plan with their salary!

"Thank you," I muttered, totally overwhelmed.

Although she smiled constantly at me, she didn't speak again as we travelled a couple of floors up in the lift. She held her palm over the door once it had opened and allowed me to walk into an open plan office. It was the place of my dreams. People dressed casually were sitting at desks or standing in front of drawing boards.

There was laughter and the smell of coffee. A couple of people turned to look at me.

"Ah, Ruby, isn't it?" one said, and I just nodded. "Come on over," he beckoned.

I stretched my cheeks as far as I could to resemble a smile. I'd frozen with fear.

All that ran through my mind was, *Get a grip, Ruby!*

"Mr. Wolfe tells me you are an exceptional draftsman. Or do we have to say draftsperson now?" An older gentleman walked out of a corner office. His smile instantly put me at ease. He had a kind face, and like a dog, I genuinely could tell if someone was nice or not.

"I'm not entirely sure that's correct. I try, but I'd love to learn more," I said, realising I was blabbing.

"Well, come on in, then."

I followed him into his office and took the chair he indicated. Then cursed myself. "I didn't bring any drawings," I said, panicking.

He waved his hand in the air. "No need. If Mr. Wolfe believes you can draw, I don't need clarification. He'd know more than anyone," he said.

I wanted to ask why, but didn't. Instead, Mike, as he introduced himself as, told me what he had in mind.

Thirty minutes in and I was busting to sign up. I would work, and get paid, for three days and study for two. I would leave college and start training through the Royal Institute of British Architecture's studio programmes. I could do online learning, therefore be at home with Grandma while I did. But the cherry on the cake? The salary and benefits. It was way higher than I would have expected, would allow me to pay Monica privately for more hours, and give up all my other jobs. I ran some calculations through my mind.

"How does that sound?" Mike asked.

"Like it's not real. What's the catch?"

He laughed. "No catch. As I said, Mr. Wolfe is very keen to have you on board. We need some apprentices, although we like to call them assistants, and you fit the bill perfectly."

"I do hope that Mr. Wolfe hasn't cajoled you into employing me," I lied. I bloody well hoped he had. This was an opportunity that would never have presented to me, normally. I didn't care how it came about.

"No. There were three candidates in the running. If I'm honest, Ruby, we prefer to give people a chance. You'll find out there are one or two who have spent time in prison, been homeless. It's Mr. Wolfe's mission in life to help others."

"He sounds like a real-life Robin Hood," I said, then laughed.

"He is."

The answer brought me up short. Was he? "Well, I hope I'm not expected to steal from the rich. I'm afraid I'd be a terrible criminal."

"You've certainly *stolen* Mr. Wolfe's heart."

I stared at him, open-mouthed. "Huh?"

"Oh, I don't mean in a... you know. I mean, he appears to be fond of you and wants to help you get to where you want to be."

I squinted at him. "*Riiiight.*"

Mike laughed. "I have some paperwork I'd like you to take home. Have a read through and if you're in full agreement, call me and we can work on a start date."

"Mike, I have to tell you I'm also a carer. I have help, but..."

He held his hand up. "Your grandma, Mr. Wolfe said. Read the document and come back to me in a couple of days. Reception will organise a car to take you home." He smiled at me.

"Do you mind if I walk?" I asked.

With a nod and a smile, they waved me off, so it seemed, and I started my journey back home.

I had one thought running through my head.

This is all too good to be true.

I didn't have time to read the documents straight away. A little while after I arrived home, Monica called to say that Grandma was ready to be collected a couple of hours later. I rushed around and batch cooked some soup, made as many easy to eat dishes as I could and filled the freezer. That and my microwave were the only things I needed in my kitchen.

Grandma couldn't eat most foods. It was as if she'd forgotten how to chew, and swallowing was also becoming a problem. I was an expert at making soups, self-taught, of course. I would cram as much goodness as I could in, but still had to rely on protein shakes for her.

I was wiping down the countertop when I heard a car pull up outside. I rushed to the door and smiled broadly. Monica was helping Grandma from the car. Although very frail, she looked rosy-cheeked. She was chatting away, mostly about Louis, and then when she saw me, she paused.

"Who is that?" she asked Monica, and my heart broke a little more.

"It's your granddaughter, Ruby."

"I don't have a granddaughter." Grandma started to get agitated.

It wasn't the first time she hadn't recognised me, but the first she'd shown fear. I wasn't sure what to do. Yet again, I cursed her dementia.

"I want to go home," Grandma said.

"You are home, Grandma," I replied, hoping the sound of my voice might settle her. It didn't.

"I want to go home!" Grandma screeched. Tears formed in her eyes.

I looked at Monica who smiled kindly at me. "How about we have a nice cup of tea, shall we?"

Grandma nodded and I stepped into the house and out of the way. I swallowed back the tears.

"Hello, Grandma. How are you today?" I heard that chocolaty smooth voice and I sighed.

"Oh, Louis, I'm so glad you're here," Grandma replied, and I sighed some more. It wasn't *Louis,* nor was it the nurse at the respite care centre she called Louis.

"Let me help you in," Sebastian said.

I watched as she smiled up at him. She allowed him to take her arm and gently lead her into the house, past me without a glance, and then to the living room.

"Smooth, isn't he?" Monica said. I nodded and frowned.

"Grandma lets *him* in the house, but freaks out about me." I knew what I said wasn't fair or entirely accurate considering I was already in the house, but my heart was hurting, and someone had to be the outlet for that.

"Come on now, Ruby. You know how this is," Monica said, gently.

I sighed once more and pushed my shoulders back. I walked into the living room and smiled.

"Hi, Grandma. I'm so glad that you're home."

"So am I. She tried to kill me," she said, pointing to Monica and I chuckled. I was off the hook. Now it was Monica's turn.

"Here, let's tuck this around you," Sebastian said as

he placed a blanket over Grandma's lap.

"He's a good boy, is my Louis," Grandma said, as she placed her palm on the side of his face.

He smiled at me. I scowled at him.

"I'll make her a cup of tea," I said, more mumbled than actually spoken.

I was standing with my back to the kitchen door when he came in. "Why do you keep turning up here?" I asked, spinning around to face him.

"*Keep?*"

"Yes, keep."

"I came to see how you'd gotten on with Mike."

"You could have called or emailed, or something..."

"I could have. I didn't. I saw your grandmother was distressed, so thought it a kind thing to help. I'll leave and make an appointment next time, shall I?"

His face was expressionless, other than his eyes. His pupils had dilated, and I saw the faintest of tics at the corner of one eye. I hoped he wasn't angry with me!

I took a deep breath. "It was kind, and thank you. The interview went well. I have a stack of things to look through and honestly, I'm waiting for the catch."

"Catch?"

"Yes, I'm half expecting someone to call April Fool, even if it's three months too early."

"No catch, Ruby. Just accept that you deserve a break and I'm offering it to you. It's easy, is it?"

I paused before I answered. "Yes. Yes, it is hard. I'm not often the recipient of kind deeds, so..." I shrugged my shoulders. "Would you like tea?" I asked in appeasement.

"No, I won't stay." He smiled and I felt like a shit, until I remembered that I really didn't know him, and it was still creepy that he just turned up.

"My meeting with Mike was great. I'll read the documents and call him tomorrow. Providing I can settle Grandma okay." I thought I ought to answer why he was standing in my house... or his house, I guessed.

"I'm pleased to hear that." He started to walk away, before he got to the front door, he turned. "You might think me strange, but I mean you no harm."

I frowned; it was an *old-fashioned* statement that I wouldn't have expected from him.

"Or a *Wolfe* in sheep's clothing," I said, laughing as I did.

He smirked, gave me a wink, and left the house without another word. The butterflies in my stomach were punching my guts in dismay that I'd let him walk out. His wink did something to them, for sure.

"Ruby?" Grandma called.

"I'm just making you some tea, Grandma," I replied and rushed back to the kitchen.

It took Grandma just a couple of hours to settle. She was happy when her favourite game show came on and we sat, holding hands, answering the questions together. It was only after I'd put her to bed that I sat at the kitchen table and read through the document Mike had given me. It was a contract and was pretty much the same as he'd said it would be with the added bonus of medical cover and a pension. I chuckled as I looked for the dental plan that wasn't there and subconsciously rubbed my teeth with my finger.

"So what's the catch?" I said, quietly. There had to be one. I decided to do some investigating.

Under my bed was an old laptop that I hadn't used in a while. I tended to do whatever was necessary on my phone, even though it was hard to read the screen. I'd needed the laptop at school but now used the more modern ones in the library. I connected to the internet via my phone and brought up a search engine. First, I typed in Sebastian Wolfe. Pages of unrelated things and suggestions for a different spelling were all I found. Nothing about him at all. That didn't surprise me. I mean, if I Googled myself, I'd find nothing.

I typed in his company name, P.I.F Group Plc. That's when it got interesting. P.I.F was a *parent* company for over a hundred others. I tried to find a map of sorts; it was quite confusing to see how the companies connected with each other. What I stumbled across were newspaper articles accusing some companies in the P.I.F group of jumping the list for government contracts and having politicians lobbying for them. Not one article actually mentioned Sebastian, however.

I began to think I might have the wrong company. How could one man own all the companies I was reading about? I wasn't up on how businesses worked, but I knew that since it was a Public Limited Company, P.I.F. had shares it sold on the stock market. That meant it probably also had a board of directors and was a big deal.

Did it matter? I had to ask myself.

I sighed and closed the laptop lid. No, it didn't matter. I should, for once, just do what Sebastian suggested. I should just accept that someone wanted to do something nice for me and take it. I was looking a gift horse in the mouth. I needed to kick my own arse if I fucked it up.

Later that night, while lying in bed, my thoughts were on Sebastian. I was curious to know what drove him to help others. Mike had said there were a couple of guys just out of prison. It wasn't often that companies of his size would give ex-criminals a chance. Not that I knew why they'd been in prison, of course. That night my dream consisted of prisoners and Sebastian chasing me through woods, even in my sleep I knew that the only outcome I wanted was for Sebastian to catch me.

CHAPTER SIX

I took the contract into college and asked to see Mr. Trent. We sat in the on-site coffee shop, and I showed him what I had.

"Wow, Ruby. How do you know this guy?" he asked, having read the contract then flicking back to the front.

"He's my landlord. Well, he owns the company that owns the house."

"And you said his name was Sebastian Wolfe?"

"Yes."

He umm'd and ahh'd and then handed it back to me. "I'll do some digging, but if I was offered that contract, I'd be jumping all over it."

"You think I should take it? That means leaving college."

"I think you should take it! Jesus, Ruby, no apprentice would get this chance or that salary, normally."

"That's what bothers me. What's the catch?" I asked.

"I have no idea. Perhaps it is simply what he says. He wants to help you. You are worthy of help, you know."

"I don't know about that. I'll call Mike and tell him I'm in," I said.

Mr. Trent was the one teacher that I wished I'd had all the way through my education. He was kind and encouraging. His attitude was, if you didn't want to learn, that was fine, but leave the classroom. He wanted to only spend his time with those that did.

I left college, my lectures finished lectures, and punched in Mike's number, hoping that muscle memory would dial the right numbers since I couldn't see them.

Thankfully, he answered.

"Hi, I've signed the contract. Do you want me to post it back?" I said, after identifying myself.

"You can bring it in when you start. I have my diary open, how about next Monday, which is the beginning of the month, so it suits our payroll." He laughed when he'd spoken.

"Next Monday is good for me. That gives me a chance to sort out my grandma."

It didn't, but I wasn't sure a delay was on offer.

I said goodbye and skipped back home. For the first time since I was a child, I had a sense of happiness bubbling away inside me. Unfortunately, a sense of fore-boding swiftly followed.

I was afraid to let myself be happy or content, even. I held back, always wary of when happiness might be snatched away. Monica had said in the past that when I suppressed the happiness, I brought on the depression.

If you think something bad will happen, then it generally will, she'd said.

I tried my hardest to focus on the start of a possible career, and the smile started to return.

I seemed to have gotten home in record time and found Grandma asleep in her chair where I'd left her. Monica would have been, but there was always that worrying period when she was on her own. Since she was fragile, I had no fear of her wandering. She was in little danger, but she would mess herself and my first job was a clean-up.

"Hello, Grandma," I called out, forgetting the lock worked. I kicked the door so hard it bounced off the wall and back at me.

"What's that noise?" she shouted.

"It's just me, Ruby."

"Come in, my granddaughter will be back shortly," she said.

I smiled at the familiar greeting. "I'll make a cup of tea, shall I?"

I headed straight to the kitchen, dumping my rucksack in the hallway, kicking off my trainers so they bounced off the wall, and pulling my hoodie over my head. My hair stood on end with static. It was one thing I loved about having a tumble dryer, the static on clean clothes.

I made Grandma a tea and warmed her some soup. I cut a bread roll into small pieces and filled a plastic tumbler with water. Grandma had all plastic, if she smashed a glass, she wouldn't realise it was sharp and would cut herself with it.

Once she was fed and settled again, I sat at the kitchen table and signed the contract. I read it again, highlighting areas I wanted to discuss. I had a bank account, but perhaps I needed a second, a savings account. With the salary I was getting, I could afford to put a little away for emergencies.

Although Sebastian had said casual clothing was the normal, I still needed to buy some more. I couldn't wear my one pair of ripped jeans and dirty Converse all the time.

I was munching on some toast, all I had in for dinner since I didn't get any money until the following day, when there was a knock on the door. A part of me hoped it was a certain someone.

I tripped over the rucksack on my way to open it. The caller knocked again.

"All right, I'm coming!" I shouted, rubbing my elbow. I opened the front door with a wince.

"Are you okay?" Sebastian asked.

"No, whacked my funny bone. What are you here for?" I asked.

"No amount of funny bone will make you smile, I take it?"

I gave him a broad fake smile and then laughed. "I fell over my rucksack," I said, pointing down the hall.

"Yes, I can see the hazards you've left in your wake."

His chuckle caused my lips to twitch—both pairs.

"What can I do for you, Mr. Wolfe?"

He held aloft a bottle of champagne. "I thought we should celebrate your new life."

"Unless you'd prefer something else," he added, and I wondered if he could see disappointment in my face.

"Not my drink, not that I've drunk much of it," I replied.

"I suspect the cheap shit you've had would turn you off."

I stared at him. Without speaking, I started closing the door. He blocked it with his foot.

"That was uncalled for from me," he said, bowing his head.

"That isn't an apology," I stated.

He didn't offer one, initially. So I kicked at his foot to move it. "You don't have any rights to force your way in here, even if you do own it," I said.

"I'm sorry, Ruby. What I said was crass and uncalled for. I'd like to share a glass of champagne with you to celebrate your new position." His voice wrapped itself around my skin, causing the hairs to stand on end, and putting me in a situation where even if I wanted to, I couldn't say no.

I opened the door fully.

"Thank you," he said, stepping inside and standing close to me.

"You know your way to the kitchen. I'll just tuck Grandma in."

I wanted just a minute to breathe. I could feel the heat radiate from him, he stood that close.

I heard him opening cupboards while I pulled Grandma's blanket up around her chin. I kissed her forehead as she closed her eyes. She wasn't in a talkative mood that evening, which happened more often than I liked. It meant she was slipping further away from me.

I turned off the ceiling light, leaving a small bedside lamp on, and gently closed the door. Before I headed to the kitchen, I took a deep breath in and exhaled slowly.

"You don't have any glasses?" he asked as I went around the kitchen, closing all the doors after him.

I picked up two. "What are these?" I asked.

He pursed his lips, then licked over his lower one. "Let me rephrase. You don't have any champagne glasses?"

"Never needed them, Mr. Wolfe. Don't have much call for celebratory drinks. But I'll be sure to visit the champagne flute store and grab some when I'm next in town." I smiled as sweetly as I could at him.

"Someone should put you over their lap," he said so quietly, I strained to hear. I near-on melted.

"I'm yet to find anyone man enough to try," I answered, waving the two water tumblers in the airs.

He snatched them from me and opened the champagne. He poured and when one fizzed up, he placed his finger in it. The bubbles subsided and I watched, mesmerised, as he placed that finger in his mouth and sucked.

He then handed me a glass. I sat, I had to, I think my legs would have given way. He came and sat opposite me.

"Do you want me to take this back to the office? I'm heading there after this," he said, waving his glass.

"Mike said to bring it in with me. Why are you heading back to work?"

"I like to work at night. I can concentrate more when the office is empty."

"Don't you get lonely?" I wasn't sure where the

question came from, but I got a sense that, like me, Sebastian was quite the loner.

"I like my own company," he replied, confirming what I thought. "Although, you're welcome to come with me. It's interesting to walk around the office when it's empty."

"I can't leave—"

"Would you, if you could?" he asked, cutting me off.

I stared at him for a moment. "Yes."

He picked up his phone and made a call. He requested assistance for a few hours and gave my home address. I frowned.

"Sorted," he said, simply.

"Whoa, hold on. I'm not letting just anyone in here. Grandma has dementia, that takes a special type of care."

"Would a specialist in dementia care be appropriate?"

"Yes, but—"

"There are no 'buts'. If you want to come with me, help is on the way. If you don't, turn the help away when they get here."

His stare was his challenge. I sipped the cold drink to cover my trembling lip.

"Blimey, this is nice," I said, and took a larger sip. He laughed. "Far better than the cheap shit I've drunk before. I might get used to this."

I turned the bottle to face me. I highly doubted I could afford it, but I wanted something to do before having to speak to him again.

I watched him watching me. I tried to be subtle about it, but his intensity was mesmerising.

"Do you always do that?" I asked.

"Yes."

I wanted to ask if he knew what on earth I was talking about? I was sure I was babbling.

"Why?"

"When I want something, I want it."

I wanted to ask what it was that he wanted, but I wasn't sure how I'd respond to the answer.

"My time is precious, Ruby. I don't like to wait around."

He placed his glass on the table and stood. He held out his hand and I took it. He walked us to the front door, and I felt like I was in a trance. It was as we opened it I saw a male nurse in blue overalls walk up the path.

"Mr. Wolfe," he said, holding out his hand. Sebastian shook it. He then pulled me forward to stand in front of him. "This is Ruby, granddaughter and primary carer."

"Hi, Ruby. My name's Tim," he said, and then handed me a folder. "All my credentials. I work only with dementia patients both in hospital and in their homes. Mr. Wolfe has asked if I'll sit with your grandma for a few hours this evening, if that's okay with you?"

We were all standing in the doorway. I didn't feel like I could go anywhere. I had Tim in front of me, smiling kindly, and Sebastian behind. I could *feel* him, his heat, and I could hear him breathing, slow and steady.

"Erm, I'm not sure," I replied, in all honesty.

"What is it you're not sure of?" Tim asked.

"This has been thrust upon me all of a sudden," I said and heard a low chuckle from behind.

"Tell him to leave, if you want to, Ruby." The voice startled me. He'd leaned down, his mouth at my ear. He moved my hair and his breath ghosted over my skin. "Although I'd rather you didn't."

I swallowed hard; my heart was racing.

I nodded. "It's fine. I'll only be a couple of hours at most," I said, aware my voice shivered. "She's asleep and usually sleeps straight through. She's not on any medication and she has water beside her. No glass, please. She's... She's fragile."

He nodded. "Mr. Wolfe has my number if you need to contact me."

I straightened my back. "Perhaps it might be best if you had mine, should you need to call, bearing in mind she is *my* relative and not Mr. Wolfe's?"

That chuckle came again and hit me straight in my core.

"Absolutely." Tim pulled out his phone, and as I was about to recite my number, Sebastian did instead. He knew my number off by heart. It irritated me no end.

"Shall we?" Sebastian said, pushing me gently forwards. I hadn't even picked up a hoodie.

I walked down the path and hesitated at the front gate. There was no car.

I wrapped my arms around myself and shivered. I then felt Sebastian place his jacket around my shoulders. He rubbed the tops of my arms. I didn't look back at Tim but heard the front door close. I was worried, hugely, but also elated. It was a sense of freedom I rarely got that coursed through me. I'd walk in the rain if I had to. I was out at night. I wasn't to or from work. It wasn't my normal and it was exciting.

"This way," Sebastian said, and when he placed his hand on my back to guide me, static coursed over my skin. Even through my clothes, I felt the shock.

He guided me to a black car. Not the same one he'd been driven in, but a sporty, low to the ground type. He opened the door for me, and I had to hold his hand to lower myself into the seat. Had he let go, I was sure I would have fallen on my arse.

I watched him walk around the car. He scanned his environment and I shivered. There was a predatory element to him that, even in the car, I could feel. But the strangest thing was, I felt protected. I wasn't prey.

"Nice car," I said as he got in. He stared at me, and then frowned. "What?" I asked.

"I was waiting for the quip, Ruby. Perhaps something about capitalism or being wealthy?"

I stared at him and then bit down on my lower lip. "I do that a lot, don't I?" I said, quietly.

"You do. Now, buckle up."

Sebastian didn't drive to the office in the same direction that I'd been before, and considering it was within walking distance, I wondered where we were going. That was until he hit the motorway.

"Fuck!" I shouted, part laughing and part screaming.

Sebastian laughed and hit the accelerator harder.

He'd put his foot down and the car had shot off so quickly, it had taken me by surprise. I laughed, and whooped, waved my arms in the air, as much as I could with the low roof, and screamed to go faster.

When we finally slowed, I was breathless. "Oh my God, that was amazing."

He laughed, and it was a natural one. His smile was broad. He whipped off his tie and threw it on the floor at my feet since there wasn't a backseat. As he undid his top two buttons, I licked my lips.

"Can you drive, Ruby?" he asked, glancing at me and catching me staring at him.

"I can, but I haven't for a long time." I'd learnt when I was seventeen and passed my test, but could never afford a car and hadn't driven since.

"Want to have a go?"

"Are you kidding me? I'd smash it up or kill us."

He laughed again. "I highly doubt that."

He pulled off the motorway and backtracked to the office. When we got there, a security guard raised a barrier and we drove into an underground car park. He stopped the car and opened his door.

"Get out," he said, commanding.

I laughed and ran around the front of the car. Only then did I see the Ferrari badge. While he stood at the side of the car, I slid into the seat. It was warm where he'd sat. I placed my hands on the steering wheel, sliding it around to feel the leather. He leaned down and moved my chair forwards so I could reach the pedals.

"Don't touch anything just yet," he said, then walked around the front and slid into the passenger seat.

"Where are the gears?" I asked.

"Automatic. You'll go too fast to change gear," he said.

I'd never driven an automatic before. "Right, see that lever? Click it down one for drive. Cover the brake gently and slowly pull away."

There was no slow with the car. We shot forwards and I panicked, slamming my foot on the brake. I laughed; Sebastian slammed his hands on the dashboard.

"Slow!" he said.

"I'm trying!" I replied.

The second time was more successful. We crept forwards in a straight line.

"Now what do I do?" I asked.

"Turn left or right unless you want to slam us into that wall," he replied.

I glanced quickly at him, too scared to take my eyes off the 'road.'

I turned us and drove a large square around the empty space. On the second round, I was confident enough to move from ten miles per hour to thirty. Even at that low speed, the car roared.

"I love the sound and the feel," I said.

"Same."

"It's that... Vibration of the engine," I said. I could feel it between my thighs, or was it the close proximity of Sebastian?

He smirked and raised an eyebrow at me. I rolled my eyes in response.

"Okay, pull over, otherwise I won't get any work done. I'll be too focused on you and vibrations."

My cheeks coloured, but I didn't respond.

I came to a halt, not in a parking spot, but randomly in front of a door. Sebastian leaned over me to press the start/stop button. He could have pointed it out, I was sure, but I think we both enjoyed the closeness. I inhaled; he smelled divine. If one could bottle power and sex, it would be his scent.

Before he moved fully back into his seat, he looked at me. His face was close to mine, I could feel his breath. I held mine. His eyes, normally a brilliant blue, had darkened and his pupils had dilated. I stared straight into his eyes for as long as I could, then my gaze fell to his lips.

He pulled back and I breathed.

"Come on," he said, leaving the car. I needed a moment to refocus, however. Finally, I joined him.

We walked in silence to a door, and he keyed in a code. We'd entered a small area. An overhead light flickered and he looked up and tutted. Opposite was another door. He keyed in his code again, and it swung open. The other side of that door was a lift and a staircase. He took the stairs, two at a time, and I struggled to keep up.

"Slow down. I only have little legs," I said, panting after him.

He stopped midway and waited for me. "You need to get fit," he said.

I paused and stared at him. "Like I have time for that! And that's rude."

"More or less rude than you've been to me? I need to

know, just for future reference, where I put my quips on our scale of rudeness."

"*Scale of rudeness?* How old are you?" I replied, chuckling.

"Thirty-five. Sixteen years older than you," he replied.

"An old man, then. And that's about mid-scale. I can do better if you'd like me to."

"You need an *old man* to keep you in check."

"I don't *need* anyone," I replied, and then started to walk ahead.

I was sure that I heard him say, *we'll see*, but when I turned around, he just smirked at me. "Stop looking at my arse, as well," I added.

"You can tell me to do a lot of things. Whether I'll comply is another matter."

I strode off, muttering under my breath, but loud enough so he knew I was doing it. His laughter echoed around the concrete chamber. Finally, we came to a landing and another door. I had to wait until he keyed in yet another code.

"Next time, can we just go in via the main entrance?"

He held the door wide and gestured with his arm for me to enter first. I stepped into an open plan office with one large corner office. The walls of which were all glass. It was a different floor than the one I'd been on before. This one was clearly his. In the corner, opposite the office, was a seating area. Plush leather sofas formed a square around a small coffee table. There were tables down one side of the room with mock ups of buildings, drawings, and it seemed to me to resemble a showroom of sorts, or a museum.

"Let me guess, another secret code," I said, looking at the keypad next to his office door. "Although, if one wanted to break in, surely they'd just smash the window."

"Two two zero seven."

"Huh?"

"The code, two two zero seven. Not such a secret. As for the glass, if one wanted to smash those, it would take a small sized bomb."

"Why the security, though? Genuine question, I didn't see anything like that downstairs."

"Because I value my privacy. I also don't want people in and out of my office."

"Except me?"

"Except you."

He stood to one side, and I keyed in the code, the door unlocked, and I opened it. It was heavy, for sure, but hinged in such a way that it swung open effortlessly.

"Make yourself at home. There is coffee or water, and a bathroom in that corner. Take a look around.

Those are some of our previous projects, they might interest you."

"What exactly do you do?" I asked.

"Property development, mostly."

"Mostly?"

"Sometimes I kill people. Being in property development is quite handy for disposing of bodies." He smirked, and the skin around his eyes crinkled.

"Ha ha. I'll grab a coffee. Do you want one?"

"Yes, please, black and strong."

He walked around a solid oak, large desk and before he'd even sat, a monitor emerged from its hiding place within the desk. He slid open a drawer and removed a keyboard.

"Impressive," I said, then left the room.

After spending about ten minutes trying to work the machine, I'd managed two mugs of black coffee. I took one back to his office. He was sitting with headphones on, the type with a mouthpiece, and typing. He typed way faster than I could have. I placed his coffee on the desk, and he looked up and smiled at me.

"Hold on, Jake," he said. "See that desk there?" he pointed to one at the furthest end of the room. "On it is a mock-up of a club, my club. It needs a total overhaul inside. Want to take a look?"

I nodded enthusiastically. Although architecture

was my primary goal, it was the interior of hotels and clubs that I wanted to work on the most. I rushed over.

On the desk was a layout of a two-story building. Whoever made the mock-up had done it to scale, which was great when it came to visualising. Also on the desk was a storyboard. All I needed to know was what the club was used for. It seemed the downstairs was the usual bar and DJ booth, but upstairs, it was different. More a lounge area with VIP rooms. Perhaps he had dancers. I also noticed a name on the storyboard. It had been put together by Amelia. The woman that paid his restaurant bill had the same name and I hoped I wouldn't have to work with her. I pulled over a stool and sat. I just looked at the downstairs first, taking the top layer of the mock-up off. The storyboard suggested it was dark in colour, perhaps dingy looking, but it was hard to get a feel for it, having never visited it before. I wasn't the club type, although I had visited one a couple of times on the odd occasion I had college friends. One of the main complaints had been how dark clubs were. It was dangerous for women.

I grabbed a pen and wrote, *women only lounge set up from the main floor and with security.*

I also noted a lack of toilets on both sides of the building, so added that. Women liked to congregate in toilets, and yet, it was often men who designed those spaces. I drew a room that was more along the lines of an old-fashioned powder room. I added sofas and dressing tables at one end, toilets and sinks at the other.

There was no space to attend to anyone who was ill. Spiking drinks was commonplace in clubs, perhaps there needed to be an area specifically for dealing with that, with a door straight to the outside for paramedics. The more I thought about it, the more I wrote and sketched.

"What's that area?" I heard. Sebastian leaned over my shoulder and pointed. He made me jump.

"Women only," I said.

"Mmm, interesting."

"It's hard to know what to do without seeing the space, so I've sketched some areas I know clubs are missing."

I pointed out the medical room, a different layout for toilets, and repositioning the bar so people didn't have to walk directly through the throng of dancers each time. Different flooring to define the spaces. Water stations where cups could be filled for free.

"What is upstairs used for?" I asked.

I heard him chuckle. The sound ran from my neck, where he was, down to my toes. I curled them in my trainers.

"That's a different sort of club. Members only."

"There's no DJ area," I said.

"No, because, as I just said, it's a different sort of

club."

"Well, unless I know, I can't visualise the space."

He chuckled some more. "Perhaps you'd like to visit it. It's open now."

I picked up my phone, knowing full well I wouldn't be able to tell the time. "What's the time?"

"Ten p.m., that's all."

"That's my bedtime," I said, laughing. "Are you a night owl?"

"Pretty much. Although I can live on very little sleep, thankfully."

I felt a distance creep in and knew he'd stood back. "So?"

"Okay, why not. I need my camera, though."

"No cameras, not this time. Perhaps I'll take you back tomorrow."

I frowned. "I clean in a strip club. I doubt you have anything in there I haven't seen."

He raised one eyebrow and did that thing. The one thing that got my insides in a knot. His tongue gently darted out to wet his lower lip before he bit down on it. It didn't seem it was a conscious thing from him, it was natural, but, boy, did it turn me on.

"Shall we go?" I said, wanting to break the moment.

I followed him back down the stairs, at a slower pace, and to the car. He waited until I had my seat belt on before he closed the passenger door and strode around the car. He pulled his phone from his pocket and made a call before he opened his door.

"Ready for this?"

"Yeah. You're making it sound like we're heading to something weird. You're not going to kill me in there, are you?"

"Maybe." He licked his lips and those brilliant white teeth flashed at me.

"I was half expecting a dental plan with my contract."

"What the fuck is it with you and teeth?" he asked, backing the car out.

"Nothing, just thinking aloud."

"Ask for one to be put in. A contract is to be negotiated, not immediately accepted," he replied, not focussing on me, but his manoeuvre.

It was my turn to chuckle. He stared at me and then shook his head.

It took only ten minutes to drive to a dingy backstreet and park outside an even dingier, black painted building.

"Looks like the bloody London Dungeon," I said, wrinkling my nose at the smell of piss as I opened the car door.

He chuckled and continued to laugh. "What did I say?"

"That's about the best description I've heard,

although I don't think we'd get away with using that name."

The club wasn't open since it was a weekday. Sebastian told me they only opened Friday through to Sunday, and then one night in the week for special DJs. However, upstairs apparently seemed to be. He picked up my hand and walked me down a side alley a little way, to a small black door manned by a security guard. Probably one of the largest I'd ever seen. He nodded at Sebastian and opened the door for him. We were met by a flight of stairs.

"Are you ready for this?" he asked. "Remember, you are only here to the assess the place for internal renovation purposes, that's all."

I frowned at him. "Strippers, that's what I'll see, isn't it?"

"You might do."

I rolled my eyes and shook my head. "Lead the way."

I followed him up the stairs to a large foyer. More security and a receptionist greeted him immediately. That area was quite welcoming and bright. I wondered how that could be since there were no windows. He didn't introduce me to anyone.

"Do you want a drink?" he asked.

"A Coke might be nice," I replied, and before I finished my sentence, a waiter appeared by his side.

He placed the order, one Coke for me, a whiskey for him.

He stared at me again. "What now?" I asked, getting agitated.

"I'm not sure this a good idea. Let's go," he said, surprising me.

"Wait. What?"

"This isn't a good idea." He reached for my wrist, and I pulled it back.

"I'm a big girl, Sebastian. Whatever is through those doors, isn't going to faze me."

The waiter appeared and I took my Coke. Eventually, he took his whiskey.

He picked up my wrist again, not holding my hand, but wrapping his around my skin, and marched me to a set of double doors.

It opened, as if by magic, and we walked in.

My heart was in my mouth, and it raced at a pace I wasn't sure my lungs could keep up with. I stood, wide-eyed, and open-mouthed at the sight in front of me.

Women were dangling from the ceiling by ribbons, some were strapped to metal circles that gently turned. All were naked.

As my eyes adjusted to the dim light, I started to see more. Couples, triples, were fucking on large beds. Orgies were all around me.

I let Sebastian take my hand at that point, too

stunned to protest. I'd known I wasn't walking into a bloody book club, but hadn't expected that.

He led me to the side of the room, where the smaller bedrooms were. Some had glass windows, some didn't. It was nicely decorated, if a sex club could be. I was actually quite impressed with some of the art on the walls.

"That's nice," I said, pointing to a picture. It was of a naked woman, back to the camera. She was kneeling, and her hands and ankles were tied with intricate knots.

He laughed. "Is that all you can say?"

I turned slowly, looking around. Some stared at us, and I felt conscious about being scruffily dressed.

"So. This is your den of inequality?" I said, quietly.

"Don't you mean inequity?"

"No, inequality. These women giving their bodies to rich old men because they can't do anything else." I snapped as my blood boiled at the sight.

There was a pause and I swear he rose in stature.

"What did you just say?" His voice was so low, and filled with such anger, it made my heart stop. His jaw clenched so tight, a rapid pulse could be seen at the side. His eyes had narrowed.

"Erm..."

"I misread you, Ruby. I didn't think you were so judgemental. I was right earlier and should have turned around and driven you home."

I wasn't sure what to say, other than I knew I'd

fucked up, and he was right. But I was too proud to apologise. He walked away, but I stood still.

"Come," he said, not even looking at me.

I ignored him. In fact, I decided to investigate further. I took a few steps in the opposite direction. It was then that I saw her.

Amelia swung from two large ribbons hanging from the ceiling. I'd seen the 'act' before, but never with a naked woman. She lowered herself and landed gently in front of me.

"I heard what you said. Perhaps you should know I have a degree in aeronautical engineering. I could work on a fucking spaceship if I chose to." Posh people swearing always amused me. But she was very annoyed, and rightly so.

Sebastian returned to my side and grabbed my arm. He held on tight to my wrist and I turned to face him.

"Don't hold me like that. You don't own me. I'm sorry, I spoke entirely out of turn. You caught me on the back foot and my mouth runs away from me when that happens."

"Apologise to her," he said.

My heart raced, more so when I saw how she acted around him. She was deferent. I apologised and she accepted. She also asked if I had any questions.

"Why are you here?"

"Because I love it. I love sex, I like to be dominated,"

and this club gives me, and many others, the freedom to practice what we love in a safe environment. These aren't all *rich old men*. Although, granted, some are. Some are also just your average Joe. See him there?" she pointed to a muscled and tattooed man. "He's a window cleaner, Ruby."

I swallowed hard, suitably chastised.

"Who... Who dominates you?" I asked, knowing the answer immediately.

She looked at him, I looked at him. He stared at her. I saw him raise his middle finger. He gently rubbed a patch of skin just beside his eye. She nodded.

"Strike one," he said, quietly. She nodded again.

He had given her a code, a message, but for what? I had no idea. She didn't say a word, and left. He still had hold of my wrist, but not as tight.

"I'm sorry, Sebastian," I said, gently.

He nodded, and then walked back, towing me behind him. We left the room and were back in the bar. He placed his undrunk glass of whisky on the tray being held by a waiter. I gulped a few mouthfuls before doing the same.

We were outside in minutes. I watched as he looked up at the sky and took in a large breath.

"Get in the car," he said, not looking at me at all.

I did as I was told.

For a moment, we just sat. "Are you angry with

me?" I asked. I didn't want him to be. For as much as I'd been rude to him in the past, being upset with me wasn't what I wanted.

"Yes."

His abruptness made me shrivel inside. I looked out of my window.

"I should take you home."

"I don't want to go home. Can we get a coffee somewhere? I'll pay," I said, trying to lighten the mood.

Only then did he look at me. "Never judge anyone, Ruby. Not until you know the circumstances."

I gently nodded. He started the engine and we drove, thankfully, in the opposite direction to home. He pulled up outside an all-night café and I waited for him to open my door. He held out his hand and I took it. It was the easiest way to get out of the car.

As I walked to the counter, he took a seat. I ordered him a black coffee, strong, and myself a latte. I paid when the drinks were ready, and then joined him.

"Ask your questions, Ruby," he said.

I had a ton, but I suddenly found I had no words. "I think I'd like to just drink my coffee, and maybe talk about the building rather than its use."

He nodded.

"As much as I love architecture, I love interiors more. It's easy to put up four walls, but the positioning of windows and lighting, flow of the rooms, that fascinates me. How to make a building work, do you know what I mean?" When I spoke about my passion, I became animated. Even my voice changed. It wasn't so sullen.

He smiled at me. "I do. It's good to be passionate about something."

"What are you passionate about?" I asked.

"Lots of things."

"That you won't tell me?" I asked, smirking.

"Exactly."

He looked at his watch and disappointment flooded through me.

"What's the time, Mr. Wolfe?" I asked, my voice low.

"It's One O'clock," he replied.

I scooted forward a little.

"I think it's time for me to head home. But..."

"But what, Ruby?"

"I'd like to go back to that club one day."

He stared at me. "For what reason?"

"Just because."

He shook his head. "That isn't a good enough reason."

"I'm curious, okay?"

My cheeks flamed. I was. I had always been curious about a more *hedonistic* sex life. It wasn't like I had a great deal of experience, although I had lost my virginity at fifteen. That was more like a fumble and thirty seconds of penetration. I had never been *satisfied* by a man.

"Do you know what curiosity killed?" He had leaned forwards towards me, our faces just a few inches apart.

"I don't want to die curious," I replied.

He didn't reply. He gulped down the remains of his coffee and stood. I took that as my cue to do the same. I guessed we were leaving. Leaving yet another half-filled drink on the table, I scrambled to follow him.

When he pulled up outside my house, I climbed from the car with reluctance. He had held the door open for me but only walked me as far as the gate.

"Can I ask a question?" I asked and he nodded. "The Amelia that signed the storyboard. Is she the same as the one in the club and with you at the restaurant?"

"Yes, why?"

"Isn't it awkward? Working with your... You know?"

"No, Ruby, I don't know. Explain."

He fucking knew; I was sure. "Is it hard working with your sub, or whatever you call her?"

He raised his eyebrows and started to chuckle.

"She said she likes to be dominated, and then she looked at you. I know what I'm talking about."

"You know what you're talking about?" he asked,

and then stepped closer to me. Only the gate separated us.

"Sort of. No, I don't, but you know what I mean."

"Yes, she's a submissive. Sometimes, when I want to, I will *play* with her. No, it's not awkward at work because we are both professionals."

"Do other people know about you two?" I asked.

"No, only you."

"And you want me to keep that quiet, I guess," I said.

"I don't care who you tell, to be honest. I like curiosity. I like that you are curious."

I thought for a moment he was going to lean down and kiss me. He didn't. Instead, he took a step back and nodded just the once before he left. I stood and watched his car leave, the tail light glowing red as he broke at the end of the road. Only then did I open the front door.

"Hi, did you have a good evening?" Tim asked. I'd forgotten he was there.

"Erm, yes. Sorry, it's late. I should have called or something. Is everything okay?"

"Perfectly. Your grandma is asleep, she hasn't woken once, to be honest. I'll be off now."

"Okay. Erm, how do I pay you?"

"You don't, it's been taken care of by Mr. Wolfe. Didn't he tell you? He's retained me on a permanent contract for you. You'll be starting work soon, he said."

"Oh, right, yes. I forgot. But I'll only be working during the days."

"I mean, my company, not just me. We'll have someone here during the day, and someone on the evening shift. Before you start, perhaps we should sit down and discuss hours," he said, and then frowned. I guessed he thought I would have known.

"Yes, sorry. It's late, I'm all over the place. I'll call you tomorrow."

I showed him out and then shut the door. I rested my back against the wood and closed my eyes.

"What the fuck am I getting myself into?" I whispered.

I looked in on Grandma and then headed upstairs to bed.

CHAPTER SEVEN

I had a fitful night, tossing and turning, and when I woke way before my alarm, I felt disorientated. I couldn't remember what I'd dreamt about, which frustrated me. Years before, when I'd had counselling, I often had night terrors and was encouraged to write them down. It was a way of discharging the image. But when I woke anxious without knowing what I'd dreamt, those took a while to get over.

I made a tea and took it in to Grandma. We had a nice routine in the morning. I'd wake her. She'd drink her tea and then I'd wash her, put her in some clothes and help her into her chair. She'd watch the television while I changed her bed or made it if it was clean. I then made her porridge. It was the only thing she'd eat in the morning, and about the right consistency for her to swallow.

Monica came and I told her about Tim. I assured her I still needed her, and she wasn't losing her job. She'd become so fond of Grandma herself.

"When I'm working, I'll be able to pay for more hours," I said.

She smiled and accepted the cup of tea I offered. "I can't do full time, Ruby."

"I know, but whatever you can do would be amazing. We can work Tim around your hours. I trust you, and Grandma trusts you. This other bloke has been thrust on me."

I told her all about the evening, excluding the club.

"Well, I think it's a good thing, to be honest. You know you'll never cope with working and caring for Grandma, and you can't pass up this opportunity. I'd be furious with you if you did." Her stern tone of voice was coupled with a smile.

"I'm not going to. I need this. I need you, and Tim. And I'm not too proud to refuse Sebastian's handout." I laughed and sipped my tea.

There had been a time I'd been way too proud to ask for help. It was only when I was at breaking point, Mr. Trent had intervened and got the school counsellor on my side. She had been the one to organise help and called in social services for me. Then had the real fight started. I had to scrap for every sliver of help I discovered I was entitled to. It was arduous and demoralising. So when a gift horse came my way, I snatched it with both hands, too exhausted to fight anymore.

Grandma called out, not for me, but for a random name. Sometimes, I'd ask her who the person was, and she'd tell me about them as if they existed in real life. It was lovely to see her animated and smiling. Other times she'd tell me they were trying to kill her, and she'd be distressed and lash out. I'd gone to college with a black eye once when she'd struck out and I'd tripped as I stepped out of the way.

I sighed. Monica smiled and went to attend to her.

I picked up the contract that was still sitting on the kitchen table. I wrote, *dental plan* on it, and laughed.

———

Later that day, after I'd attended a couple of lectures, although more to say goodbye to my teachers, I went through my wardrobe. I couldn't afford new clothes and had become a dab hand at sewing up tears and repurposing items. I'd even altered and redesigned some of Grandma's clothes. She had a trunk in the loft, full of outfits I imagined she would have worn in the forties and fifties. Occasionally, I'd rifle through and sell off some to retro stores. I decided to do that. I climbed into the loft and grabbed a handful of items. There was a retro store nearby that would take all I'd let them have. Why I didn't take the entire trunk, I wasn't sure. It didn't feel so disloyal, I guessed, if I only took a few items at a time. Next to the retro shop was a charity shop and I hoped I might be able to find some trousers and perhaps some footwear in there.

I called out to Monica that I'd be back in an hour and left the house.

"Oh, these are lovely, Ruby," Darcy said. She held up dress after dress. "You know this one's Chanel, don't you?"

I nodded. Grandma had a lot of designer items, especially handbags.

"I'm going to keep this one for myself. Let me price them all up for you."

Darcy offered me fifty pounds for the Chanel even though I knew it would be worth more, and another one hundred pounds for the rest. I took the money. She wasn't trying to rip me off, it was what she could afford, and I didn't have the time nor inclination to sell it myself. I headed next door.

I loved to rifle through charity shops. I'd found many a bargain before. In fact, I was sure most of what we had in the house had come from one charity or another.

I held up a pair of black trousers, new and still with the tag. I then found a rather nice blue shirt. It was a man's but small and I was sure it would look good with the trousers. I found a pair of flat black shoes, only slightly scuffed, a largeish tote that would do for carrying my lunch to work, and a dress. I only owned one dress. I had, in the past, I'd had loads. But since being on my own with Grandma, clothes hadn't been a priority. I was super excited, however, to find a beautiful red coat.

It was woollen and military style, with a slight flare at the bottom. I tried it on. It was slightly on the large side, but that didn't matter. I did the gold buttons up and then the belt. I looked at myself in the mirror. It was flattering, for sure. It highlighted my waist. I'd always been slim and that was simply from not having a ton of food to eat. I wasn't ever hungry, though. I guess I'd learned to ignore the grumble in my stomach.

I stuffed my purchases in a creased old plastic carrier bag and headed back home. I sighed as I rounded the corner and saw the now familiar black car. As I walked towards it, Sebastian stepped out.

"People are going to talk," I said.

"Let them."

"I've been clothes shopping," I said, holding the bag aloft.

He frowned. "Where?"

"The charity shop. Where do you think? Don't get money for designer from the government, you know."

"Yes, I do know. I lived on it myself."

He had briefly told me about his childhood, but not in any great detail.

I came up to him. "So, what do you want?" I asked.

He raised his eyebrows at me. "That's a polite greeting, considering I'm just about to authorise a total redecoration of your house."

"Then let me rephrase. Hello, Mr. Landlord, oh Gracious One. I bow down in full appreciation of you doing what the law says he should." I bowed theatrically, but then slipped. I landed on my knees and reached out to grab his trousers for support.

He looked down at me. I looked up at him while I knelt at his feet.

He smirked.

"Oh, for fuck's sake, I slipped. Help me up," I said, scrambling on his clothes for assistance.

"Oh, I don't know. I kinda like you at my feet," he replied, but he did reach down so I could take his hands.

"I'm sure you do, but it won't happen again."

"Want to put a wager on that?"

I looked sharply at him.

"Fifty pounds," I said.

"You sell yourself way too cheap. Five thousand pounds."

"You're on," I said, shaking his hand. I knew I'd never have to pay. He laughed. "Coffee?"

He followed me into the house, and I emptied my bag on the kitchen table. While I made coffee, he held up each item.

"I love the coat, but the rest is shit," he said.

"It might be shit to you, but it will do me until I get paid and then I can get some nicer clothes," I said. I refrained from reminding him what it was like not to have any money.

"I'm going to take you shopping. Come on," he said.

"Err, no you're not. I've been, that's it. I want a drink, and I'm hungry. And Grandma needs her lunch sorting."

I could have reeled off any number of things, and I knew it would make no difference whatsoever. As soon as he pulled out his phone, I was done for. I tried to snatch it from him, but he held it aloft, and I was too short to grab it.

Monica came into the kitchen. "What's going on?" she asked, laughing.

"He's trying to call someone, and I don't want him to. I don't want to go shopping."

Monica laughed more and looked at Sebastian. "You really think you're going to get her to do a clothes shop?"

"See, I told you. I don't do shopping," I added, pouting.

Sebastian made a call. "Tim is sending someone. Thank you, Monica, for the heads up, but she isn't working in my office in those. You have five minutes. Put on some decent underwear."

He turned and walked from the kitchen, taking his coffee with him. I heard him greet Grandma as he sat with her. Monica and I just looked at each other.

"Put on decent underwear?" I asked.

"You can't try on clothes in shabby knickers," she replied.

"Who the fuck is going to see what knickers I have on? Can you believe that arsehole?"

"Go get showered, tie your hair up, and put on some decent underwear," she said, laughing.

I stomped up the stairs, grumbling that I was a fucking nineteen-year-old, nearly twenty, and could do what I wanted. I did, however, shower, put my hair up, and slip on the only decent pair of knickers and bra that I had.

"Would you like to choose my clothes?" I shouted while I stood in front of my wardrobe pondering on what to wear.

I nearly jumped out of my skin when an arm reached over to grab the one dress hanging there.

"What the fuck?" I shrieked, covering myself with my arms.

He sighed and rolled his eyes. "I'm not looking at you."

"Why are you in here?"

"Because your five minutes were up, and I don't like waiting."

"Too fucking bad," I said.

"And I don't like foul language," he added, standing way too close for my liking... Or rather, it was for my liking.

I cocked my head to one side and raised my eyebrows. "What will you do about it, then?" I challenged.

"Put you over my knee and spank the shit out of you."

He didn't smile or smirk, and although I wasn't sure if he was serious or not, there was something that made me want to unleash all the *foul language* I could.

Then he did that thing. He rubbed the side of his eye with his middle finger. "Strike one, Ruby."

I swallowed hard, my stomach flipped, and I wanted to cross my legs to quell the throb between my thighs.

"How many strikes do I get?" I asked, my voice husky.

"Three, no more."

"And when I get to three?"

"You'll see, I guess." He handed me the dress. "Put this on, now."

I slipped it over my head, grabbed the first pair of footwear that came to hand and a hair band. As I was following him down the stairs, I bunched my hair on top of my head. Of course, being the untamed curls that it was, it fell all over the place.

"Ah, you look nice," Monica said.

"Thank you. I don't know what's happening," I said, shrugging my shoulders.

"You're going clothes shopping," she answered. "Go, gift horse and all that," she added with a whisper. "I'll wait here until someone arrives."

I sat at the bottom of the stairs and laced up my boots.

Sebastian was waiting in the car, impatiently I thought. He tapped his fingers on the centre arm rest.

"Don't you have better things to do?" I asked as I slid in beside him. The door closed automatically.

"Yes."

"Then why aren't you doing it?"

"Because you need clothes."

He said it so matter of fact. I shrugged my shoulders and settled in my seat, crossing my seatbelt over my chest.

"I don't like this dress, it's too short," I said.

"Yes, it is."

He was looking at my legs. The dress had risen to my upper thighs. I tugged at it, hoping to cover a little more skin.

"I don't like those boots, they're too manly," he said.

"Yes, they are," I replied, smiling sweetly.

We soon pulled into the underground car park of my worst nightmare, a shopping centre. The driver stopped by the doors and Sebastian climbed out. I sat and sulked. He opened the door and held out his hand. I slowly took it and was yanked from my seat.

"Do you have to pull me around?" I asked.

"Only when you don't respond quick enough."

"Jesus, anyone would think you're my dad," I said, smirking at him.

He led the way, still holding my hand. He did that a lot, held my hand. There were times when I thought it might mean something, and others, like then, when he just held it so I didn't lag behind.

"Slow down, will you?" I asked.

"Sorry, I hate shopping."

"So do I. So why are we?" I asked.

"Because. Now get your arse in there." We had stopped outside a department store.

"You actually trust me to pick out some clothes? And how do you think I'm going to pay for them?" I was back to having my hands on hips to show how serious I was.

"No," he said, laughing. "And I am. Now get in. There's a private shopper waiting for us."

He pushed me forwards, and we walked towards the women's clothes section. We stood for a minute, neither of us sure where to go.

"Ah, Mr. Wolfe?" We heard. I turned first to see an older lady jogging over. "Is this your daughter, Ruby?" she asked.

I had to bite down hard on my lower lip to stop from laughing. He looked like thunder had struck. His glare had her shrivel.

"No, she is not my daughter," he said, his voice low and stern.

"Oh. Oh, I'm sorry. Erm..."

"She needs work clothes, a casually dressed office environment. She also needs some evening wear and smart restaurant clothes. And shoes, please don't forget the shoes."

"I can pick—" I started. He glared at me, clearly pissed, and I shut up. I couldn't, however, stop my shoulders from shaking.

"Oh, for fuck's sake, let it out, Ruby," he said, sighing.

I laughed. I laughed so hard tears rolled down my cheeks. The shopper stood totally bemused.

"Better?" he asked when I used a tissue he held out to wipe my eyes.

"Yes, Dad, thanks." I was off again.

He shook his head. "Where do I wait?" he asked, brusquely.

"Follow me," the shopper said. She was obviously confused.

We walked through a door and into a seating area. Champagne was on ice, and beside it was soft drinks. He was invited to sit; I was invited to follow her into a cubical. I was asked to remove the dress and then she measured me. I guessed that was the reason for the decent underwear. She asked me what my favourite styles and colours were. All I could do was shrug my shoulders. I didn't have any, I'd told her. She gave me a robe to put on and told me she'd be about a half hour.

There were magazines and we were offered tea and coffee. He took the coffee and I opted for a soft drink. We were then left alone. I sat, swinging my legs, and looking around. The robe was too long, and my hands were halfway up my sleeves. I waved my arms. He sighed.

"Do you do this a lot?" I asked.

"Shop?" he asked, and I nodded. "No. I have someone come to the house."

"How did she know to expect us?" I asked.

"I called her from your house. What do you think I do?"

"I don't know. You just say something and then it happens."

"That's the way it's meant to be," he said.

"Not for me, it doesn't."

He looked at me. "That changes now, Ruby."

For a moment I was silent. "Why, Sebastian?"

"Why, what?"

"Why me? Why are you doing this for me?" I asked, clarifying.

"Because I want to, and I can."

"I mean, I'm super grateful and all, but I'm still waiting for the catch."

"No catch. I've said that before. Something tells me to do this. Maybe you're my redemption, my ticket to heaven, since I've been such a selfish prick most of my adult life." He laughed and then picked up a magazine.

"I can't imagine you ever being selfish," I said, meaning it.

"You don't know me," he replied.

"Will I ever?"

He lowered the magazine but was stopped from answering by the return of my shopper. She wheeled in a rail that held an array of clothes. One caught my eye. A bright red sequined dress, mid length with, I assumed, a halter neck. I stood and walked over to it, running my hand over the material.

"Try that on first," Sebastian said. He leant forward in his chair.

I pulled it from the rack and the shopper followed me to the changing room.

"You'll need to remove your bra," she said, standing at the open cubical.

"Yes, I sort of got that. If you don't mind...?"

She stepped back and I closed the door. When I slipped the dress over my head, I felt a million dollars. Closely fitted to my curves, it was stunning. I'd never worn anything like it before.

"Come out when you're ready," she said.

I opened the door and shyly walked to a pedestal in front of a large mirror. I stood on it, facing the glass. I saw Sebastian looking at me. He caught my eye and very slowly nodded. His appraisal pleased me. I turned my focus back to me and reached up to pull the band from my hair. After fluffing it, I let it fall down my back. I heard a strange noise and looked at Sebastian again. He stood and walked over. He moved the hair that had fallen over my shoulder, exposing the deep V at the front of the dress.

"Shoes," he said, still looking at me.

The shopper opened a box and pulled out a pair of red high-heeled shoes. I was sure I'd never be able to walk in them. He took one and tapped my thigh. I lifted my leg, and he placed the shoe on my foot. There was something erotic about the way he held me, more so when I had to lean on him while he placed the other shoe on. He was the one kneeling behind me. He looked at me in the mirror for way too long before he stood. He licked his lower lip and circled me.

"We'll take these," he said.

The air was hot, heady, and I wanted to fan myself.

He circled me again, studying me, licking his lips as if he was about to pounce. It was only the shopper, concealing a cough, that brought him back to the present.

I tried on trousers and shirts, flat shoes, and another midnight blue, full-length dress. That one slinked over my body and because it was satin, it caused my nipples to pucker. He noticed that, of course. Another pair of high heels accompanied that dress.

By the time we were done, I had added smart jeans, some polo shirts, and jumpers. I refused a new coat. I loved the red one and fully intended to wear that.

"Bag all this up, please," he said to the shopper as I handed the last item from the dressing room. I slipped on my dress and Dr Marten boots and joined him. He handed her a credit card.

We followed her to a till and I nearly fell on the floor when it rang up the total. He'd spent over three thousand pounds on me. I opened my mouth to speak.

"Strike two," I heard quietly. I looked at him. He had two fingers stroking the side of his face.

"I didn't say anything," I whispered back.

"You were about to. Be happy."

I was, in fact. I couldn't stop smiling at the thought of the new clothes. I then felt a pang of dismay. Other than work, I had nowhere to wear the dresses. Maybe that would change. Perhaps there would be work outings I'd be invited to.

I took his hand in mine as he paid and squeezed it. He didn't look down, but squeezed back. I leaned in close.

"Thank you. Honestly, I know I'm a bitch most times, but I really do appreciate what you're doing for me."

He took back his card and the receipt and then smiled down at me. He gave me a wink and I all but melted inside.

"I'm still not paying you back with sex, though. You can keep asking," I said, then grabbed my bags and walked off.

"Strike three," he called out, and I laughed.

I jogged back to the entrance and slid into the car before he got there. The driver took a call, and I noticed Sebastian walking towards the car, also on the phone. I started to get excited, but also worried. I wanted to know what happened after strike three but didn't at the same time.

He slid into the seat and didn't look at me, let alone speak.

The car pulled away. I sat and stared at him; he looked forwards. He must have known I was looking at him, I'd turned in my seat to face him.

We drove past my house, past the office, and out

towards Kent. I panicked a little at that point. I sat straight in my seat and looked out the window. Eventually, we pulled up at metal gates and waited for them to open.

A tree lined drive led towards a large modern house. The car stopped outside. Sebastian opened his door while the driver opened mine. I went to gather the bags.

"Leave them," Sebastian said, and it was the first time he'd spoken since we'd left the store. His voice was gravelly.

I did as I was told and stood by the car, not sure what to do.

"Come," he said.

I didn't want to, but my legs had other ideas. I walked towards him, and the driver carried my bags to the front door. He opened it, not Sebastian, and placed them in the vast hall. I followed Sebastian in. The hall was cool and white, with a marble floor and grand staircase to one side.

When the driver closed the front door behind him, we were left standing in the vast space together. He stared at me.

"What's the time, Mr. Wolfe?" I whispered.

"One O'clock," he replied.

I took one step closer to him.

"What's the time, Mr. Wolfe," I asked again.

"Four O'clock," he said.

I took four steps. My body was touching his. I looked down, keeping my eyes closed.

"What's the time, Mr. Wolfe?" I whispered.

"Dinner time, Ruby."

He grabbed my chin and raised my face. He lowered his and I struggled to regulate my breath. I dragged in air to fill my lungs. He hadn't restricted my breathing in any way. It was desire and want that crushed my lungs. My hands shook as he stared at me, his face angled so close to mine. I closed my eyes as his lips met my cheek gently. He dragged them across to my neck, using his tongue to taste me. I moaned, then, giving in to the sound that had been building in my chest.

My legs started to shake, more so when he ran a hand up my back and fisted in my hair. He pulled, forcing my head backwards.

"Look at me, Ruby," he demanded.

At first, I couldn't. He pulled my hair harder, jolting me. I mewled; a sound I'd never heard from myself before. I looked at him.

"I gave you warning, didn't I?" he whispered.

I nodded causing a pull on my scalp.

"How many?"

"Three strikes," I replied, my voice hoarse.

"Are you aroused?"

"Yes."

"Punishment arouses you," he said, as if he knew that for fact.

I started to shake more. My stomach was flipping a triple salchow.

"You arouse me," I confessed.

His lips crashed on mine so hard he nearly forced me off my feet. I had to take a half step back to balance. His tongue demanded mine. His hand tightened further in my hair, and I moaned into his mouth. That spurred him on, I guessed.

His kiss was deep, claiming. I could hear him breathe through his nose, feel his chest rise and fall against me. Only then did I raise my arms and wrap them around his neck. I grabbed his hair, and it was more for something to hang onto. My legs were going to give way.

He bit down on my lower lip, and I thought he'd drawn blood. He crushed me to him, holding me tighter. Just his mouth was close to bringing me to an orgasm.

Then he stopped.

He took a step back and wiped his mouth with the back of his hand. I saw a smear of blood, not knowing if it was his or mine. I panted, desperate to catch my breath.

He shook his head. "I can't."

I was shaken. My legs quivered and I blinked rapidly.

"You need to go," he said.

I bit down on my sore lip to stop from crying.

What the fuck had just happened?

He turned away, keeping his back to me, and I saw him take a deep breath and exhale slowly. He straightened himself, pulled himself upright, before slowly turning back to face me.

"What did I do?" I asked, quietly.

"You're too young, Ruby."

"I'm nineteen!"

"I'm old enough to be you dad, remember?"

"So? I'm not a child, for Christ's sake."

"You. Are. Too. Young."

"And yet you want me," I challenged.

He nodded.

I pulled my dress over my head; he closed his eyes.

I slipped off my bra; he opened his eyes.

When I lowered my knickers, he stepped towards me.

"I'm on three strikes, Mr. Wolfe," I said, aware that my voice was sultry, but it wasn't intentional.

He grabbed me then, forced me back against the wall and turned me away from him. He held my wrists above my head, and I held my breath.

He slapped my arse.

It stung. It brought tears to my eyes, and a pulse

between my legs. I was instantly wet, enough to feel it between my thighs.

He slapped my arse again.

I moaned and rested my forehead on the wall. I'd never been spanked before. I'd read it, watched it online. It was different, experiencing it, of course. My skin stung, it was a heat that spread not only over my skin but down between my legs. His palm stayed connected with my arse and he gently rubbed. It didn't do anything to ease the soreness, but it was pleasurable.

Sebastian used his foot to kick at my ankles, and I parted my legs.

"Strike three," he said, and then spanked me again.

That time, it was lower. His fingers covered my opening, and he held his hand there, teasing my clitoris. I was done for. I came, arching my back towards him. I felt liquid run from me, drip down my thigh, and I wanted to die of embarrassment.

He rubbed at my opening, coating his fingers, and then lowered his head to my neck. "Good girl, Ruby," he said.

There was something in the way he spoke such simple words that had me wanting to please him.

When he pulled his hand away, I felt bereft. "No!" I said.

"You don't tell me what to do," he whispered. "But

don't worry, I'm not finished with you yet. What time did I say it was?"

My stomach lurched, and because I didn't reply as quickly as I guess he wanted me to, I got another spank.

"Dinner time," I said.

He turned me to face him. "Beautiful," he said, rubbing his thumb under my eyes to catch the tears that had settled there.

He lowered himself to his knees, holding my hips. "You wanted me on my knees, Ruby, and here I am."

Before I could respond, he had buried his face in my pussy. He sucked on my clitoris, sending shockwaves through my body. He held the sensitive nub between his teeth, slowing biting down until I screamed out.

I fisted his hair, tightening my grip with every lick, suck, or nip. Sweat rolled down my back, my hair stuck to my skin, and my legs started to shake again.

"No," I said, pushing his head. The orgasm that was building was intense, the ache in my stomach from the last one hadn't subsided.

He paused. "No!" I said, and he chuckled.

"You don't get to say no, Ruby," he whispered, and his breath soothed the heat.

"Shouldn't I have a safe word?" I panted out.

He chuckled. "Safe words are for pussies. Trust me to know what you can stand, okay?" he said, looking up at me.

I hardly knew him, but I trusted him explicitly. I wasn't sure why, I just did. I nodded. He continued his feasting of me.

When I came again, I wanted to slide down the wall. Instead, he stood, and he picked me up. His face glistened with my come and I ran my tongue over his lips, tasting myself. He walked us up to his bedroom.

He placed me, very gently, on the bed and then pulled his shirt over his head. He slowly undid the buckle of his belt and slid it through the hoops. He placed it on the bed. He kicked off his shoes and then removed his trousers. He was naked underneath.

"Condom," he said, pointing to a cabinet beside the bed.

I reached for one and tore the packet open. "I... I've never put one on before," I said, holding it.

He took it from me, and I watched as he rolled it down his cock.

He crawled up my body, holding himself above me. "I'm going to fuck you now. Is that okay?" His mouth was near mine and his voice a whisper over my lips. I nodded.

He held his cock near my entrance, gently teasing me. I wrapped my arms around him and scraped my nails down his back. I parted my legs further, ready for him. When he pushed inside me, I thought I'd die. He was balls deep and still.

"Move," I said.

"What did I say to you before?" he asked, still holding himself above me.

I stared at him and then smirked.

"You. Don't. Get. To. Tell. Me. What. I. Can. Do." He slammed into me on each word.

He fucked me like I'd never been before. Admittedly, I'd only had sex a handful of times and it wasn't particularly enjoyable, but the emotion and feelings he produced were addictive. I wanted more and more. I wanted harder and deeper.

Time spun around me. I came, and then I came again. I wanted to curl up to ease the ache. He wouldn't let me. It was a delicious pain that throbbed through me. He kissed me hard, then softly, he nibbled on the skin of my neck and shoulder.

I wrapped my legs over his, dug my nails into his skin, which earned me a hard bite, enough to break skin, I was sure.

I was sore. I ached. I had lost my voice. My throat scratched with every dragged in mouthful of air.

Finally, he came, and granted me some relief.

Sebastian slid to the side of me and lay on his back. We didn't speak for a little while. Eventually, he propped himself up on his elbow and removed the condom. He placed that in the bin beside the bed.

"Okay?" he asked, gently.

"More than," I said, chuckling.

"Did I hurt you?"

"Yes, but not enough."

It was his turn to chuckle.

"Can I tell you a secret?" I asked, turning on my side to look at him. He nodded as he pushed my hair from my face. "I've never had an orgasm before. I've just had three and I don't know if that's normal or not."

He didn't laugh or smirk. "I'm glad I was able to do that for you, Ruby. There is no normal where sex is concerned. If you liked it, it's normal. If you didn't, then say."

"I doubt I could have stopped them," I said, and I knew my cheeks were flaming. I didn't talk about sex normally.

"I have a lot to teach you, don't I?" he whispered.

"I want you to teach me," I replied. "But now, I think I need to go home. I need some time to process."

He smiled at me, kissed the tip of my nose, and slid from the bed. He headed through a door and then called me. He'd turned on the shower and beckoned me under. He stood in front of him soaped a sponge. He washed me, then he dried me and once he'd done that, he slathered on a cold cream over my arse cheeks.

"You look fucking amazing with my handprint on your arse," he said.

I twisted my body to see in the mirror. "Jesus!" I said, catching a glimpse.

He dressed and then ran downstairs to collect my clothes. Once I was dressed again, we walked out of the house. He carried the shopping bags. To the side, were garages. He told me to wait while he collected his car.

I wished he hadn't driven as fast. I didn't want to get home, but I knew I needed to. Soon, we were there, and I sat for a moment.

"I feel guilty," I said, looking at the house.

"Why?"

"Because I've been enjoying myself and I should have been looking after my Grandma."

"Are you not allowed to enjoy yourself?" he asked, gently.

"No, not really."

He didn't reply. He left the car and opened my door. I took his hand and stood. When he opened the boot to retrieve the bags, a tear slipped from my eye.

"Why the tears?" he asked, walking with me to the front door.

"Thank you for today. Can you return those?" I asked, pointing to the bags.

"Why would I want to?"

"Because this isn't my reality," I said, placing my hand on his chest. "This is," I added, turning to the front door.

"Why can't you have both?" he asked.

I sighed. "I don't deserve to have both. You don't know what I've done."

He stepped closer to me. "Are you sure about that?"

"You can't know. No one knows."

"I know a tortured soul when I see one. One that mirrors mine."

I shook my head, opened the front door, and stepped in. He didn't attempt to hand me the bags, and I wasn't ashamed of the tears that flowed down my face.

"Thank you for today. I really do appreciate it. I guess... I guess I'll see you at work."

He nodded. "I'll keep these at mine for when you're ready."

I closed the front door.

It wasn't Tim on duty that night, but someone new, Emma. I guessed she'd heard me and kept her distance. It was only when I was making tea that she appeared.

"Hi, Ruby," she said, startling me.

"Sorry, I was making tea. How is my grandma?"

"She's sleeping. She woke once and asked after you. I told her you were sleeping, too. That settled her."

"Thank you. I can carry on from here," I said.

She nodded and returned to the living room to grab her bag.

"You know, carer breakdown is the most common

thing I see as a professional carer. If you don't look after you, you're no good to your grandma."

I didn't respond and she left, not before telling me that Jim was on the following morning, and he'd be there at eight. I thanked her.

I cried that night, really sobbed. I let out all the pent up upset and sadness I'd been holding in for years. I buried my face in my pillow to quell the noise. No one knew what I'd done.

Killing my mother was something I'd take to my grave.

CHAPTER EIGHT

We had a new person come to look after Grandma the following morning and I started to worry about the number of new faces. I called Tim.

"I'm super grateful, and all, but I wonder if we can keep to the same people? Grandma was a bit upset this morning because she's not doing too well with all the changes."

"Of course. We do need to sit down and go through your exact requirements. We haven't done that yet. How about I pop along later today?"

We agreed on a time, and I set about to clean the house. I had a sense of needing to make up for the time I spent enjoying myself the previous day.

I thought about Sebastian as I worked. More so about our sex. My body ached for him, and I knew it would take all my resolve to keep my distance. I hoped I wouldn't have to work on the club interior. That way, I could avoid him and Amelia. I wasn't sure, having seen her naked, I could face her again. I had three days to get myself together.

Once the kitchen was spotless, the living room clean and Grandma's bedding all in the wash, I set about cleaning upstairs. I was a clean freak and I think that started as the only way of controlling my environment. My parents, before settling in a house, would camp on beaches, in fields, and communes. I had no control of where I was, or where I'd even wake up the following morning. I scrubbed the bathroom until the skin around my fingernails cracked and bled. I bleached everywhere so much that my eyes watered. When I was done, I tackled the bedrooms. Although the mould had been treated in Grandma's old bedroom, it was yet to be redecorated. I decided to rip up the old carpet and dispose of all the furniture. It wasn't needed anymore.

I called a charity and arranged for them to come and inspect and then collect the furniture. It wasn't antique, but still in good condition. Most of it had come from the charity in the first place. I shifted what I could, cut up the carpet into manageable pieces and hauled them downstairs.

Sweat coated my neck and I grabbed my hair to hold it on top of my head. I wanted some cool air to wick away the moisture. When I heard a car drive slowly past, I turned. It was his car. I sighed.

The car stopped, but it wasn't Sebastian who climbed out, it was the driver.

"I shouldn't be here, but I wanted to tell you that Seb is like a bear with a sore head today," he said.

I frowned at two things. First, why he was telling me this, and second, at the shortening of his name. Sebastian had told me all his *staff* called him by his surname only.

"I'm sorry about that," I said, not really knowing what to say.

"Save my skin and call him?"

I shrugged my shoulders. "I don't know what you mean?"

He smiled. "He's a miserable fucker when you're not around, or he's not around you."

"I've met him a handful of times. I can't imagine I've affected him that much," I replied, chuckling at the absurdity of that.

"Ruby, you know that isn't true. As I said, I shouldn't be here. He'd go fucking mad if he found out."

"I'm confused. I haven't seen him every single day since he... you... tried to drown me. What's different?"

"What's different is that he doesn't think he's going to see you again."

"He told you that?" I asked.

"Yes. I don't just drive him around, we're family, just not blood."

He climbed back in the car and left, leaving me even more confused than when he'd first arrived. I didn't even know his name.

However, a small smile crept over my lips. So, he was missing me, was he? We'd only seen each other the previous evening. I swallowed that smile back down. It wasn't my fault he was moody, and I believed I had been right to put a stop to whatever it was happening before it got started.

Sadness washed over me, though. I was always meant to be alone. I knew that. I just wanted to get on with my life with as few complications as possible.

By the time I'd finished cleaning upstairs and had the second load of washing in, it was time for Grandma's lunch. I heated some soup and buttered some bread, then took it in on a tray. I offered the carer some, but she'd brought her own, she'd told me. I also reminded her she could make herself a drink whenever she wanted. She followed me back to the kitchen.

"Your grandmother is lovely. She's been telling me all about Spain," she said.

"You understand her?" I asked.

"Yes, I took Spanish at school. I'm hoping to move there and become a language teacher. I'm just doing this before uni starts."

I smiled. "That's nice. It's a lovely country."

"Do you miss it?"

I paused. *Did I?*

"I miss elements of it," I said, which was true.

I didn't miss the drugs and drink. The parties and orgies.

I didn't miss the lack of love and attention from my parents.

I didn't miss the moving around, sometimes in the dead of night because rent hadn't been paid.

I did miss the house that my grandma eventually bought, so I had a place to settle.

The carer left when Tim arrived, her shift over.

"This was all a little rushed, so we didn't confirm a proper care plan with you," he said. "Perhaps we could do that now?"

I nodded and offered him a coffee. He sat at the kitchen table with a bunch of forms.

"Before we do anything, I have to know how much this is going to cost. I start work on Monday, but I'll be paid monthly," I said.

"The fee has been taken care of. I assumed you were aware of that?"

I tried to keep my face neutral. "I wasn't sure."

"We've been asked to give you as much cover as you require. The invoice is sent to Mr. Wolfe's secretary."

"Okay. So how do we go about this?"

We detailed my working hours, and I scheduled in the times that Monica would be sitting with Grandma. At first, I declined any help in the evenings, but after Tim pressed the matter, I agreed to three nights per week and then any emergency cover as needed. As Tim had said, I might have to work late sometimes. I might just want a night out with my new work colleagues. I chuckled at that one, knowing it to be highly unlikely.

I signed the documents and kept a copy. I had a huge file of documents about Grandma, and I added it to that.

When Tim had left, I just sat for a while. Grandma dozed in her chair, and I turned the television down so as not to disturb her.

I contemplated texting Sebastian a thank you, but that would break the 'no contact' rule I'd put on myself. I'd email instead, it felt more distant.

Hi, I just wanted to say that Tim came today, and we sorted the contract. I don't expect you to cover the cost. Once I'm working, I should be able to do that. Perhaps we can make arrangements that I pay you back?

I'd pressed send before I read it back. I hadn't meant to leave the email on a question, encouraging a response... Or had I?

I closed the laptop lid and left it on the table.

Back upstairs, I prepared my outfit for the Monday.

I'd wear the trousers and blue shirt I'd gotten from the charity shop. I still had some money left over from selling the dresses and wondered if I ought to add another pair of trousers. I felt bad for getting caught up in the clothes shopping moment and then asking Sebastian to return the items. Maybe I should have brought them home to return myself. Although he'd paid on a card, so I'd need that for a refund, anyway. It had been pretty irresponsible of me, I thought. And irresponsible wasn't what I did, generally.

I cleaned the shoes, disinfected the inside and left them on the kitchen table to dry off. I chuckled. Grandma would curse me for leaving shoes on a table, something to do with bad luck she'd say. I'd often reply that my luck couldn't get any worse.

That night I had a terrible nightmare. I was in the woods, and I was lost. It was dark and I couldn't see. My eyes hadn't adjusted to the lack of light. I was trying to feel my way around. I would hear a chuckle, his voice gently calling me, but I knew it wasn't because he wanted me. Or maybe he did, but it was scary. I tried to run, and I'd bump into trees, fall over bushes. I could see my house in the middle, the one I'd drawn, but I never seemed to get there. Nothing I did got me closer to the house. His voice would bounce around, echo, sometimes close, sometimes far away. I couldn't determine if I was running to or from him. I was both terrified and aroused in my dream. I wanted to get to him, knowing he would likely kill me, but hoping he'd fuck me instead.

I woke, startled, out of breath, and with the sheets tangled around my body. I kicked them off and lay still, taking in deep breaths to stop my hands from shaking.

"Shit," I whispered, finally.

I swung my legs over the side of the bed and shivered. I wanted to splash some cold water on my face, but the chill in the room had already cooled my skin. I placed my hand on a radiator and felt the coldness, perhaps the heating had gone off? It shouldn't have been that cold.

I grabbed a jumper and slipped it on, then crept downstairs. I didn't want to wake Grandma, but I needed to check she would be warm enough.

After satisfying myself that she was okay, I decided to check the boiler and then make a hot drink to take back up with me. The lights were on, suggesting the boiler was working, so I'd have to leave it until the morning to figure out why the bedroom was cold.

I made a tea and as I passed my laptop, I picked that up as well. It was highly unlikely I'd get straight back to sleep and maybe reading something might clear my mind of my dream.

Once I was back in bed, with the jumper still on, I opened the laptop. My email account was still open, and

Sebastian had replied. I hovered over it, not wanting to read, but knowing I couldn't ignore it even if I tried.

Good evening, Ruby. It's late. I imagine you're in bed. There is no need for any form of repayment. I wanted to do this for you, and I won't be returning the clothes, either. They are yours to do what you will with. I'll have them delivered to you over the weekend. I understand your hesitance, but I'm here if you need me. Always. Sebastian.

I read it a couple of times. *Always*. He had said he felt compelled to look after me, or words to that effect, but I wasn't sure I believed that. You don't just bump into someone and need to pay for them! Although, I didn't feel like a charity case with him. What he'd done and continued to do came from a good place, and like I'd said, I wasn't going to refuse the help I needed.

But did I need the clothes? Yes and no.

Did I need him? I didn't like the answer that immediately popped into my head.

I'm awake. I had a nightmare, my usual one, but you were in the woods this time. You were chasing me, and I didn't know if you meant me harm or not. I kept running towards a house, the one I drew, but I never got there. I made a cup of tea and I'm going

to read, take my mind off it. Thank you for the clothes. I will accept them, I need them. Not so much the party frocks, but they might be nice to play 'dress-up' in sometimes.

I pondered on whether I should send the reply for a few minutes, and then I did. Maybe I'd regret that, perhaps not.

Maybe you need to make your dreams more realistic, achievable. You chasing something and never getting there suggests one of two things. You don't actually want to. Or it's just too far away to grab right now. Small steps, Ruby. You will get your house in the woods one day, but perhaps you need to place something in front of that house. Something smaller, something you can achieve quicker. Seb xx

He'd shortened his name and added two kisses! Perhaps I was overthinking it, since I was an over-thinker, but he had said *something smaller*.

He'd made his name smaller. Was he suggesting that I could get to him quicker than my house in the woods?

I was aware the house in the woods was a metaphor, of course. Not that I'd turn down a house surrounded by countryside. It symbolised my place of peace, of acceptance of my life, I believed.

It was also a place of forgiveness. I needed to forgive myself of my sins to really be able to move on life.

I turned the laptop off so I didn't respond, and drank my tea. I tried to clear my mind of all thoughts of woods and houses and Sebastian. Although that was hard to do. When I settled back down, I must have drifted off pretty quickly. I didn't remember dreaming when I woke the following morning.

———

I hated the weekends more than weekdays. I'd had college to keep me occupied when Grandma was sleeping, which was a lot, or watching her tv shows, which was all the rest of the time. The house was clean, the bed linens washed and ironed. I had a cupboard of clean towels, fluffy and not rough and scratchy for once. All I had to do was bag up the carpet left in the front garden, and maybe I'd start to get some nice winter flower beds going. I wasn't a gardener, but Grandma liked to look out the window and see colour. The grey road and dirty red bricks of the opposite houses weren't very enticing.

Once I had her settled in front of the television, I pulled on my red hoodie. I had a bundle of rubbish sacks and I started to screw the cut-up carpet into them. It wasn't as easy as I thought it would be. Some bags tore, and I swore, getting more annoyed at my stupidity, thinking I was doing the right thing by removing the carpet in small sections. I knew I could call the council and ask them to remove the carpet for a fee, but I wasn't sure they'd do that in a bundle of black sacks.

"Do you need help?" I heard. I didn't need to look to know who had spoken.

"No, I've got this," I said, panting as I stomped on a larger piece of carpet that wouldn't bend.

Sebastian stood by the gate and watched me. I snuck a glance. He wore jeans and a polo shirt; I was sure he should be cold. He sipped from a takeout coffee cup, holding another in his hand. At his feet were the bags of clothes.

"Okay, I'll just watch then," he said, smirking at me.

I continued to fill the bags, double bagging when they split, cursing under my breath, and wiping sweat from my eyes with the cuffs of my sleeves.

When I had the last bag done, I stood, placing my hands on my lower back to stretch it out. "Shit," I said.

Then I finally turned to look at him fully. He held out the cup. "I imagine it's cold now," he said.

I reached out for it; I didn't mind cold coffee. "Why are you here, Sebastian?" I asked, gently.

"Because I might not be *your* reality, but you're mine."

I stared at him, and then gently shook my head. "I don't get it. You could have all the Amelia's in the world.

You're wealthy, good looking, great at... you know. I'm just me, a poor woman trying to make ends meet."

"Oh stop with the *woe is me* crap, Ruby," he said, and his tone startled me. It also pissed me off.

"The what?" I asked.

"Yes, you're trying to make ends meet. We've all been there, but there is nothing *poor* about you. You are courageous, talented, good looking, great at sex, I'll say it for you, and I don't want all the Amelia's of the world."

He hadn't said he wanted me, though, I realised.

"I'm good at sex?" I asked, raising one eyebrow.

"I fought so fucking hard not to come within minutes of being inside you. No one has made me feel like that before."

I looked up and down the street. "Shush, for fuck's sake," I said in an angry whisper.

He laughed. "I'll ask again. Do you need help?"

"You've stood there fucking watching me, Sebastian. It's done now."

"What are you actually doing?"

"I wanted to get the upstairs bedroom ready for redecorating. Remember that part? It hasn't happened."

"You need to get on your landlord."

"Get *on* or *get on to*?"

He winked. "I'll have someone here in the week. Can I come in? It's cold out here."

I sighed; I knew I should have sent him on his way. I smiled and led the way back into the kitchen.

"This is cold," I said, pouring the coffee down the sink. "I'll make a fresh one."

"You need a coffee machine," he replied.

"No, I don't. I have a kettle, that's good enough for me."

I made two coffees and placed the black on in front of him. He looked at it as if I'd just served up dog shit in a mug. He sniffed it and then took a sip.

"Good enough for you, is it?" I asked sarcastically.

"No, not really. But it's hot and wet." He stared at me; his eyes narrowed as he focussed in.

"Don't do that," I said, sipping my coffee and waving my arm.

"Do what, Ruby?"

"Or that."

"Give me a clue here," he asked.

"Don't narrow your eyes, or get all throaty, seductive," I said, stumbling over my words.

"Why?"

"Because I'm not in the mood. This is wrong. I'm too young, remember?"

He slowly shook his head. "And you decided you weren't. You also asked to return to the club because you're curious, remember that?"

I screwed my eyes shut. I had, hadn't I? "Well..." I had no reply, really.

"I have your clothes, and I want to take you out to dinner tonight. I promise that I'll return you back here. There is a great restaurant that has opened, and if it makes you feel any better, I've been invited but I have no one to go with. I don't like to dine on my own."

"Oh, so I'm the fill-in, am I?" I asked, knowing that wasn't what he meant at all.

"I can't win with you, can I?" he replied and sighed.

I slid my hand over, so my fingertips touched his. "I was joking, badly, it seems. If I can get cover, then yes, I'd love to come with you."

"Good. I'll collect you at seven. Now, what else needs doing before I leave?"

"I need help to get the furniture down for the charity to collect," I said, cocking my head and smiling.

"Fuck me, I didn't anticipate manual labour today," he replied, and then winked again. "Come on, can't sit around here drinking coffee."

While I dragged a chest of drawers to the hallway, he took apart the bed. He then moaned at me for dragging the chest of drawers and removed the drawers from their runners. It certainly made it a little lighter.

He took the front end, and I stationed myself at the back, and we carried it down the stairs. We placed it in the front garden, then stacked the bed on top. The wardrobe was the problem.

"Leave that. I'll have someone come tomorrow to get that out," he said.

"Tomorrow is Sunday," I replied.

"And? Every day is a work day if there is work to be done."

When we were done, I walked him to the front gate. He paused and stared at me for a moment. He then raised his hand and placed it on the back of my head. He closed his fist around my hair and pulled my head back. Despite not wanting to respond, I moaned slightly. He leaned down.

"I told you once, you don't get to tell me what to do, and telling me I can't have you is something I'm not familiar with."

"Do I have a choice?" I whispered. His mouth was so close to mine, I felt my words being sucked in with his inhalation.

"Always."

"It doesn't feel like it."

"Look me straight in the eyes and tell me to leave you alone. To never see or contact you again, ever. Your job is safe. You said I wasn't your reality, but then I'm in your dreams. Maybe I'm meant to be. So tell me!"

I stared at him and opened my mouth. I felt his

tongue dart out and lick across my lips. "I'll see you at seven," I replied.

"Good girl. Wear the red dress."

His kiss was fierce and claiming. And I let it happen. Whether he was my reality was something I'd need to figure out another time. When I was with him, I wanted him.

CHAPTER NINE

Milly was sitting with Grandma that evening. I liked her, more importantly, Grandma did. Although she thought Milly was her granddaughter. I bathed, shaved off all unwanted hair, plucked my eyebrows so badly they ended up wonky, and I had to infill with a pencil, and moisturised my whole body. I had the one pair of decent knickers that I put on and then slipped the dress over my head.

As before, I loved it. I loved the way it clung to my body, how it shimmered when I moved. More so, I loved the way it made me feel. I felt way older than my nineteen years... I pulled myself up short. It was my birthday! I was twenty years old that day, no longer a teenager. I fought back a tear, no one would have sent me card anyway. Grandma wouldn't have remembered, of course.

'Shit," I said, annoyed at myself. I didn't do emotion. I rubbed my eyes and then started to apply some makeup.

I hadn't worn makeup in years and what I had was cloggy and old. I used a little concealer and then rubbed it off. I didn't have any blemishes or dark circles to conceal. I swiped some mascara over my lashes and some gloss over my lips. I guessed the one thing I could thank my mother for was good skin. I had a few freckles over my nose that were more pronounced in the summer when I tanned.

I slipped on the red shoes and stared at myself in the full-length mirror. The shoes extended my legs, defined my calf muscles. I was sure I'd turn an ankle and hoped that we didn't have to walk far. I decided I needed a bag and opened a chest to grab one of Grandma's. I'd pop some flip flops in for when the heels became too much. Then I was ready.

I grabbed keys and my phone. Sat with Grandma for a few minutes before I heard the roar of an engine outside. I knew it would be Sebastian without having to look.

"Have a good evening," Milly said, and I kissed Grandma on her forehead.

"You look just like my Ruby," she said, and I thanked her.

There was a knock on the front door, and I took a deep breath before opening it. Sebastian stood there in black trousers and a black shirt. No tie and no jacket.

"You look like a gangster," I said, chuckling.

"And you look amazing, too," he replied.

"Sorry. I'm digging the goth look," I said, waving my hand over his body.

"Get in the car, Ruby," he said with a sigh.

He held open the Ferrari door and I slid in. "What about the seats?" I asked before he closed the door.

"What about them?"

"Won't this scratch the leather?"

"So what if it does?"

He closed the door and I waited until he'd opened his. "You are very much into disposable, aren't you?"

"Huh?" He looked at me as he started the engine.

"You're very... So *what if it does?*"

He frowned at me. "What on earth are you on about now? If the leather gets scratched, then it gets scratched. I don't sweat the small stuff, Ruby."

"A cow died for this," I replied, pushing my luck a little.

"R.I.P that cow. Now's lets go eat steak to make ourselves feel better about its demise."

I giggled at his response. He started to pull away as I was putting on the seatbelt.

"Oh, it's my birthday today," I said, not sure why I wanted him to know.

He slammed on the brakes, and I lurched forward.

"Why didn't you say?"

"I just did. I only just remembered."

"You only just remembered?" He turned to look at me.

"Erm... Well, I shouldn't have said anything. It's not important."

"Of course it's important. It's your birthday. I would have liked to have known."

"Sorry, do you need my menstrual schedule as well?"

"No, there's nothing more erotic than the thought of fucking you while you're bleeding. So if you tell me, I'll get hard and that won't be comfortable."

I held up both hands and shuddered.

"Now, put your seat belt on. We're going to celebrate your birthday."

He pulled away so fast I slammed into the back of the seat. He laughed while I grumbled.

We pulled up outside a swish restaurant with a doorman. It had blacked-out windows, so I couldn't see inside. I couldn't make out the name, either.

"What does that say?" I asked, looking up.

"I have no idea. Apparently, it's a *thing* just to have a symbol."

"No good if someone is googling for it."

I waited until he opened my door, and he held out his hand for me to take. He helped me stand, and I was extra glad. It was hard enough to get out in flats, let alone heels. I stood and looked up at him. I still only came up to his shoulders. He closed the door and locked the car, leaving it on the yellow lines.

"You'll need to hold my hand," I whispered.

"Scared?"

"No, I can't walk in these things," I replied. "And scared. I don't remember the last time I ate out in a place I wasn't working."

He squeezed my hand as we entered.

"Mr. Wolfe," someone said, and a shortish man come running over.

He greeted Sebastian with an enthusiastic handshake. Sebastian didn't look overly amused. "Come. I have a wonderful table for you."

He first led us to one in the middle of the restaurant. I watched as people turned to look and stare at us.

"Somewhere a little more private?" Sebastian asked.

"Of course, sure, sure," came the reply. The man scuttled off in front of us.

We came to a more suitable table along the wall. "This is much better, thank you," Sebastian said.

The man pulled my chair out for me, and I sat, smoothing the sequins as I did. I crossed my ankles, a throwback to when Grandma would correct my posture as a child. I recalled her words.

Una dama nunca cruza las piernas, solo los tobillos, she'd say.

"What's funny?" he asked, taking the seat in front of me.

"I just remembered something my grandma used to say. *A lady never crosses her legs, just her ankles.* She used to get mad at me for slouching."

"A wise woman. I don't want you to cross your legs, either."

I squinted at him. "For posture reasons?"

"No, for accessibility," he said, and then laughed.

I was handed a menu and was glad! I used it to fan my face.

"Would you let me order for you?" he asked. I squinted at him again. "I want you to try things I don't think you would have."

"What if I don't like them?"

"Then you don't like them."

I placed the menu down on the table. "Okay."

He smiled. "It pleases me that you trust me, Ruby."

"Well, I'm super glad about that." I reminded myself I needed to lower the sarcasm notch just a little.

A waitress came by, and he ordered a bottle of white

wine. He looked at me as he did and I nodded, pleased to have been included in at least what I drank. He also asked for a bottle of mineral water.

"I do wish I'd known it was your birthday," he said.

"Why? What does it matter? I don't think I've ever celebrated a birthday. I only know the date because I have to renew my passport and visa," I replied.

"Visa?"

"Oh, I wasn't born here. I have dual nationality, though, and can work here. My mother was English, and my father was Spanish."

"What happened to your parents?"

A shiver rolled over me. I shrugged my shoulders and looked around the room. He reached forward and covered one of my hands. "Sorry, I shouldn't have asked."

I smiled and nodded my thanks.

"We're very much the same, Ruby. Cut from the same cloth, just a decade apart." He chuckled and I joined in.

"Does it bother you? I mean, people do think I'm your daughter?" I asked.

"No, I don't care what people think, only what they do."

"It's a defence mechanism, isn't it?" I added, quietly.

He was stopped from answering by the return of the waitress. She poured a small amount of wine into his glass, and he tasted. He kept his gaze on me while he sipped. Then he simply nodded. She half filled my glass, then his, before returning the bottle to an ice bucket.

"Shall I pour the water?" she asked.

"No, leave it there," he replied. No please or thank you offered. "What?"

"You are rude sometimes," I said, chuckling.

"Says Miss-fucking-Rudeness personified." I laughed and he smiled. "Yes, sometimes I am. I don't mean to be. I'm a demanding man, I guess."

"I guess we are cut from the same cloth in that regard."

"What do you demand, Ruby?" he asked, lowering his voice.

"Honesty and loyalty, nothing more."

"That's the least you should expect, isn't it?" he asked.

"If I don't *expect*, then I can't be let down," I replied. "What about you?"

"The same, I guess. Honesty is important to me, but I also understand some secrets can't be told."

"Are you a one-woman man, Sebastian?" My voice had lowered.

"Yes... And no. It depends."

"On what?"

"On who I'm with and what the *relationship* is. Not every relationship I've had requires monogamy."

"What do you do for fun?" I asked, changing the subject as the image of Amelia sprung to mind.

"Fun? Mmm. I drive fast cars, sometimes around a track. I fuck, I like doing that," he said, starting to rub his chin as if thinking. "I read."

I wasn't expecting that one. "You read? What?"

"Books, Ruby. You should try it. It's therapeutic."

"I didn't see any books in your house."

"You saw a hallway and bedroom, that's all. Perhaps we'll have a tour after..."

I raised my eyebrows. "You said you'd take me home."

"And I will, if that's what you want."

The waitress took his order, he didn't consult the menu once and I wanted to heave at his suggestion of oysters. "Try everything once," he said, noticing the look on my face.

"What have you not tried, then?" I asked, leaning forward on the table.

"Lots of things, but this isn't about me," he replied. He moved closer, his body position mirroring mine.

"Okay, I'll try," I said, lowering my voice.

"Good girl," he whispered.

"I like it when you say that," I whispered back.

"If it wasn't for your sarcasm, you'd make a good submissive," he replied, probably a little louder than I would have liked.

I chuckled as the couple on the table next to us looked aghast.

"What *is* a submissive? Like, what do you do to them?"

"You are curious, aren't you?"

"Yes. But don't get the wrong idea, I don't want to be one."

"So, what *is* a submissive? In real general terms here, because it's not a straight forward answer, but it's a person who wants to be led, guided, told what to do. A sub is someone who obeys."

"What do they get out of it?"

"Sexual pleasure. There are people that live a sub and Dom lifestyle, I don't. And there are people that like to take on those roles for their sexual pleasure. You got pleasure from being spanked, didn't you?"

Wide-eyed, I looked around. Thankfully, no one had heard that comment.

"But I bet you also got pleasure from the anticipation. You ran when you knew you'd earned three strikes, yet no one had told you what that specifically meant. For some, the anticipation of what comes if they don't obey is the ultimate thrill. That's where you'd fit in."

"And for you?" I asked, becoming slightly breathless.

"I like the power. I like to know that I am pleasing you in every way you desire without even knowing what it is that you want. I get pleasure from you doing what I ask of you."

"Are there any books that you've read that would explain it to me?"

"Perhaps, I'll have a look."

"I think we need to also change the subject," I said, laughing, and waving my hand in front of my face to cool me down.

"Exploring your sexuality, your desires and wants, is what you should be doing, Ruby," he said, then sat back.

"Well, right now, I'm going to either explore the inside of the toilet bowl or hump your leg. The oysters are on the way."

His laughter was not only infectious but caused all the surrounding tables to look over and smile.

The waitress placed a metal stand in the middle of the table. She then laid a silver salver full of seafood on top. Some looked delicious, others, not so. We had a large finger bowl to share and extra napkins.

"There's something special about eating with your hands," Sebastian said.

"Mmm, says the man who didn't have to scrape around the floor for food, I bet. I'll have the luxury of a fork if that's okay."

"I told you before, don't judge me. You don't know what I've gone through myself."

Suitably chastised, I nodded my head by way of an

apology. "So, how do I do this?" I asked, picking up an oyster.

He gave me a choice of items to add to the oyster, I chose red wine vinegar. He then ate one himself. Well, I say ate, he tipped it down his throat.

"So you don't actually *eat* them?"

"Sort of. Just put it in your mouth, let it sit there for a moment, then decide to chew or swallow."

"Sounds rude," I replied, but then did as instructed.

I wasn't sure at first. I think it was the texture, a snotty like substance that sat on my tongue. Until the taste kicked in. I chewed and then swallowed.

"Wow. It's like... It's like fresh seaside air. Salty, but not like the sea."

It was hard to articulate, but I wanted another.

"Wait," he said, and then stood. He moved his chair, so he was beside me, not opposite.

He picked up an oyster and dressed it. He then held my chin, tilting my head up. "Open," he said, quietly.

I closed my eyes and opened my mouth. He poured the oyster in. Before I could close my mouth, his lips covered mine. His tongue joined mine and he kissed me while I swallowed.

"Wow," I said, when he pulled away.

He smirked at me. "More?"

"Oh yeah." I nodded.

I ate another two oysters, opting to leave him at least

one. And then we moved on to the clams and crab. He cracked the shell of the crab and dug out the flesh with his fingers. He offered those to my lips, and I sucked them in. He fed me the clams and licked the juice that ran down my chin.

"People are going to talk," I whispered.

"Let them."

"You're quite the exhibitionist, aren't you?"

"Not normally," he replied, chuckling.

With our starters finished, he moved back to his original place. I'd rather he stayed put but didn't tell him so.

The second course was a delicate white fish, samphire, and spinach, with crushed potatoes.

"I thought we were getting the cow," I said, looking at the plate.

"If you want cow we can order it," he said.

"I'm kidding. This looks good."

As we ate, he told me a little about his businesses.

"I worked three, four jobs, and I was homeless. I saved as much money as I could until I could get into a hostel. I fucking hated it there. Drug addicts, drunks, paedophiles praying on kids."

He paused, taking in a deep breath, the memory obviously painful.

"Anyway, I worked day and night, did whatever I could, sometimes not even legal, to get money. Eventually, I had enough to put down a deposit on a rundown house, but I knew I'd never get a mortgage. Then I met my benefactor. A man called Simon Morton. A successful man who offered me a way out. He backed me, he funded the renovation of the house and I did all the work; I went to night school to learn how to build things and called in contractors when I couldn't do it. Eventually, I had a house that I sold. I paid him back with interest. I didn't make a lot of money, but I learned a great deal."

"What happened next?" I asked.

We ate and talked. He told me that Simon then funded the next project, and the one after that, until he'd sold a property for such a profit, he no longer need Simon's money.

"Sadly, he died, a few years ago now. By then I owned five, could have been six, properties I rented out. He left me some money, but I gave it all to charity. He also left me a letter. He told me that one day, when I found the right person, I was to do the same. I had the ability to change a life, like he had done for me."

"Is that me?" I asked.

"No, there were others that came before you. You, Ruby, you're different. I don't want to help you because I feel I ought to, because that's what Simon would expect of me. I want to do it for very different reasons."

"What reasons?"

"Another time. Now I want to know about you."

"There isn't much to tell. My mum died, she was a drug addict and alcoholic but I loved her. My dad sold our house and fucked off with the money."

"See, cut from the same cloth."

"What about your parents?" I asked.

"I don't remember them. I was in care for most of my childhood."

"Have you ever been curious about them?"

He sighed. "Not really. I've got this far without them."

"What about marriage, kids?"

"I thought we were talking about you?"

He had finished eating and laid his cutlery down to top up our wine.

"I think I'd like to get married, but that's probably more about stability. I'm not sure on kids, though," I said, honestly. "Maybe we've both seen the worst of society. Why on earth would we bring children into that?"

I saw the flinch, the rapid blink, and knew I'd said the wrong thing.

It was fleeting, though. He raised his glass to me and smiled. "To curiosity," he said.

I wonder if sex was where he felt the most comfortable, where he felt safe, which was why he brought it all back there when things got awkward.

With the table cleared, we opted for coffee instead

of dessert. I didn't think I could fit another thing in my stomach,

"You can dance it off later," he said.

"What do you mean?"

"It's your birthday, the evening isn't over yet."

"I don't do clubbing, if that's what you mean. More so in these shoes. If I dance, I'll kill myself," I said, laughing.

We asked for the bill and didn't look at it, he just laid his credit card on top. While I finished my coffee, he paid.

"Come," he said, holding out his hand. Once again, we were watched as we left the restaurant.

His car was where he'd left it, and without a ticket. "See, gangster. Only the mob would get away with no parking tickets," I said as he opened the door.

"We don't use that term in the UK, Ruby," he replied, then slammed the door before I could respond.

I was still straightening my dress and buckling up when he started the car and pulled out into the traffic. It was heavy, thankfully, so there was no roaring around. He drove for about ten minutes, until we pulled into a familiar alley.

"I thought..." I wasn't sure what I thought, but I hadn't expected that.

"Trust me."

He left the car, opened my door, and we walked in.

Instead of climbing the stairs, we headed through another door, one I hadn't noticed before.

Music blasted, the floor throbbed with the beat, and people danced. It was my worst nightmare. I clung to his side, burying my face in his arm. I didn't do crowds.

"It's okay, just walk with me," he said. I scuttled along beside him.

In my peripheral vision, I saw a lift. It opened and we stepped in. Only when the doors shut did I look up and take in a deep breath.

"I told you, I don't do clubbing," I said.

"And we're not."

The lift took seconds to open to a mezzanine floor. There were floor to ceiling glass panels, which deadened the noise. I could look down on the club below, but not have that throb in my chest from the speakers. However, there was a small dancefloor, a bar, sofas, and booths. And there were people, but ones much older than the teens downstairs. It was a club, but way more refined. Sebastian unhooked a red rope and ushed me in. It led to a private booth. A waiter came immediately and placed water, soft drinks, a bottle of whiskey, and wine on the side next to a large bucket of ice and glasses. He left us to help ourselves.

"This is much better," I said, running my hand over the smooth velvet of the couch.

"I want to watch you dance," he said, and his voice had taken on that husky tone.

"What if I can't? That would be a let-down," I chuckled while also feeling extremely self-conscious.

"Then sway. Move. Do something. I want to watch you in that dress."

"What about other people?"

"They'll be leaving soon."

"You're going to chuck them out just so you can ogle me?"

"No, they will voluntarily leave to head upstairs. It's what they do."

I glanced around. "Everyone looks... normal," I said, leaning close to him.

"What did you expect them to look like? I believe you saw some of them naked just the other day."

"Oh, fuck," I replied, lowering my gaze so as not to catch anyone's eye.

"Drink," he said, and he handed me a glass of wine. He poured himself a whiskey.

As predicted, people started to leave. It wasn't a mad rush, some stood and walked away, others finished their drinks. Sebastian called over the waiter.

"Music, then shut this place down. I want some privacy. You can head upstairs or take an early night."

"Of course, Mr. Wolfe."

He left and started to turn off the main lights. It left

just a subtle glow from the booths. Music drifted around the room. It wasn't the thump thump of club sounds, but the kind one could sway their body to.

Sebastian stood. "Dance for me," he said, holding out his hand.

I chuckled nervously. I didn't dance. Well, I could, but not brilliantly I didn't think. But I could move my body in a way he'd like. I'd auditioned to cage dance at the club I cleaned but had backed out at the last minute. My nerves just wouldn't let me, despite the money I could have earned. He took my hand and led me to the middle of the floor.

He didn't leave, initially. He wrapped his arms around me and nuzzled into my neck. We swayed from side to side, he placed his leg between mine. He ran one hand up and down my bare back, causing the hairs to stand on end and me to shiver.

We danced for a couple of songs until the tempo changed. He then stood back. He watched me for a few seconds, then walked to the edge of the dance floor. He pulled a chair over and sat.

I had danced on my own, normally when I was hoovering, but that was a shake of the butt type dance. However, with Sebastian watching me, I wanted to dance. I wanted to move my body in such a way it aroused him. I was doing what he asked of me, what his sub would do. I was obeying, but, and I smiled at the thought, it was I who held the power. I could make it good, or not.

I chose good.

I lost myself in the music. I closed my eyes and kicked off my shoes. I danced like I hadn't danced before, just moving in time with the music. I sang the words I knew. I felt him behind me, his hands on my hips and his breath on my shoulder. I leaned back into him, and we swayed together. He slid his hands up to my waist, dragging my dress with them. I didn't care.

I had zoned into a place I hadn't ventured before. It was just about me, feeling the music. It was just about him, feeling me.

He moved my hair over one shoulder and kissed the other. I could feel his erection through his trousers pressing into the small of my back. I wished I'd kept the shoes on, I would have felt him against my arse. I reached behind me, placing one hand on his cheek, he turned and kissed my palm. I wanted more.

I turned in his arms and placed my hand on his chest. I stared at him, not saying a word as I walked him back to the chair and he sat. I slid my knickers down and stepped out of them, I then straddled his lap.

While he fumbled with his zipper, I held his face and kissed his lips. I took what I wanted, what I needed, and I felt no shame about it.

When his cock was free, I lowered. The sigh that

left my body was one of full contentment. I felt full and for a moment, I sat still. When I moved, it was slow. I wanted to feel him at my very core, deep and hot. He held my hips and stared at me. He didn't blink, neither did I. His lips parted and ran his tongue over his lower one. I wanted to suck that tongue into my mouth. Instead, I kissed his neck, I trailed my tongue up to his earlobe and gently bit. When he moaned, I moved faster, slamming myself down on him harder and harder. I kissed his throat when he threw his head back. I bit his skin as he had done mine, leaving a mark. He grabbed my arse, digging his fingers into my flesh, bruising me, and then he stood. It took me by surprise at first. I wrapped my legs around his waist. Still inside me, he walked to the glass panel. He fucked me against it.

I had no idea if anyone could see us, and I didn't care. In that moment, nothing mattered but him, but us.

He slammed me so hard I worried the glass might give way. My dress scratched against it. Sweat beaded on his forehead and ran down his temple. I licked it away while he groaned more.

I was desperate to come and by the way he bit down hard on his lower lip, so was he. He tried to pull out, I tightened my legs around him. I needed to feel him pulse inside me, give me all he could.

When he came, he growled out my name. It was the most erotic sound I'd heard. He lived up to his name. He bared his teeth, he narrowed his eyes, and while he pumped inside me, he sunk those teeth into my shoulder.

I couldn't catch my breath, and when I lowered my legs, they shook. I buried my face into his chest, his shirt damp with his exertion.

"Ruby," he said, gently, but with a husky tone.

I shook my head. I didn't want to look up. I wanted to stay where I was.

He stepped back a little and I felt his fingertips under my chin. He lifted my face. A tear left one eye and he kissed it away.

"That was amazing," he whispered.

I smiled gently and nodded. I didn't think I'd find my voice for a while.

He tucked his cock back into his trousers and then pulled me to his chest again. He just held me, and I felt his come start to seep out.

"I need to clean up," I said, and chuckled.

He stepped back and I crossed my legs. He laughed. "Wait here," he said.

"I'm not sure I can go anywhere right now," I replied, also with a husky voice.

He headed to the bar and returned with a wad of napkins. "Crass, but all I could find."

He stood staring at me. "Turn around," I said.

He still stared at me. "Are you kidding me?" he

asked. He snatched the wad from my hand and shoved them between my thighs. He cleaned me and I held on to his arms.

He returned the wad to the bar and deposited it in the bin. I walked over to where I'd left my underwear and shoes. I slipped them all on.

When he returned, he cupped my cheeks with his hands. "*You* are amazing," he said.

"Did anyone see us?" I asked.

He shook his head. "One way glass."

I closed my eyes and sighed with relief. "I didn't think we were going to do this."

"All I promised you, Ruby, was that I'd take you home. I didn't make any mention of not fucking you. But, in this instance, I think it's you who fucked me."

I giggled. "I do need to go home, though."

We walked in silence back down to the car. It was a cold night and I shivered while he opened the door. I was grateful that the engine produced enough heat almost instantly to take off the chill. Too soon, we were outside my house. I could see that Grandma's side light was on, she'd been put to bed. That pang of guilt washed over me.

"Don't over think it, Ruby," he said, quietly.

I nodded. "Thank you for a wonderful birthday. It's probably the best I've ever had."

He didn't speak and I missed him when he left the

car. He walked me to the door but declined my offer of coffee.

"I think we need some space, don't we?" he whispered, and I nodded. "Although soon, I want you for the whole night, Ruby. I want to fall sleep beside you, wake up next to you."

Tears filled my eyes knowing how unlikely that was to happen. But I nodded anyway. It would be a nice dream to have.

He kissed me gently on the lips and wished me a good night. I stepped inside and closed the door.

I walked into the living room and gently woke Milly. She had dozed off in her chair. She apologised profusely; I waved that apology away. It was okay to doze, I told her. She collected her bag and left.

Alone, all I could do was think. I could smell his aftershave on me. I could feel his come still on my thighs. I felt the sting where he'd marked me. I headed for the bathroom. I needed a bath to calm me, hot water to soothe me. And then I needed the sleep of the dead. Exhaustion had washed over me.

———

Sunday was uneventful initially. That was until lunchtime. I heard a knock on the door and opened it to see a beautiful bouquet of flowers. I took the flowers into the kitchen and opened the card.

Happy belated birthday, Ruby. Thank you for last night. I won't see you today, but I wanted to wish you good luck for tomorrow. I will call tonight, if that's okay. Seb xx

Again, that shortening of his name and two kisses. I didn't think I could call him Seb; he was a Sebastian to me. He was too full on for a nickname.

The temptation to call him or text was strong, but I waited until he called me, as he'd said. I wondered if there was a reason he couldn't see me, yet I appreciated that. Time spent with him was intense and when he'd said we needed some space, I'd agreed wholeheartedly. I also had to consider that we'd had unprotected sex. I was on the pill, which is why I didn't care that we had no condom. I also believed him to be healthy, but it wasn't a conversation I was comfortable having yet knew I'd have to.

Sebastian called me that evening. I had been in bed for about an hour just reading a book I'd found on a bus some time ago.

"Hi," he said, when I answered.

"Hey, how are you?" I asked.

"Lonely, how about you."

I chuckled, assuming he was joking. "In bed. How about you read a book, that's what I'm doing."

"How about you read to me," he replied.

"I can't, it's rude."

"Even better," he said.

I giggled. "I'm too embarrassed."

"Then I'll read to you. Wait there."

I heard a rustling, movement, and then he was back on the line. "Let me tell you about Little Red Riding Hood," he said.

His voice was seductive, for sure. He wasn't talking about a little girl in a red cloak, but a woman in a red dress and high heels. She was walking through the woods to Grandma's cottage, and she heard him whispering to her. He told me what the whispers were.

I shivered as he detailed all the things we'd done sexually, and all the things he wanted to do, I guessed. Little Red Riding Hood was desperate to get to the cottage because she knew that was where the big bad Mr. Wolfe is.

I closed my eyes and listened.

"She's desperate to get to him, Ruby," he said.

I slid my hand down my stomach and under my knickers. I could feel my wetness as I slid my fingers across my opening.

"Tell me more," I asked breathlessly.

He told me what happens when Little Red Riding Hood gets to the cottage. How he first undresses her, sliding the red dress over her head and she's standing naked in just the heels. He circles her, licking his lips, deciding what part of her body he wants to ravish first.

I moaned and slid two fingers inside me.

He detailed how he licks over her body, lowering himself to his knees before devouring her pussy. How he loves the taste of her, and how he intends to claim her as his.

I could feel my stomach tighten as my orgasm built.

Sebastian then told me how the big bad Mr. Wolfe fucks Little Red Riding Hood. And I came.

I moaned and called out his name. My cheeks flamed with heat and embarrassment. I'd never had phone sex before.

I sighed as I came back down to earth and turned on my side. He chuckled, gently.

"Was that good?" he asked.

"Yes. It's the first time I've made myself come," I confessed.

"I'd like to think I had a little part in that," he replied, chuckling.

"You had a big part in it. I wish you were here."

"I can be."

I shook my head. "No, I think I need to sleep now."

"I need to work. Sweet dreams, Little Red Riding Hood," he said, and then disconnected the call.

That night I did dream, but there was nothing sweet about them. It was him in the woods, calling me, and my panic wasn't because I was trying to run away, but I was trying to run to him. It was him that was just out of reach, not the cottage. I ran while wearing the red dress and heels. I didn't fall once. I just never quite got to him.

I woke more frustrated than ever.

CHAPTER TEN

Monica was downstairs when I woke. I could hear her clattering around in the kitchen preparing Grandma's breakfast. I grabbed my phone and cursed, yet again, that I couldn't see the time. I reached for my alarm clock and then sighed. It was okay, there was still five minutes before it would go off. I switched it off and climbed from the bed.

"You're early?" I called down.

"I know, sorry, did I wake you? I was up with the larks so thought I'd get here early. Then you can just concentrate on getting ready for your first day. I bought some pastries as a treat."

I laughed. "I love you, you know that, right?"

I headed to the bathroom and ran the bath. I piled my hair on top of my head, there wasn't the time to wash and dry it, that shit took an hour. As I washed, I recalled the previous evening's conversation with Sebastian. I had no idea what was going on between us. The sex was amazing, and, yes, he'd taken me for dinner, but it wasn't a relationship, I didn't think. He was a lot older than me. Could we even have a relationship with that age gap?

I dried and dressed in some of the clothes Sebastian had bought. I felt smart, for once. I'd spent too many years in shabby second-hand clothes. I didn't bother with make-up other than some mascara, and then headed downstairs.

"Wow, look at you. Give us a twirl," Monica said.

I laughed, holding my arms out, and turned on the spot.

"You look so different. So... grown up, even though you are one."

"Why, thank you," I replied, bowing. I picked up Grandma's handbag and emptied it of the flip flops. I'd use it as a lunch bag as well. "I should buy a flask or a water bottle."

"I'm sure you can get coffee and water in the office," she replied.

I sat and accepted the cup of tea she offered, nibbling on one of the pastries while she tended to Grandma. My stomach was a flutter of nerves. I wasn't the confident person some thought me to be, which is probably why I covered that up with sarcasm. I looked at my bitten nails, ones that had never been painted. I started to worry that I would stand out as the charity case. Then I remembered the ex-cons and the alcoholics. I imagined they would have felt the same on their first day as well.

I made a sandwich and placed that in my bag with my phone. I'd buy a new phone with my first pay packet, I vowed. I then sat with Grandma for ten minutes. She wasn't in a happy mood, so Monica ushered me out. It was best sometimes, that I left the room. Not for Grandma, but for myself. I found it hard, I was finding it harder, to cope when Grandma wasn't good. She was also lashing out at me more frequently. On their last visit, Social Services had encouraged me to think about putting her in a home. I wasn't sure I was ready for that.

"I'm off now," I called out, and after received good lucks from Monica, I left the house.

It was a half hour walk to the office, which I didn't mind. Thankfully, it wasn't raining, but I did pull my red coat tightly around me. There was a chill that suggested we might have bad weather on the way. Maybe I'd invest in an umbrella as well.

I arrived at the office twenty minutes before I was due to start. I was greeted at reception by name, which was a surprise and asked to sign in. I was told I'd be given my security badges at some point during the day and would I mind standing for a photograph.

I posed against a white wall, unsmiling as instructed. Two headshots were taken, and I was given a look to approve. They were headshots for a security card, I didn't think I'd need to approve them.

"Yes, they're fine," I said.

"You'd be amazed how many I have to retake sometimes," Sally, the receptionist, said.

She had told me she'd worked on reception for three years now. She was chatty and bubbly, the perfect type for her role. But she was too happy for my liking. I was always wary of people that were nice. I guessed I was always waiting for the catch.

"If you want to have lunch together, just let me know," she added, and then walked me to the lift.

"Second floor," she said, when it arrived.

I nodded my thanks. I had remembered where to go from my interview.

My nerves got worse the closer to the floor I got. When the doors opened, my hands visibly shook. I took in a deep breath to steady myself.

"Ruby, hi, you're here," I heard. I looked over to see Amelia. She smiled and walked towards me. "You're working with me to start with. Is that okay with you?"

I nodded. It was awkward and I tried to look at nothing but her face. Not that she was naked, of course.

"Let's go get a coffee, shall we?"

I thought that meant we'd head to a kitchen, instead we took the lift back down and walked the short distance to a coffee house.

"Elephant in the room, and all that," she said, after we sat.

I laughed and sighed. "I thought I'd feel awkward, but I don't now."

"Good. We can work well together. We can play together if you want to," she replied, and I really wasn't sure what she meant. "Mr. Wolfe and I have a professional working relationship; I want you to know that. What goes on outside the office always stays outside the office."

"Do other people know about... You two?"

She reached over and placed her hand over mine. "There isn't a *you two*. I want you to understand that. You're free to have any kind of relationship with him you want."

"I'm not sure we have a relationship," I replied, and laughed, not that it was funny.

"He seems to think so. And others do, too. There are some in the business that frequent the club as well."

"I don't know what he thinks, to be honest. But I'm not a sub, or whatever. He might need you for that." Again, I laughed, but it was more from uncomfortableness than anything else. I certainly wasn't up for a threesome or sharing, not that I believed I had him to share in the first place.

"He'll only ever do what you give him permission to do."

She sat back and sipped on her coffee.

"I don't understand that. Aren't you the one that must obey and all that."

She laughed, she did think my comment funny, I guessed. "Oh, Ruby. You've a lot of learn. We have all the power. We decide what we will tolerate or not. We set the rules. We allow them to be dominant."

"I don't know that I get any of that. I'm not sure I want to."

I just wanted to get on with my life in as uncomplicated manner as possible. However, I was starting to believe that wasn't going to be possible. I smiled and shook my head. "I'm still coming to terms with what I've fallen into, to be honest."

"He's enigmatic, isn't he?"

"And mysterious," I added.

"That's addictive," she said.

I worried, then. What if he didn't want her anymore because of me, and she was addicted to him?

Somewhere in my head, I told myself to stop doing my usual and overthinking.

"So, work," I said, needing to bring the conversation back to my level.

We finished our coffee and walked back to the office. As we crossed reception, Sebastian exited the lift. He was with another suited man. He stopped and smiled at us.

"My two favourite women," he said. I bristled, but Amelia bowed her head.

He stared at me; I glared back. He raised his middle finger and rubbed beside his eye. Slowly, I smiled.

He left, chatting to the man beside him.

"Phew," Amelia said, fanning her face.

I raised my eyebrows. "What stays outside and all that?" I reminded her.

"Not him, the other one. Now, he's hot."

I laughed as she linked her arm in mine. "Let's try and find out who he is," she added.

"No, let's not. Let's go get work done before I get fired before I've even started."

———

The first project, as I thought, was the nightclub. Amelia and I went upstairs to Sebastian's floor and sat at the desk with the mock-up. I detailed some of my ideas and she readily agreed. She was an architect by qualification, and like me, preferred to design the interior layout than the outside.

We took what we needed back to our floor, and she

gave me a station next to hers. I had a desk, a drawing board, a laptop that I could take home, and a mobile phone. It was the latest iPhone that would sync with the laptop so I could work on either. I placed my bag on the desk.

"Wow, that's a vintage Dior, isn't it?" she said, picking up the bag.

"No idea. It's one of many that my grandma owns. She has a trunk of designer dresses from the forties and fifties. I sold some to a brilliant retro shop."

She looked aghast. "You have no idea what this is worth, do you?"

I shook my head. "This bag would probably cost around ten thousand pounds to buy."

"No way!" I took the bag from her and studied it. "She has loads of these!"

If only I'd bloody known, we might not have struggled so much. I chuckled and placed it on the floor. Perhaps I'd take better care of them now I knew.

Amelia left me to redesign the downstairs. I felt she was better placed on the upstairs than I was.

Mike came over to check on me a couple of times and asked to meet me at the end of the day. I was so engrossed in what I was doing that I hadn't noticed the time.

"Lunch?" I heard as Sally walked across the room. I

hadn't wanted to have lunch with her, but felt I couldn't say no.

"Erm, okay. I've bought a sandwich."

"Great, so have I. We can sit in the park for a half hour."

I picked up my bag and we left together. We grabbed a coffee from a vendor and crossed the busy road into the park. It was actually nice to get out and although it was chilly, it was refreshing.

"I like to come and sit here during the day. Gives me a break from the lighting," she said.

"The lighting?"

"Yeah, you have... What are they called? Those daylight bulbs. I don't have that downstairs. The light flickers sometimes and it gives me a headache."

"Have you reported it?" I asked.

She shook her head as she took a bite of her lunch. "I will do, when I get round to it."

She told me she lived in a basement apartment, shared it with her brother who also worked at the company. It seemed they could only afford the apartment in London if they shared. The more she talked, the more I liked her. She asked me a few questions about my life, and I found it hard to respond. I gave only the basics. She didn't give the usual, *oh I'm so sorry,* that always infuriated me. She simply nodded and listened.

"We ought to get back," I said, noticing we'd been sitting for a half an hour.

We had one hour for lunch break, but I didn't feel I could sit outside for that length of time. We wandered in and went our separate ways. I travelled up in the lift on my own. I was smiling when I returned to my desk. There was a note left informing me that I had emails to address. I didn't recognise the writing, obviously. I turned on the laptop. I saw a notification that I had emails and I clicked on it. I was immediately taken to the company's internal email server.

Good morning, Ruby. Please take note of your company email address.

It wasn't signed by anyone, and I assumed it was automated. It was followed by one from Mike that detailed my course with start dates.

A third was from HR, wanting a stack of personal information that I replied with.

I sat back, smiling. I had a company email address! Maybe at some point, I'd get business cards as well.

I had a look through the computer. There was a bespoke client programme that needed a password I didn't have. I assumed that would be something Mike would tell me if I needed to know.

I went back to my drawing board and sketched. By the time I noticed people leaving, I had half the downstairs done. Amelia wandered over.

"Wow, Ruby. That's fantastic," she said. "I wish I could draw as well as that."

"Erm, thank you. I don't know if it's what you wanted or not," I said, feeling uncomfortable taking the compliment.

"It's exactly what I wanted. I hadn't thought about that bathroom concept. That will set us apart from other clubs. And the medical room!"

I explained that, although there would be some loss of space from the dancing area, the DJ booth could be made a little smaller and some of the booths lost. I hadn't realised, however, that the booths made a ton of money. They had to be booked in advance at a minimum of two-hundred and fifty pounds per person, plus a minimum bar spend.

I agreed to work on replacing them somewhere else.

"I think Mike wants you. I'm off now, so I'll see you tomorrow. It's great to have you here, Ruby," she said, and smiled warmly at me.

I closed the laptop and headed over to Mike's office. I knocked and waited for him to call me in. When he did, I opened the door and then came to a halt. Sebastian was sitting with Mike. I hadn't noticed him come onto the floor at all.

"Hi, you wanted to see me?" I asked.

"Yes, take a seat," he said. Sebastian said nothing but lounged on a sofa against the wall.

I looked at him and then immediately back at Mike.

"How was your first day?" he asked.

"Great. I like working with Amelia. We agreed to split the club, I'd do downstairs."

"Was there a reason for that choice?" I heard. I looked over to Sebastian who smirked at me.

"Yes, I felt she'd have better knowledge of upstairs than I would," I answered sternly. He had said he didn't care who knew about him and her, after all.

He chuckled. "Right answer."

I turned back to Mike. "I replied to the email from HR, and I noticed a client programme. Is that something I need access to?"

Mike slid over a small booklet. "Company rule book, and all the passwords you need. You're right, all the clients are on there. You need to input a name and project number; the client will come up and it's important that anything you do is noted on there. We charge by the hour or part of. So if you take a call, note it down."

I nodded. "Who is the client for the club project?"

"I am," Sebastian replied.

"Is your name and project number in the system?"

"Of course. So be sure to add what you've done today."

I nodded.

"It might help to print out the course details, you

have a couple of months before you need to start. I didn't think it wise to have you start mid-course, so you'll be joining in January. You'll be there Monday and Tuesday, here for the rest of the week. I understand you have suitable cover at home, but remember, Ruby. If anything happens, we do employ a work from home policy here. You should remember to take your laptop home with you."

"And set up the new phone. We don't want you being late anywhere," Sebastian added.

"Laptop, check. Phone, check." I laughed as I spoke.

"Amelia is extremely impressed with your drawing skills, and she's one of our best. I think you're going to do very well here, Ruby," Mike said.

"I hope so. I want to do well. You've... both given me an amazing opportunity."

Sebastian stood and as he did, he buttoned up his jacket. "I'll run you home, Ruby."

"I can walk. It's a half hour, that's all."

"It's pissing down outside," he replied.

I looked through the window to see dark clouds rolling in.

"What's the time, Mr...." I stopped when I got to his name.

"It's nearly six. You really do need a watch," Mike said, laughing.

"Blimey, I lost track of time."

"See you tomorrow," Mike said.

I stood and followed Sebastian from the office. I collected my bag and the laptop and hurried after him.

He was silent in the lift going down and I wondered why. He strode across the reception and to the door that took us down to the parking area.

"Slow down, will you?" I asked, sternly.

"Ah, yes, little legs," he said, smirking.

"Not so little they can't—"

He paused on the last flight of stairs.

"They can't, what, Ruby?"

"Nothing, a poorly timed joke."

He stepped up one step, so we were face to face.

"Wrap around my waist? Is that what you were going to say?"

I blushed and blinked rapidly. "Erm, no. I was going to say run away from you if I had to."

"Liar." He ran his fingers down my cheek.

I chuckled. "Yes, okay. I'm a liar."

"I don't like lies, Ruby." He used two fingers to stroke beside his eye and I swallowed hard.

I nodded. My heart started to race but before I could gather my next thought, he turned and continued down. I all but slumped against the wall.

"What the fuck?" I whispered. He paused, but then continued.

I followed him into the car park and over to where he'd parked his car. I hated empty car parks at the best of times, and just following behind him was giving me the shivers.

"I could get murdered back here and you'd never bloody know," I said, my voice echoing around the cavernous space.

"I highly doubt you'd be quiet if anyone tried, Ruby," he replied.

"What if they covered my mouth first? Huh?"

"Then someone would see you and call me."

"Oh, that's okay then. I'd be dead, but at least someone called you."

He chuckled and stopped. I stopped still a little distance away.

"Well?" he said.

"What?"

"I'm waiting for you to catch up."

"Oh." I started to walk again.

He opened the passenger door, and I slid in, smiling sweetly at him as I did.

He rolled his eyes and sighed.

When he got in, he sat for just a minute. Then he turned to me. "Did you have a good first day?"

"I did, thank you. I'm going to love it there." I was honest with my answer. "Although, what do you think Amelia meant when she said we could play together?"

He blinked rapidly; his eyebrows shot up. "She said, what?"

"Something like, we can work well together, or play together. I can't remember the exact words."

He didn't reply for a moment.

"Oh!" I said, as it dawned on me. "OH!"

He then leaned forward. "I don't share, Ruby," he said.

"Oh fuck, or not fuck, actually. Jesus. What do you mean?"

"Exactly what I said. You're mine. I don't share you with anyone."

"I'm...?" My head was spinning. What the fuck was he on about?

"OH!" I said, realising exactly what he meant.

He pressed the start button, and the sound was deafening. We roared from the garage. He didn't drive me home, though. He hit the motorway and cursed repeatedly at the level of traffic.

"Erm, you're going the wrong way," I said, pointing out the passenger window.

"I know where the fuck I'm going," he snapped back.

I wanted to giggle. But then remembered I was on two strikes already. I clamped my mouth shut, sucking in my lips, and then covering them with both hands.

He glanced at me, angrily. I closed my eyes tightly. I

wanted to laugh and knew it would be the exact wrong time to do so.

Instead, he weaved in and out of the traffic until he had a clear run ahead and put his foot down.

We whizzed past signposts, and I had no idea where we were. By the time he slowed, tears were leaking from my eyes.

"Let it the fuck out," he snapped.

I looked at him and shook my head rapidly.

He sighed. "Let it out Ruby," he repeated, a little gentler.

I laughed. I squashed my hands into my lap, so I didn't pee on his leather seats, and laughed hard.

It was a laugh of hilarity and partly astonishment. When embarrassed, I laughed. When on the back foot or scared, I sometimes laughed. I think, what was bursting from me was a combination of them all.

He slowed the car, and eventually indicated to pull into a service station.

"Oh, coffee," I said looking at the drive-through.

He didn't drive through.

"Oh," I said, looking at it behind me.

"The car is too low. We'll go in," he said.

He parked the car and took his time climbing out and opening my door.

"I need to pee, badly," I said, bouncing from foot to foot.

He slowly shook his head in exasperation, I thought.

"I'll order then," he said, and strode off.

I jiggled while I followed and then ran to the loos.

When I returned, he was sitting at a table and looking out the window. He actually looked a little lost, forlorn even.

He looked up as I approached and then smiled when I sat.

"I'm sorry for laughing. I do that when I'm embarrassed, or... whatever," I said.

He slid a coffee towards me. "Accepted."

"But it is a bit mad, isn't it?"

"What is, Ruby?"

"All this, her playing with you, you playing with her, her wanting to play with me, not allowed to, and all that stuff." I made it sound like we were in a primary school playground.

Finally, he chuckled. He frowned and smiled, then shook his head. "Yeah, fucking mad."

He reached forwards and took my hand in his. "I get jealous, and I have no rights over you. You're free to do what you want."

I looked down at our joined hands, then back at his face. He didn't look his age, he looked much younger.

"I like that you get jealous and maybe I want you to have a right over me. I know what I want, Sebastian."

I'd spoken so quietly, that when he didn't reply, I

thought he might not have heard. I looked down at my coffee cup, knowing my cheeks were alight.

"Do you understand what you're asking for?"

I looked up. His head was cocked to one side.

"Not really. But I want you and that's what you are."

He picked up my hand and kissed my knuckles. "Do you trust me?"

I nodded. "I do."

"Do you consent to be with me in all my guises?"

I had no idea what he meant. "I do."

"You'll give yourself to me, and me only?"

I wanted to sigh. "I. Do." I added an eye roll for effect.

He smiled, and it was a wicked smile that showed those white straight teeth. If I'd have seen canines, I wouldn't have been surprised.

"Does all the, *I do's* mean we're married?" I asked, giggling.

"In all but a signature on paper," he replied, and I was stunned into silence.

CHAPTER ELEVEN

Sebastian had dropped me back home with a promise to call later. I had hoped that he might stay for a while, but he'd said he had things to do. He didn't detail what that was, of course. I changed into my sloppy clothes and sat with Grandma. She held my hand and told me about her day.

She'd been to the shops with Fredo. He'd been so lovely to her, bought her silk stockings, she said. Of course, there was no Fredo, or shop visit, but I went along with it. Fredo was a soldier apparently and I got that we'd slip back into the war. She'd been a teen then, in her nineties now. I dreaded the day I'd lose her, which is why, I guessed, I'd hung onto her despite it being so hard for me. She told me about the *woman* that sat with her. Asking me if she was her daughter. I wasn't sure what to say to that. I nodded as tears sprang to my eyes. Grandma smiled, it seemed to please her.

I made her dinner and washed her. By the time I had her settled in her bed, it was nearing nine o'clock, late for Grandma, and I was starving.

As if he could read my thoughts, I received a text.

Are you hungry? Seb xx

I replied immediately. **Starving!**

I'll be there in ten.

I placed the phone on the kitchen table and sat. I needed to add a screensaver, I thought. I had no idea how to do that. Perhaps a nice picture of Sebastian would be good. But then I didn't want people at work to know about us, not that I really knew what we had still.

I sat and pondered. My life had been turned upside down by Sebastian Wolfe, and I knew so very little about him. I had no idea what kind of a relationship we were having. I'd committed myself to him, but had he to me? Yet he knew very little about me, also.

"Stop overthinking," I said to myself, and stood. I needed to just take life as it came and see where I ended up.

Sebastian arrived promptly and I chuckled as I answered the door. "Are you ever late?" I asked.

"No, why would I be?"

"No reason." I stood aside and let him in.

"How's your grandmother?" he asked.

"Sleeping now, but she seems more talkative, more engaged but still in the past. She spoke tonight for about twenty minutes and hasn't done that in years." He stared at me. "Yes, I know," I said, answering his silent message.

"I'm sorry, Ruby."

I nodded gently. I'd read that, often, people perked up before they died. Grandma was on her last legs for sure. She'd used up all her lives multiple times over. It was just a matter of time now. I planned to talk to Monica about it in the morning.

"I have food," he said, holding a bag aloft.

"Good, because I could eat a donkey's arse," I said, taking the bag from him.

"What a peculiar term," he said, and laughed.

I emptied the bag of its contents and grabbed a couple of plates and forks. It smelled divine and when I opened a lid, I closed my eyes and wafted the scent towards me.

"Japanese," he said.

"What is it?"

He detailed the dishes as I helped myself from each pot. He reached into the bag and retrieved some chopsticks. I shook my head at the offered pair, I'd never get anything into my mouth with those.

"I won't be able to sleep now, eating this late," I said, and chuckled.

"I can think of plenty of things to do if you get bored."

I raised my eyebrows at him. "I'm sure you can."

"We are pretend married now, remember?"

"Mmm, I did say, *I do*, didn't I? So, what do you suggest, Mr. Wolfe? I wash and iron your shirts?"

He shook his head. "I have someone to do that."

"Perhaps, shine your shoes?"

"I buy new ones when these dull."

"Hold you while you sleep."

He paused. He looked over my head. "I've never had someone do that for me," he said gently.

"Are the nightmares why you work at night?" I asked.

He'd never told me he had nightmares, but it was an easy assumption considering his traumatic childhood. I didn't believe anyone was a night owl by choice.

He didn't answer and I let him be.

When we'd finished eating, he stood. He leaned down to kiss the top of my head. "I have to go. Chase those nightmares away," he said.

I stood and wrapped my arms around him. "Wait," I said. I ran to a drawer in the kitchen. "A key, in case you want that holding," I said, placing it in his palm.

He cupped my face and rested his forehead on mine. He kissed me gently on the lips before he left. I didn't walk him to the door, I couldn't. I was full of emotion and sadness. I'd just seen a glimmer of the real Sebastian Wolfe and he was broken.

I wasn't sure of the time I felt a dip in the bed. I rolled over and wrapped my arms around him. He kissed me gently and then fell into a deep sleep. I held him all night, or at least until I fell asleep myself in the early hours of the morning, I guessed. When my alarm went off, I was alone. I knew I hadn't dreamt it; he'd left a worn shirt over the end of the bed. I picked it up and held it to my nose. I inhaled his scent, his aftershave and rubbed the soft cotton material on my cheek. He'd also left a note. I picked up the piece of paper left beside the alarm.

Thank you. Seb xx

I smiled and slipped the note inside the drawer. I had Grandma to see to, and a job to get ready for.

———

My first week flew past. I enjoyed every minute of it. Some days I saw Sebastian, and some days I didn't. A couple of nights he crept into my bed in the early hours and was gone before I woke. I didn't mention it, but I did wash and iron his shirts. On the Friday, Sebastian surprised me in the office.

It was mid-afternoon and dress down Friday, apparently. I was wearing jeans and one of my new t-shirts. I had chalk smudges on my hands and face. I'd been playing with various colour schemes, and I liked to do that with chalk as it was the closest to paint colours.

I saw him enter the floor and he strode across to me. He leaned down and kissed my cheek.

"Hi," he said.

"Hi, yourself. Should you have done that at work?"

"Why not, they all know we're an item."

"Do they? And an item? I appear to have been demoted from the pretend married, I see," I said, pouting my lips in mock distress.

He chuckled. "Well, let's up to pretend marriage. I want you to stay the weekend with me."

"I can't, Sebastian," I said, gently.

"You can. Between Monica and Tim, they're covering the weekend. Monica agrees you could do with the space."

"Are you organising my life behind my back?" I asked, smiling.

"Isn't that what you agreed to?"

"I did. And wow, thank you. I'll be wracked with guilt, of course."

"I have something that can ease that for you," he whispered. I shook my head and laughed.

"I'll collect you in an hour. We'll swing by yours so you can pick up some clothes. I've bought all your favourite toiletries to keep at mine, so you don't need to bring any of those."

I raised my eyebrows. "How do you know...?"

"I've been in your bathroom, Ruby. Of course I'd know."

I saw Amelia walk over. "Hey, you two," she said. She'd been to the club to take photographs for us.

Sebastian seemed uneasy, and I frowned at him. "Do you think we can grab a coffee? The three of us?" she asked.

I waited for Sebastian to answer. "Sure, why not. Wash up, Ruby, we'll leave now."

"I can't just *leave*," I said.

Amelia laughed. "He does own the company, darling. I'm guessing that's all the permission you need."

I left them to head to the toilet. I needed to wash my hands. A pang of anxiety struck my chest, although it wasn't quite jealousy. I wasn't sure why Sebastian felt uncomfortable, and that made me feel... uncomfortable.

We walked to the coffee shop that seemed to be a company favourite. I waved to a colleague I recognised, who was sitting with his laptop open. He waved back.

"Okay," she said, and she took a deep breath in. "I feel like I need to say this, and I really hope that it's okay."

"Say what, Amelia?" Sebastian asked and whether

he knew it or not, his voice had lowered. I saw her gently shiver, but then correct herself.

"I wanted to say how happy I am for you, Sebastian. You've found a wonderful partner in Ruby and, although I'm sad and a little jealous, I wanted to ask you both to just give me a little time to come to terms with it."

I hadn't thought for one minute how Sebastian and I being together would affect her. I'd always assumed it was just a super casual fuck buddies thing. I didn't consider whether she had feelings for him. I was also aware that, for the first time in my presence at least, she'd called him by his first name.

"I always told you it wouldn't lead to anything permanent," Sebastian said, and I placed my hand on his knee hoping he'd get my message. I wanted him to soften his tone a little.

He glanced at me. "Thank you, Amelia, and I'm sorry. I should have thought more about your feelings when I was talking about him," I said, nodding towards Sebastian. "That wasn't very thoughtful of me."

She smiled. "I appreciate that, Ruby. I knew it wouldn't lead anywhere, but a girl could always hope. I can also assure you, nothing changes when I'm at work. I'll still be my usual professional self, Mr. Wolfe." She'd reverted to using his surname and, I assumed, to reinforce her pledge of professionalism.

Sebastian stayed silent and I didn't think it was because he didn't care. From the frown, I got the impression he simply didn't know how to react. This was new territory for him, I imagined.

"Will you still be visiting the club?" I asked.

"Of course! I have a lifetime membership," she replied, laughing.

"Do you need me to find you someone else?" Sebastian asked, finally contributing something.

"I would, If you agree to that, Ruby?"

"Of course," I answered wondering why she needed my agreement.

"I trust you, Mr. Wolfe, so I'll wait for your direction. Thank you, both, for letting me talk this frankly to you."

I reached over and took her hand in mine. She smiled at me and then quickly wiped away a tear. "Take care of him, Ruby. He needs a good, strong woman, and I know that's you, regardless of your age."

Sebastian opened his mouth to speak, and I squeezed his knee again. I got the impression he didn't like her statement.

Amelia stood, saying she'd see me on Monday morning and reminding Sebastian that they were to meet the contractor as well. He nodded, confirmed he had it in his diary, and then she left.

"Well, that was hard," I said.

"Why? I never promised her anything. I don't get the dramatics, to be honest. And why the fuck were you squeezing my leg?"

"Are you that blind to love?"

"Oh, give it up. She isn't in love with me!"

"Maybe not *you*, but she is in love with the dom side of you." He frowned at me. "She's in love with the person you are when you're with her, intimately, at least. And I think, perhaps with you, Sebastian as well. I was hoping you'd soften just a little when you spoke to her."

He frowned some more and gently shook his head. He didn't get it at all. "Let's go home. I can't be doing all this shit."

I chuckled as he chugged down his coffee, knowing full well that wasn't the case. He wasn't angry or irritated, he was confused.

When we arrived back at my house, Monica was sitting with Grandma.

"You're home early," she said.

"I got let out for good behaviour," I replied, chuckling.

She held out her hand to Sebastian who took it. "It's a pleasure to meet you, Monica," he said.

I narrowed my eyes at her when she pretended to swoon.

"I want to sit with Grandma for a few minutes, is

that okay? I can get a cab over to you if you want to go," I said.

"I'll wait."

He strode off to the kitchen and Monica and I went into the living room.

"I don't know about leaving her for a whole weekend," I said, quietly. I picked up Grandma's hand and held it. She ignored me and continued to watch her programme.

"When did you have a weekend off, Ruby?" Monica asked.

I shrugged my shoulders. "Never, I guess."

"So you deserve it. You've met someone that clearly dotes on you, you're entitled to a life outside being a carer."

"What about the age difference?" I asked, looking at her.

"What about it? You're not a child. If you were mid-teens, I'd be calling the police, but you're twenty, and way older in the head. You're an adult, he's an adult. You're not being coerced, are you?"

"No, not at all. If anything, I'm the one pushing, not him."

"Then take this opportunity of a weekend away."

"I don't want to fall for him," I whispered.

"You won't be able to control that, I'm afraid."

"What if I do, and he doesn't feel the same way?"

"You won't be able to control that, either. But you'll deal with it. Stop overthinking, Ruby."

"I fell in love once," I heard. I turned to see Grandma looking at me. "If you have a chance, Ruby, you take it with both hands. I'm off soon."

Both Monica and I stared at her. There had been times where she'd been totally with it, but those times were few and far between.

"It's me, Grandma, Ruby."

"I know, dear." She turned back to the television.

Tears rolled down my cheeks. Monica took my other hand and stood. "Time to go," she said.

I let her lead me into the kitchen.

"What's happened?" Sebastian said, concern lacing his voice.

"Grandma just spoke to me. Like, to me, Ruby. Not a carer."

He frowned.

"Her dementia is such that she doesn't really know who Ruby is. However, every now and again, she'll remember. She just did," Monica explained.

"What did she say?" Sebastian asked.

"She told me that if I have a chance, I'm to grab it with both hands and that she'll be off soon," I replied. My voice hitched with emotion.

"Oh, baby," he said, and wrapped me in his arms.

I felt secure, safe, and warm. The most comfort I'd

ever felt in that position. My heart cracked just a little knowing it probably wouldn't be forever.

I packed an overnight bag with some clothes, and we left. Monica waved me off with a promise to call me regularly. She refused to do so hourly.

I fretted the whole journey.

"Sit still, will you? You're making me twitchy!"

"You leave your only family member alone for the weekend and see if you sit still," I snapped back.

"She's not alone. She has twenty-four-hour care."

I snorted and turned to face the window, ignoring him. He reached over and took my hand in his. I let him.

We arrived at his house and once again, I marvelled at the outside. It was Georgian in design, but not of the period. It was sympathetically done with a grand entrance and circular drive. I hadn't taken much notice when I'd been there before, so as I exited the car, I stood and looked.

"I designed this myself," he said, coming to stand beside me.

"You did a good job. It's very symmetrical," I replied.

"I didn't want ultra-modern, but not period either. Somewhere in between. Come on, let me show you around."

He led me inside to the cool marble hallway. "I know this room," I said, chuckling.

He left my bag at the bottom of the stairs and then showed me around. There was a sitting room, which doubled up as a library. I remembered him telling me he liked to read. It looked a lovely place to chill out with large sofas and footstools, a cuddle chair, and fluffy rug in front of an open fire.

"This room is gorgeous, and very tidy!"

"I'm a tidy person," he said, chuckling.

He showed me into a snug that doubled up as a home office, there was a downstairs loo which was about the size of my bathroom. We walked into a large kitchen with a walk-in pantry and utility room off to the side, then through to a huge sunroom.

"This is amazing," I said, walking to the doors. I opened them onto a terrace and looked down his garden. There were woods at the end, and I shivered. It looked familiar.

"There is nothing scary out there, Ruby," he said quietly as he stood behind me.

"It looks like the woods of my dreams."

"All woods look the same. I hunt out there, I've walked every inch of it."

"What do you hunt?"

"Deer. Rabbit, sometimes. Whatever takes my fancy."

I didn't like the thought of hunting animals for fun, if he ate the meat, however it didn't bother me.

"We'll take a walk over the weekend. Now, let me show you the rest of the house."

There was a formal dining room which he said had never been used and invited me to think up a way to use it. He preferred to eat at the breakfast bar that looked out through the sunroom.

Upstairs, I'd been to his bedroom, of course, but there were three further bedrooms, all en-suit and with dressing rooms.

It wasn't the largest house, but certainly not small either. It was perfect for him. The colour scheme suited him, too. Muted greys and taupes coupled with off white marble floors. It was his dressing room that I had the most envy for. He had picked up my bag and when we walked into the room, he'd set it on a central table. It wasn't just a table however, it had drawers underneath and the top was glass. Under the glass were watches, a large selection.

"One for every week of the year?" I joked.

"Nope, investment pieces most of them. I don't trust my money in banks," he laughed as he spoke. "I've made some space for you," he added.

One side of the room was bare. "I don't think my couple of t-shirts, a pair of jeans, and a pair of trousers warrant all that space," I said.

"Maybe you can move some other clothes in here,

permanently. Then you haven't got to drag this bag back and forth."

"I don't have enough clothes to double up, but thank you." I reached up on my tip toes and kissed his cheek.

I unpacked my bag, all the contents except underwear fitted on one shelf with two items on hangers. I stood back to admire my handy work.

"They look lonely," he said.

"I'm sure they'll cope."

"I'll fill the space if you don't want to."

"I don't want to, and neither should you. It's a waste having two lots of clothes. Now, were you going to make me a coffee since you're the host?"

He chuckled and we walked back down to the kitchen. He fiddled with a coffee machine, and I was presented with a latte. He sat beside me.

"What do you want to do this weekend?" he asked.

"I don't know, other than the obvious."

I smirked at him, and he raised an eyebrow.

"Explain, Ruby," he said.

"I want to explore some things. You said you have books I could read. Maybe you could do that with me."

I was desperate to overcome my awkwardness, but I knew the pitch of my voice had risen.

"I like the sound of that," he replied. "When do we start your lessons?"

"Whenever you want me in class, Mr. Wolfe."

He took my coffee away and picked up my hand. I slid from the stool, and he led me back upstairs.

"No lesson this afternoon, Miss Montando. Just a warm up."

He grabbed the hem of my t-shirt and lifted it over my head. Then he unclipped my bra and slid it from my shoulders. His hands ran down my sides and I shivered at his touch. When he reached the waistband of my jeans, he slid his fingers underneath and then round to the front. He kept his gaze on me at all times. He unzipped and wiggled them down over my hips dragging my knickers with them. I toed off my trainers and stepped out of the clothes.

I stood naked while he took a step back. He appraised me. "You don't know how beautiful you are, do you?" he said, his voice low.

I pulled my hair from my ponytail and let it fall down my back and over my shoulders.

"I want to undress you," I said, stepping towards him.

I slowly unbuttoned his shirt, kissing his chest as I exposed each section. I undid the cuffs and then slid my hands over his shoulders pushing the shirt off his back. He was muscular, and he had scars. I traced my fingers over them wondering how they'd gotten there. Although I'd seen him without clothes, I hadn't studied his body. And that's what I fully intended to do.

I reached for his belt, unbuckling it, and lowering the zipper of his trousers. He kicked off his shoes and I slid the material down to his ankles, falling to my knees as I did.

"I bet I wouldn't get to my knees for you. I guess I lost," I said, looking up at him and taking his erect cock in my hands.

His moan was gentle, yet it hit me bang in the chest. I licked over the head of his cock, tasting pre-cum, before opening my mouth and guiding him in. He fisted my hair, holding my head as I rocked up and down his shaft. I sucked and tasted him. I licked. When he pulled at my hair, I stood.

"You'll make me come," he whispered.

"So?"

He smirked and then pushed me back down again. I sucked his cock until he came in my mouth. I'd never done that before, it was revolting, but like the good girl I wanted to be, I swallowed it down and tried not to gag.

"First time," he said, as I stood and my eyes watered. I nodded and he laughed.

"An acquired taste, I'm sure," I said. "I owe you five thousand pounds," I added, laughing.

"No, Ruby, I owe you, and much more than that," he whispered, before kissing me.

Sebastian picked me up and laid me on his bed, he climbed on and held himself above me. He kissed my forehead, my nose, my chin and then down my chest. Small butterfly kisses down my stomach and then across my hips. He avoided all the places I was desperate for him to go to. I tried to push his head towards my crotch, and he chuckled.

"In my own time, Ruby," he said, sternly.

He continued his kissing down the inside of my thighs. That tickled and I squirmed my legs away from his touch. He looked at me, and without a word, slipped from the bed. He walked into his dressing room and returned. In his palm were leather cuffs with chains attached. His stature had changed, I was sure. He was taller, bulkier, and his eyes were dark. He licked over his lips as he stared at me.

"Give me permission, Ruby," he said, so quietly I only just heard.

I nodded.

"Give me permission!" His harsh tone startled me.

"I do," I said.

He cuffed my wrists and ankles to the bedposts, and it was only then that I noticed black painted hooks on each. I hadn't seen them before; they'd blended in with the black bed frame.

"Now you can't squirm," he said, tightening the chains. "And you are mine to do with as I please."

My stomach flipped multiple times.

He ran his fingers over my body, heat and ice

collided, my skin goose bumped, and my hairs stood on end. It was the lightest touch and it had me wanting more.

He stroked over my hips, my inner thighs, again avoiding the places I wanted him to be. He laughed at my frustrated moans.

He pinched one nipple so hard, I tried to twist away. "Go with it, Ruby," he whispered.

I tried. I lay as still as I could, panting, and then holding my breath. While he did that, he sucked the other into his mouth. One was full of pain, the other of pleasure. It was a collision of sensation and my brain struggled to keep up with it. When he released the nipple and a prickling feeling returned, he took it between his teeth. I cried out. I pulled at my arms. He sucked until the blood returned and it was the most delicious sensation. Wetness pooled between my thighs, and I was desperate to close my legs, to get some pressure on my clitoris to ease the ache. I arched my back off the bed.

"Please," I said.

"Please, what?"

"Do something, anything. Touch me." I felt close to tears.

He ignored me. He moved to the bottom of the bed and ran his tongue over the top of my feet, up my legs, circling and nipping my skin. When he got to my pussy, he placed just the tip of his tongue on my clitoris.

"Fucking hell!" I screamed, trying to force my body closer to his mouth.

His breath as he chuckled, whispered over my heat.

"Bastard," I added in a whisper.

"Strike three, Ruby."

I closed my eyes and held my breath, waiting.

When it came, it was... I had no words. His palm connected with my pussy and the delayed sensation confused me. I lay still, shocked. Then it hit me. A wave of heat flooded over me, rolling up my body and settling on my neck and cheeks.

He slapped my pussy again. That time it was instant. I felt such a wetness I wasn't sure if I'd pissed myself or not.

The third slap was pure torture. It wasn't painful, it was the fleeting skin on skin contact that I didn't like. I needed his hand on me, his fingers inside me. I begged him with tears rolling down my cheeks.

"Please!"

He gave me what I wanted. He inserted two fingers, then a third. He hooked and gently rubbed over my G spot, or what I assumed it was since my orgasm was almost instant. I raised off the bed, rigid, as I came. Before I came down to earth, he replaced his fingers with his mouth. He sucked and licked that orgasm from me. It was his to claim, and I willing gave it up. He held my hips, digging his fingertips into my skin to keep me from moving while he took what he wanted. I was powerless to do anything about it. Then I got it.

I understood what Amelia had said. It was giving it all up to him. It made it the most pleasurable thing I'd ever experienced. Allowing him to take what he wanted from me, resulted in him also giving me what I desired.

When he raised his face, it glistened. He ran his tongue over his teeth and stalked up my body. He lowered his head, but not close enough.

"Clean me," he said, gravelly.

I raised off the bed as far as I could, and I licked over his chin. Then his lips. He closed his eyes and dragged in air through his nose.

When he pulled his head back, he stared at me. I could feel his cock at my entrance, and although I wanted to reach down for it, I couldn't. Without guiding, he slammed into me, then stilled.

He did it a second time, holding himself so deep inside. His cock pulsed as I tightened my muscles around him. He kept his stare on me the whole time. His piercing look had me paralysed on the bed. The only thing I could do was to gasp in a breath each time he did move.

Then he fucked me, so hard and fast, then slow and deep. I gripped the bedding, when what I wanted was to tear at his skin. I raised my chest off the bed and closed my eyes when his intenseness became too much to look at.

I shed tears when I came again. A thumping orgasm that ripped through my body so much so, I saw stars behind my eyelids. I lost track of time, but the room had darkened, the evening had drawn in.

When he came, I was ready for it. I ached and I wanted to hold him.

"Let me go," I whispered when he slumped over my body.

He reached up and unclipped the cuffs from my wrists. I wrapped my arms around him and held him to my body. Sweat coated his skin and he panted with exertion. His face was nestled in my neck, and I ran my hands over his back, gently scratching the skin. I felt his come gently seep from me. I listened as his breathing slowed and he rested. I wanted to wrap my legs around him as well, cocoon him, but they were still restrained. Instead, I held him tight.

I kissed his shoulder and eventually, he turned his head and kissed my cheek.

"Thank you," he whispered.

"I just laid here, so not sure what you're thanking me for," I replied.

"For just lying there and let me do what I wanted."

"Ah, okay. Then I accept your thanks. I would like

the use of my legs back, though, I'm leaking all over your nice silk bedding."

He chuckled and slid to the side. He stretched and sighed, propping himself up on his elbow to look at me.

"Any time tonight would be good," I said.

He sat up and uncuffed my ankles. He then stood. "No, don't go," I whined.

"Up, shower, then we eat."

He walked towards the bathroom, and I reluctantly followed.

A shower was a luxury I rarely had. He didn't have a bath, just a huge, four-person shower with two waterfall showerheads. He set the temperature and dragged me in.

"Hot, hot hot," I squealed, trying to duck out.

"Stop being a wuss. You need the heat to soothe your skin."

"I know my skin and it's currently telling you to fuck right off with that bullshit."

He stared at me. "Strike one."

I bit my lower lip to stop from giggling and gingerly stood under the jets.

"Good girl."

My stomach flipped, despite it already having a workout that would be befitting an Olympian.

"No you don't," I said, slapping it.

Sebastian laughed. He grabbed me around the waist,

and I squealed as he placed me in front of him, forcing my upper body towards the wall. I placed my hands on the tiles to balance.

"No," I said, laughing. He stilled.

"Yes," I then said.

He entered me from behind and even though sore, it still felt like heaven. The water ran over our bodies, he held my hips as he fucked me, and I was sure I'd see double bruises there. I loved every second of it.

CHAPTER TWELVE

Sebastian was in the kitchen and preparing something for us to eat. I had taken longer to shower because I needed to wash my hair. It was still wet and piled on top of my head. I hadn't bought a hairdryer, and he didn't own one. He told me to make a list of the things he needed to buy.

I stood in his dressing room with a towel wrapped around me and realised, I hadn't packed any pyjama's or something to lounge around in. I opened drawers and found a pair of sweat pant shorts. They'd do. I had to roll the top over a few times. Once they almost fitted, I grabbed one of his t-shirts. It was grey with *Nirvana* on the front. I had no idea what that meant, of course, but assumed it to be a band.

"Baby, you are never leaving this house," he said, stalking towards me. "These look good on you."

"Shall I tell you something?" I asked, as he lifted me and placed me on the steel counter. He nodded. "When you stayed that first night, you left your shirt. I slept with it the second night so I could feel close to you, could smell you."

I lifted the t-shirt to my nose. Since it was clean, it didn't have the same scent, but it was still there. A very faint hint of his aftershave.

"If you moved in with me, you could have that all the time," he said, stepping between my thighs.

I placed my hands on his cheeks. "If only, but for now, that's a nice dream to have. Can you imagine what my landlord would say if I tried to give up my contract early? I'm sure there would be a penalty."

"He'd probably want to spank that gorgeous arse of yours," he replied, turning his head and kissing my palm.

"Can I ask something?" I said, and he nodded. "Is three strikes always a spanking?"

He laughed. "No."

"What else is it, then?"

"Whatever I want it to be." He kissed my nose and stepped back. "Now, food. I have steaks."

I slid from the counter and offered to help. While he prepared the steaks, I made a salad. His fridge was so well stocked and mostly with fresh food. I grabbed a half-drunk bottle of wine and held it up.

"It's white, we're having steak."

"So? Can't we drink what we like when we like? Let's break the rules," I said, teasing him.

He shook his head and smiled; I poured two glasses after opening multiple cupboards to find them. We sat in the sun room and ate. I liked watching him eat. The only way I could describe it was that he ate *manly*. He tore into his meat and chewed it hard, I thought.

"What?" he asked, seeing me stare at him.

"I like the way you eat."

He laughed and shook his head. "You are entertained by the strangest things."

"I'm entertained by you."

He gave me a wink and while we continued to eat, he told me about the house. He wasn't pretentious about it, he'd just wanted enough space for himself. I reminded him of the four bedrooms, and he laughed again.

"It was either take over the whole floor just for myself, or have additional bedrooms. One day, I'll sell this so..." He shrugged his shoulders and then placed his cutlery on his plate.

I finished my meal and took both plates to the sink.

"Do you want more wine?" I asked. I picked up the bottle and took it back to him.

As I stood beside him to pour, he placed his hand around my hips.

"It feels good having you here," he said.

"It's a beautiful house, one of my dreams. And for now, that's where it will have to stay," I replied, ignoring his meaning.

I grabbed my phone from the kitchen counter and texted Monica. I wanted to know Grandma had settled down okay. She replied immediately to tell me Milly was there and yes, she went off to sleep easily.

"Come and sit, Ruby," Sebastian said. I followed him into the sitting room.

He sat on the sofa, and I curled up beside him. "This is nice," I mumbled.

He wrapped his arm around me. "It is. It's odd, too."

"Why?"

"Because I've never done this before," he said.

"How many partners have you had? Maybe we need to have *that* conversation as well," I said.

"Partners, as in long term? None. I haven't wanted one until now."

I looked up at him. "Until now?"

He kissed the top of my head. "Until now. As for your other question, I'm clean. I can show you my latest health certificate."

"I don't need to see anything. I'm on the pill, so no worry about babies."

"I know. I saw it in your bathroom cupboard." I snuggled down again. "So, how many partners have you had?"

"None," I replied, and chuckled. "I've only had sex with two other men... Boys, really, I guess. I haven't had sex in a few years. Does it show?"

He laughed and pulled me closer.

"I have a plan," I said, and laughed before I divulged it. "Let's have sex in every room of this house, and then outside as well. I've always wanted to do that, although it's a bit cold, isn't it? Or maybe we'll forget the outside—"

"Ruby, shut up," he said, then leaned down to kiss me.

We slid down the sofa and I lay on top of him. He placed his hands down the back of my... his shorts and cupped my arse cheeks. I kissed his face, moving around until I found his lips.

We lay like that for a while, just talking. Sharing our favourite songs and movies. I rested my chin on my arms crossed on his chest.

"Was your childhood really awful?" he asked.

My heart fluttered. "I can't say it was awful, not compared to yours. My parents were hippies, I guess. There were too many drugs around. Grandma gave my dad some money to buy a house in Spain because she worried about me. But that just gave them a base to party from. I ingested cocaine once. I was born drug and alcohol dependent, apparently. It stunted my growth," I said.

"Really?"

"No," I replied and laughed. "The drug and drink part is real. My mum was short. You know, I can't really remember what she looked like now."

"How did she die?" he asked.

I didn't speak for a little while and then I sighed. I pushed myself off him and sat on the edge of the sofa beside his stretched-out body.

"Maybe I need to tell you something, before this goes any further."

He shuffled up. "What do you need to tell me, Ruby?"

"I... I helped her die. I killed her."

I didn't look at him and it was the first time I'd ever spoken the words out loud to anyone before. Although I suspected my dad knew which is why he had disappeared.

"Do you want to tell me about it?" he asked, calmly.

"Erm... You're not likely to call the police, are you?"

"You've just admitted to killing someone. Perhaps you should have asked me that before."

I looked at him. He offered me a smile. "Tell me what happened."

"She wanted to take her own life. I knew it. She had no choice, Sebastian. She couldn't get clean, and she was dying anyway." Tears started to fall, and I hiccupped. He sat up and wrapped his arms around me.

"Take your time, but tell me. Let it out," he said.

"She wanted to die. She said it was the only way she could keep me safe."

"Did you understand what she meant by that?"

"Yes. I was getting more exposed to their lifestyle. She believed if she wasn't around, it would end. So I thought. I scored the drugs for her, Sebastian. I cooked up the heroin."

He was silent, just looking at me. "You didn't kill her, Ruby. She killed herself. You wouldn't have known what you were doing," Sebastian said quietly.

"But I did. I knew exactly what I was doing. And that makes me guilty in Spanish law. My dad dragged me away in the middle of the night and let the police just find her."

I took a few deep breaths and lifted the t-shirt to wipe my face.

"I heard when they found her, they started to look for me. My dad didn't even bury her. I don't know what happened to her body."

"That still doesn't mean you knew what you were doing. Or that you intended to kill her. You were a child fucked up by her parent's behaviour." His voice became sterner.

"The police pulled in the dealer, and he told them that I'd scored the drugs to kill her. The police wanted to speak to me."

"You were underage, Ruby."

"They didn't care. So we ran again. My dad said he was going to sell the house and we'd move countries. He disappeared and I've never seen him since. He sold the house, leaving me homeless. That's when Grandma came to my rescue again. I was twelve, Sebastian. Old enough to be charged as a juvenile in Spain."

"Charged with what, Ruby? You didn't do anything wrong!" There was a level of exasperation in his voice.

I looked up at him. "I injected her. It was me that did it. Her hands shook so much she couldn't get the needle in. I took it from her and did it myself. I killed her."

I broke down then and he hugged me tight. He rocked me as I wailed, letting out eight years, more even, of pain and anger, of loneliness and hunger. I had been dirty, I'd seen things I should never have seen, done things a child should never have done. I'd had no education until I was a teenager. I told him all this while he comforted me.

"Shush, baby. It's okay. It's okay," he repeated.

Spent, I slumped against him. "I can go home now, if you want me to."

"Are you kidding me? You and me, Ruby, we're more alike than you think we are." I looked at him, waiting for him to continue. "What you did was a mercy. You gave your mother the release she needed, and you saved your own life in the meantime. It was a form of self-defence. I've killed in cold blood. For real, Ruby. I've murdered, willingly and knowingly. You haven't."

He showed no emotion at all. I placed my hands on his cheeks. "You can leave me if you want. I won't tell you all the details because it's way too gory, but I was abused, and I killed one of my abusers when I was twelve years old. I took great delight in it, Ruby. I went to juvenile prison for seven years. It was *only* seven years because the police and social services knew they'd let me down, so I guess I did a token time away. When I was released, I became homeless."

"You killed to save other children, didn't you?" I asked.

"I killed because I hated with such passion that if I hadn't acted on my desire, Ruby, I would have gone mad. Other children didn't figure. *I* wanted him dead for *me*. I wanted to see the pain on his face as he bled out, and I took great pleasure in it. I stabbed him, multiple times. I washed my hands in his blood, Ruby. Thankfully, the police thought I was fighting him off, I was charged with manslaughter."

I closed my eyes and rested my forehead on his. "I should be scared of you," I whispered.

"Are you?"

I shook my head. "No, but I should, shouldn't I?"

"I can't answer that, Ruby."

"What does it say about me, I'm not? I'm not scared of you at all."

"It says that you're a courageous woman who sees beyond what you're told."

"I guess so."

"So now we know the worst in each other. How do you feel?" he asked.

"No different. When I'm with you, I feel safe and secure. I feel comfort for the first time in my life. I feel at peace. I feel like I belong somewhere."

"Good." He held me tighter.

"How did it feel?" I asked him. "To watch him die."

"Pleasing. How did you feel?"

"Sad, but relieved. She just went to sleep and didn't wake up. I waited with her, and then my dad came in."

"What did he do?"

"He beat me for using all the drugs."

He stiffened beside me.

"I don't know where he is, I suspect somewhere like Cuba, somewhere he can speak the language. And now, I don't care. I did for a long time. I wanted my money, wanted what was due, but now, I don't think it was ever about the cash. It was more about him not benefitting from her death."

"You don't need him, and you certainly don't need that money," he said.

Sebastian stood and pulled me to stand beside him. He looked at me, tracing my face with his eyes.

"You're so young, so wrong for me. But so very right. I have a feeling you're doing to be my downfall."

"Let's just keep the *right* bit, please?"

He picked me up and I wrapped my legs around his waist. I buried my head in his neck and he carried me up to bed.

The sheets were ruffled and damp from our previous stay, but I didn't care. He laid me down so gently, and I slid off the shorts, pulled the t-shirt over my head.

He was gentler and slower. Taking his time to pleasure my body, to kiss and lick every inch of me. I did the same to him.

I woke to a sound. Sebastian had walked into the bedroom wearing shorts and a very sweaty t-shirt. I stretched to relieve myself of the gentle ache.

"Good morning," he said, leaning down and kissing me.

"Eww, you're all sweaty," I said, after grabbing his t-shirt to pull him closer.

He laughed. "You didn't moan about that last night." He winked and then pulled the t-shirt over his head. He threw it at me, and I flicked it to the floor. "I'm taking a shower."

I wasn't sure if that was an invitation or not. I rolled to my side and grabbed my phone. It had run out of battery, and I cursed.

"Do you have a charger?" I called out.

"Just place the phone on the nightstand, it will charge."

"It's on the nightstand," I called back.

"Then check the plug is switched on."

I looked down the back of the cabinet and switched the plug on. Instantly, my phone started to charge. I lay on my side looking at him through the open bathroom door. We hadn't spoken again about our confessions, but I had a sense of lightness about myself. I felt cleansed, talking and sobbing had been cathartic. I also felt exhausted. I stretched and yawned again, noticing notifications flash up on my phone.

I picked it up to see a missed call from Monica. My heart stopped as I called her.

"Ruby, darling, I'm so sorry—"

"She's died, hasn't she?" I asked, just as Sebastian walked back into the room.

"She has. She went in her sleep, Ruby."

"Oh no. Oh God. I wasn't there," I said, my voice shaking.

"She wouldn't have known if you were, darling. I've called the doctor and he'll be here shortly."

"The doctor, why?"

"Maybe you should have Sebastian bring you home?"

"I will."

I cut off the call and looked up at him. He had come to stand beside me, and now he knelt, cradling me to his chest while I cried again.

"I wasn't there, Sebastian."

"It's okay, baby. Remember what she said to you?"

I nodded. "I need to go home," I said, my voice croaking.

He stood and held his hand out to help me up. We both dressed and silently, he drove me home. When we got there, an ambulance car stood outside, and behind it, a black van.

I rushed in. Grandma was in the living room. She looked like she was just asleep. I fell to the floor beside her bed and grabbed her hand. She was cold. I held it and cried. I apologised for not being there when she died. Monica rubbed my back while Sebastian dealt with the doctor and undertakers. I had no idea what to do, but Monica had called the necessary people. Grandma had pre-paid for her funeral years ago and always made sure, when she was more with it, that both Monica and I knew what to do.

I was glad she'd made the calls; I wasn't sure I could have. While I sat, Sebastian and Monica dealt with everything. Eventually, Sebastian came and sat with me.

"They need to take her now, baby," he said, quietly.

I nodded and stood, leaning down to kiss her forehead. I didn't like the feel of her, but there wasn't much I could do about that.

I waited in the kitchen, unable to watch, while the undertaker took her out. Watch her be put in the back of black van. The doctor spoke to Monica and then came to sit with me.

"Ruby, I know this is going to be a very sad time for you. I want you to know she went peacefully; we can see that. She was ready to go, and you have done everything ever asked of you. She had a good life and you should be proud of what you did for her. I'm just a phone call away if you need any help."

I nodded. He'd been a great doctor for Grandma, she'd liked him. I'd never been sick so had never seen him in that capacity. I could hear Monica and Sebastian talking, but I just sat staring into space. I'd cried my tears. I was at peace with her death, it was a blessing and one we had been waiting for. But I felt so unbelievably sad.

"Sebastian wants to take you home," Monica said, kneeling in front of me.

I nodded. I didn't want to stay in the house without her. I couldn't face seeing her empty bed.

"Shall I come and help you after the weekend?" she asked.

"Please, I don't think I can do all that alone."

She hugged me and then stood. She hugged Sebastian and I was surprised to see him hug her back. He didn't appear to do affection with strangers. Then it was just us.

"Shall I get you some more clothes, baby?" he asked.

"I guess so. I'll come with you."

Together we walked up the stairs. I stood just outside the empty room that had once been Grandma's.

"I'll have to tell the landlord not to bother redecorating now," I said, and gave him a small smile.

"I know the landlord will do whatever you ask of him," he replied.

I patted his chest then walked into my bedroom. I placed my hairdryer on the bed along with a brush designed for my extra curly hair, and some pyjama's.

Sebastian grabbed some of the new clothes he'd bought and added them to the pile. I didn't own a suitcase so packed it all into two tote bags. I also grabbed a tatty old teddy that sat on my pillow. It was the only thing I had from my mother.

He locked up the house and we walked down the path. The neighbours were out, leaning on their fences and gossiping, wondering what was going on. I ignored them all. I'd never spoken to any and they'd never shown an interest in Grandma before then.

We climbed back into Sebastian's Ferrari, and I gave them the finger as we drove off.

"What do I do?" I asked Sebastian when we arrived back at his house.

"Did she have a funeral plan? A will, maybe?" he asked.

"A funeral plan, yes. No will, I don't think. She wouldn't have had anything to leave. She spent all her money on a house for my parents."

I slumped onto one of the kitchen stools and rested my head in my hands. While I was glad she'd finally passed on, for her sake, I wasn't ready. My life was finally coming together. I might have been able to save to take her on a little holiday. For the past year, she hadn't left the house. I had to keep reminding myself, she wouldn't have known any different.

Sebastian came and sat beside me. He placed his hand on my back and the heat from it seeped through my skin. He comforted me.

"I already feel lost. I mean, I know I have a job now, but looking after her is all I've known for years."

He didn't speak but let me ramble on.

"Shit, I need to call Mike," I said.

"I've done that. You're entitled to some leave, Ruby."

"Not really, though, am I? I've only just started. I'll make it up somehow."

"Ruby, I own the fucking company. If I say you can have some leave, then you can."

"That's not the point, they'll hate me because you're showing favouritism."

"I show everyone favouritism, I'm a walking fucking charity where that company is concerned. Everyone gets what they deserve. If they don't deserve it, they don't get it."

I sighed. "I knew this day was coming. I'm not sure I'm ready for it, though."

"Well, baby, it's happened. I'll take care of everything until you're ready to take over, okay?"

I nodded. I had never been dependent of anyone

before, but I wanted him to take care of me, to take over for a little while.

"I think I might lay down for a bit, is that okay?"

Crying had exhausted me.

"You don't need to ask. Since we're pretend married, you can do as you please, and treat this house as your own," he said, giving me a gentle smile. I knew he was trying to cheer me up, and he did, a little.

I placed my hand on his cheek. "Plenty of women lucked out where you're concerned, didn't they?"

"I don't know what you mean?" he said, helping me slide off the stool.

"You're not the big bad wolf, you're a kind hearted and loveable Labrador in disguise."

He raised his eyebrows. "Can I be a mastiff? Please let me be anything other than a soppy Lab."

I chuckled and reached up to kiss his lips.

"Loveable, huh?" he whispered.

"Loveable."

I walked upstairs and fully dressed, climbed under the duvet.

The curtains were still drawn from the evening, and I lay in semi-darkness, thinking. My grandma had been so feisty in her day, a leader in women's rights in Spain. She'd fought Franco's rule and the level of fascism she hated. I know my father had called her revolutionary. That thought took me to my father. I had no way of contacting him, assuming he was still alive, to tell him. But then, did he deserve to know anything since he'd abandoned us both?

Thoughts whirled through my head, memories of my time with Grandma. I chuckled at the blasted blanket I'd now be able to wash. She'd knitted that blanket when she was a teen, although I couldn't be entirely sure. It was so old, it might not survive a wash. I let a few tears fall as I recalled my life with her, and I wished her well in her next.

I started to think about the future. Maybe I'd downsize to a flat. With my brain whirling, I began to mentally list the things I knew I needed to do. I'd need to call the benefits office to let them know she'd died, call Tim so he didn't send anyone to cover Monica. There was a ton of things to do, and I was lying in bed hiding away from it all. I pulled the duvet up over my head. I'd deal with it all tomorrow, any other day other than now.

Some time later I felt the bed dip and Sebastian pulled back the duvet. "You'll suffocate under there," he said. He had made me a coffee and he placed it on the cabinet.

I shuffled up and picked up the mug. "Thank you," I said and sipped.

He ran his hand over my head, trying to tame my wayward curls. I imagined they were standing on end.

"I need a haircut. And I'll need to get a dress for Grandma's funeral."

"We can shop tomorrow, if you want."

I shook my head. "I can shop. You can't keep buying me stuff."

"I can and I will."

I didn't have the energy to argue with him, and there wasn't much point. He'd more than likely get this own way.

"You will come with me, won't you?" I asked.

"Are you kidding? Of course I will!"

I sighed again.

"Do you feel bad you weren't there?" he asked, gently.

"No, not really. As Monica said, she wouldn't have known. I'd have liked to, for my sake, but there's not much point in worrying about something I can't control."

"What about your father? Do you want me to find him?"

"Find him? I've been trying for years. No, he didn't care about us."

"I'm quite skilled at finding people," he said, still smoothing my hair.

"I'm sure you are, but no. I can't imagine Grandma would want him there. Before her memory went, she told me she hated him. It surprised me, she'd never disliked anyone before."

"Then we won't bother."

I sipped my coffee again and we fell into silence for a couple of minutes.

"I have no one left now," I whispered.

"You have me, and Monica."

"You'll both leave at some point," I said, not looking up at him.

"I can't, we're pretend married, and I don't fuck about with pretend marriage." He gave me a small smile. "As for Monica, I highly doubt she'll never speak to you again. She's like a mother to you."

"Pretend married," I said, and chuckled. "It's okay if you want to get pretend divorced, though. I'd hate for you to think you were stuck with me."

"If you're trying to get rid of me, I'll be forever wounded," he said, placing his hand over his heart.

"Nah, I'll keep you around for a little while. You're the only one who can make me smile."

"And scream. And call out my name. And come like never before. Don't forget all those things."

"You are quite conceited, aren't you?"

"Yeah. I like to big myself up from time to time. Now, come and eat something."

I climbed from the bed and followed him downstairs.

He'd called for a takeout, which was sitting on the side. I hoped it hadn't been there for a while, no matter the situation, I was always hungry and ready to eat. I put it down to the days when I never knew when I might eat next, so grabbed whatever I could, whenever it was available.

Sebastian plated up his favourite Japanese meal, and I tucked in. "I'm beginning to love this food," I said.

"Good. I'll take you to a Japanese restaurant I like tomorrow if you feel up to it."

I shrugged, not sure I wanted to be all 'dolled up' and out. "Or we can just curl up here and not see the world until we have to?" I suggested.

"We can do whatever you want," he said.

"Whatever?"

"Whatever."

I laid my fork down. "I know I've asked this before but, why me? You could have any woman you want."

"I don't want any other woman. I want you. It's quite simple, Ruby. I saw you soaking wet, standing on the pavement, furious with me. You are beautiful when you're angry, and you stirred something inside me. I wanted to know more about you."

"Did you see a *project*? Someone needy?" I asked, genuinely curious.

"No. I saw someone feisty. Someone who would challenge me, not roll over and give in at the click of a finger. I need that."

"I think I rolled over pretty quick," I replied and sighed.

"You did what you did because you wanted it. It wasn't to please me, or to get me. That's the difference."

"Do lots of women throw themselves at you?"

"They have."

"Why?"

"You, Ruby, are so bad for my fucking ego! Maybe because I'm good looking, successful, wealthy, fucking ace in the sack."

"Well, yes, you are all that, but I don't think I'd throw myself at you just because of it."

"Why do you, then?"

"I *don't*!" I shot him a stern glare before defrosting it into a small smile. "But if I did, it would be because under your ego there is someone like me," I said, quietly.

"Both orphans, huh?"

I nodded.

"Finish your food," he said.

"And, this sounds strange, but it's nice to have someone take control for once. I don't know if you know what I mean, but all I think about the next bill, the next meal, how to afford the basics like Tampax, even. With you, I don't need to think. It's... It's refreshing. But I don't want you to think that's all I'm about... I don't know how to explain this very well."

He stared at me. "Maybe you would make a good

sub after all. But only if you learn to shut up when told. Although, I suspect you might struggle with that." He was joking, of course, and trying to keep me smiling.

I rolled my eyes and shook my head. "Seriously, I don't want you to pay for me, but it's nice to think I'm not in this alone. That I have someone I can talk to, for once. It's been a lonely existence until now."

Sebastian picked up my hand. "You're not alone, Ruby. I'm here, and I'm going nowhere."

CHAPTER THIRTEEN

The following day, Sebastian took me back to the house. I'd said I wasn't going to be there, but his talk of funerals had me wanting to find her documents. The funeral home had Grandma, and I'd realised they'd have no way of getting in touch with me. I'd needed to call them with my new mobile number.

I also wanted to pick out a nice outfit for her. One of her dresses from the trunk in the loft.

Sebastian panicked when I used the old wooden rickety ladder to gain access to the loft.

"For fuck's sake, Ruby. Get down and let me get in there," he said as I was halfway up.

"I've climbed this ladder more times than I've had hot dinners with you, so be quiet, you're putting me off."

"Be quiet?"

"Yes. Be quiet. I'm concentrating. One of these treads is dodgy..."

"Get the fuck down now, Ruby." He snapped, and I giggled. Not because it was funny, but because I knew I wasn't getting down and it was annoying him.

He reached up for me. I scooted upwards and launched myself into the loft hatch. "See, I'm up, all fine."

I walked from beam to beam across the loft until I reached the trunk. I sat for a moment and rifled through. Towards the bottom was a dress wrapped in tissue paper. I smiled and brought it to the top. It was Grandma's wedding dress. I'd seen it before, of course. It was a beautiful lace dress she'd made herself. I sat and remembered her telling me, pieces of lace had been woven by her mother and her grandmother. It would be perfect to go with her.

"Can you take this and be careful with it," I said leaning out of the loft.

"I tell you know, Ruby, when you get down here, I'm... I'm going..." He shook his head and sighed. "Pass it down!"

I handed down the dress and then proceeded to climb out. Sebastian had climbed halfway up the ladder to 'cradle' me in case I fell. I highly doubted the ladder would hold us both if I slipped and landed on him, but I figured it best not to mention that. When my arse was at his face height, he sunk his teeth in to it.

"Ouch! What the fuck!"

"If I tell you to come down, I mean it. When are you going to learn to do as you're told?"

"When I'm dead. I'm okay, aren't I? Stop acting like a bloody drama queen and you need to move, otherwise we're both going to fall. This ladder wasn't built for two."

"You are on so many fucking strikes, Ruby."

"Goody, now move, please?"

He lowered to the hall floor, and I looked at him before I took the last step down.

"How many strikes?" I asked.

"Too fucking many," he replied.

"Should I go back up and hide?"

"You should get your fucking arse off that ladder before I whip it!"

"Oh, you look quite cross. Have you still got hold of Grandma's dress?"

I knew I was pushing him, but his buttons were so easy to press, I couldn't help myself.

"Get. Off. The. Ladder." He stepped towards me and grabbed my wrist.

"All right! Blimey, it's just one more step."

As I spoke, the tread gave way and I thumped to the floor. It was a matter of inches, but you'd have thought

I'd fallen over the banister the way Sebastian was flapping.

"See! That could have happened while you were up there." He pointed to the hatch.

"But it didn't. *That* happened when I was one rung up a ladder. One rung! Do you think you might be over-reacting just a little? Plus you've probably left a bruise on my arse, so that must count for one strike."

He grabbed my wrist and dragged me towards him. He then picked me up and threw me over his shoulder.

"Watch the dress!" I called, as he dropped it on the floor.

He stepped over it and walked us into my bedroom.

"You can't just do one fucking thing I ask, can you?" He let me fall to the bed and leaned down over me, his hands either side of my head. "One thing, that's all I asked."

"Okay, I'm sorry. I didn't think it was important," I said, and then bit down on my lower lip.

"Go on, fucking laugh."

I giggled. "You're all cave man and I kinda like it," I said, laughing more.

He silenced me with a kiss.

I wrapped my arms around him and pulled him closer. My legs were dangling off the bed and when he lifted up, he pulled my sweatpants down.

"No underwear?"

"I didn't have time."

"All the better for me." He pushed my t-shirt up and dragged my bra under my breasts.

He released his cock from his jeans and positioned himself at my entrance.

"No foreplay?" I asked.

"You're fucking dripping, Ruby. And no, this is purely for *my* pleasure."

With that, he slammed into me jolting me across the bed. He grunted with every thrust, and I didn't think I'd ever felt him as deep. Perhaps the position, standing and leaning over me, offered him depth. Whatever it was, I wanted more.

I could feel my stomach knotting and I moaned in pleasure. Sebastian grabbed my t-shirt and raised it to my neck.

As I was about to come, he pulled out.

"No!" I said, reaching for him.

He placed a hand on my chest holding me down while he pleasured himself. He came over me, and when he'd milked every drop from himself, he smeared his cum over my breasts and then pulled up my bra.

"Do not wash that off," he said, standing up.

"What? No way! You're going to leave me all frustrated?"

"Yep. Maybe you'll learn to listen to me."

My mouth opened; part shock, part dismay. "You bastard!"

"Back to strike one, Ruby."

I wrenched my t-shirt down, feeling his stickiness beneath it. "You bloody bastard. And I'm going to keep saying it until you decide to fuck me in punishment. Didn't plan for that, did you?" I laughed, a little manically.

"You're assuming I'll fuck you, of course. I make the punishment up as I go along. No rules, Ruby. That way you don't get complacent." It was his turn to laugh.

"Well, I don't like your fucking game anymore."

I stood adjusting my clothing. As I did, he placed both hands on my cheeks and leaned in close. I could feel his breath on my skin.

"Tell me to stop, then."

"You said we didn't have a safe word, or whatever crap that was." I pouted but stood still, enjoying the feel of him so close.

"Tell me to stop. It's as simple as that. And I will."

I stared at him.

"You are fucking stunning when you're angry," he said, then he lowered further and kissed me.

I reached up to wrap my arms around his neck. Of course I'd never tell him to stop, no matter how frustrated I got. I was enjoying the game.

"I might pretend to divorce you. I'm sure it's a thing,

withholding conjugal rights or something like that," I whined when he broke the kiss.

"I think you'll find the right to divorce if you withhold my *right,* applied to men only back in the day. You won't deny me, Ruby, you'd be way too frustrated within hours."

The conceited bastard gave me a wink and a kiss to my forehead. I slapped his chest, hard, and he pretended to be wounded.

"Come on, let's go home. I might need another wank," he said, chuckling.

I stomped after him. He carried the additional clothes he'd gathered for me, while I held Grandma's dress. I laid it down in the boot of his car and he gave me a hug and kissed my temple as he closed it.

"I was mean earlier, I'll make it up to you," he said.

I smirked, remembering what I'd been told. I had all the power.

"I shouldn't be laughing or enjoying myself," I said, suddenly.

He smiled gently at me. "I wanted to just give you a moment of distraction while we were here."

I think I fell in love with him, then. Not that I told him..

We headed to the funeral home, and I handed over the dress. I was asked if I wanted to see her, but declined. I'd rather wait until she wore the dress. We went through the plan she'd already put in place and all that was left was to decide where the funeral left from. I knew it had to be my house, but I hated the thought the neighbours would be looking on. It was stupid. I knew I hadn't made any effort to get to know them, either, but I needed to vent some frustration, and they were the perfect targets.

"You can leave from my house," Sebastian said.

I shook my head. "No, that's silly. It's fine, we'll leave from the house."

With the details finalised, all that was left was for me to provide some information for an Order of Service and choose hymns. Grandma was Catholic yet had chosen a cremation. She wanted her ashes to be taken back to Spain. Of course, when she'd made these wishes she'd been of sound mind and she'd the money to afford it. I would do it, however. I would take her back to Spain and scatter her where she wanted, it just might take some time for me to afford it.

We drove back to Sebastian's mostly in silence. I was tired and emotional, but it wasn't from the funeral visit. An empty gnawing clawed through my body.

"If someone is denied an orgasm, how does it make them feel?" I asked, not looking at him as I spoke.

"Emotional, frustrated, obviously. Sometimes angry, which is always fun. I don't want to sound like a prick asking this, but do you know what happens to your body when you climax?"

I didn't want to look at him. "Of course..." What was the point of lying? "No, not really."

"So, there is a build-up of endorphins, blood flow increases, and muscles tense. Your orgasm is your body contracting to bring that all down to normal levels. If you don't, it stays put for longer. So, effectively, you experience your orgasm for longer which isn't particularly pleasant."

"So why do the denial thing?"

"I don't, usually. And you'll find out later what happens when you're given your release after being denied."

His voice had taken on a wicked tone. I finally looked at him and he glanced back at me. His eyes had darkened. He licked his tongue over his teeth.

"You look like you're gonna eat me," I said.

"I am."

He put his foot down on the accelerator and I was thrown back into my seat.

We didn't make it to the bedroom. We barely made it to the front door. He parked the car and was out, leaving his door open. He wrenched mine, and before I even had my seatbelt off, he was pulling me from the car.

I laughed, getting more tangled up. By the time he'd

said, *fuck's sake*, three times, I was out of the car and standing on one leg. He shook his head, clenched his jaw so tight the grind of his teeth was an audible snap. He picked me up, again, and threw me over his shoulder. I reached down, I wasn't being dragged around without a fight, and gripped his arse cheeks. I dug my nails in through his jeans, he didn't make a sound. I thought about giving him a wedgy but knew that to be a risk too far. Instead, I grabbed his jeans and hung on.

We got just inside the front door before he let me down. I stood staring up at him, wide-eyed, trying to look innocent. His chest heaved and it wasn't exertion, it was him trying to control himself.

He pulled my T-shirt over my head, and I stood still. His face had taken on a different look, I frowned, trying to work out what had changed. His eyes had darkened, but that wasn't unusual. He was tense, that, also, wasn't unusual. It was the frown, I thought. I reached behind me to unhook my bra, the material peeled from my skin. I let it fall to the floor. He took a step back and while he did, I removed my sweatpants. I stood completely naked in front of him.

Heat rose on my chest and settled in my neck. The air charged. He didn't speak, he didn't blink, even. He just stared at me. It was if he'd gone into a trance, while a need to touch him took me over. It was unexplainable. Perhaps it was his intensity that drew me closer. I took the couple of steps to him, he didn't move.

I placed my hand on his chest, feeling his heart beat rapidly though his T-shirt. I wanted skin on skin. I bit down on my lower lip, sucking it into my mouth as I gripped the hem at the sides. I looked at him and he gave a slight nod. I slipped the T-shirt over his head.

I placed both hands on his chest, his muscles flexed, and his heart thumped hard.

I ran my hand down to the waist of his jeans, again, I looked up at him and he nodded.

I was asking permission, I knew that. It hadn't been premeditated at all. I'd fallen into a role he wanted. All that had prompted me to do so, was his stance, his silence, and the need that radiated from him. I hadn't seen it before. It was a look of pure want in his face. The frown, the grinding of the teeth, it was frustration. He was holding back; I wasn't sure I wanted him to.

An overwhelming need to ease that washed over me.

I fell to my knees, undoing his jeans and sliding them down his legs. He stepped out of them, kicking off his shoes at the same time. I cupped his balls, and he ran both his hands through my hair, pulling off the band holding it in a ponytail.

I slid my hand up and down his shaft, his skin was silky to the touch, and I could smell myself on him. It aroused me. When I tasted his cock, I moaned.

I opened my mouth, and he slid in. He held my head while he fucked my mouth, rocking his hips into me. I fought my gag reflex, but tears streamed down my cheeks. I looked up at him, he stared down at me. He then closed his eyes.

"You are beautiful," he whispered, and I thought I saw a small tear leak from the corner of one eye.

I sucked hard, I rolled his balls in my palm, scraping my nails across the skin behind them. I wanted to pleasure him. I wanted to learn how to do so in a way he wanted. When he came, I swallowed it down. I didn't like it, I just wanted whatever he would give me.

His body shuddered and when I looked at him, he had his head thrown back and his eyes closed. He hadn't uttered a sound. I stayed on my knees until he finally looked at me. He crouched down and cupped my face. He opened his mouth to speak but before he did, I kissed him. I took what I wanted from that moment on.

When he'd hardened again, I pushed him to his back and straddled him. I held his cock at my entrance, teasing myself, and then I lowered. I rode him hard and all the while I flicked the tip of my finger over my clitoris. I needed to orgasm, badly.

I totally got what he'd said. The denial had made me ready way too quickly, and I came so hard, I doubled over, holding my stomach. My muscles clenched and clenched, and I had no control. I cried out, shedding tears. I wanted it to stop. I didn't want it to stop.

"Fuck me through this!" I said, my voice gravelly and low.

He flipped me to my back and did as I asked. Sweat poured from his forehead, running down his chest and dripping onto me as he pounded over and over. All I could do was wrap my legs around his waist and lift my shoulders from the floor. I needed to curl up. I needed him inside me. I had no idea what I needed, just that I wanted it.

When I finally came, I felt liquid gush from me.

"Oh fuck," I whispered, unaware of what was actually happening, but knowing it was the second time it had.

"Baby, go with it," he whispered.

Gently I straightened my body, and my stomach muscles eased. The most amazing feeling of pleasure washed over me. My skin tingled, my fingertips and toes had gone numb as if all my blood was rushing to my core. I felt lightheaded and I saw not only stars, but black dashes flash across my vision. He lowered himself until his mouth covered my pussy and he drank from me. He licked and sucked, nipped, and teased. He moaned and the sound vibrated my clitoris. He breathed in heavily, exhaling hot air. Despite wanting to, I couldn't push him away, I had no strength left.

When it was finally over, I lay limp. And I cried.

"What was that?" I sobbed.

Sebastian stood, he grabbed his jeans and slid them on. Then he reached down and picked me up in his arms. He cradled me to his chest, and I cried some more.

He carried me to his bedroom and gently laid me on his bed. I curled up, foetal position.

I heard taps turn on and the smell of something sweet and calm. After a few minutes, he came to pick me up again, and that time, he placed me gently a bath he'd run.

He sat by the side wafting the water over my body. I lay with my eyes closed. Calmness, but also extreme tiredness washed through me. Peace settled in my chest, and I gently smiled. I must have drifted off, because when I woke, I was naked in his bed and the sun was setting.

CHAPTER FOURTEEN

When I woke, Sebastian was lying beside me. "Hey, baby," he said gently.

"What time is it?" I asked, stretching.

"Just coming up to seven. You've been asleep about four hours," he replied.

"Bloody hell, have I? Have you been here all the time?"

"Not all the time. How do you feel?"

"I didn't like that," I said, gently.

He nodded. "Okay, I won't do it again. I promise."

"But I also liked it. And I don't want to like it," I replied, and then hiccupped as the tears started to flow.

"Okay," he said, slowly. "I will do it again, but only if you ask me to."

I chuckled and snuggled closer to him. "I don't know

how I feel, to be honest. Other than exhausted and... Sated? Is that really a word? I feel content and my body feels calm. I have no idea what I'm saying. I know I don't want to lose this feeling and I will."

"What is it that you don't want to lose?"

"The calm and peacefulness I feel with you. My brain isn't running a million miles an hour. I can actually think nothing and just be comfortable being led by you. I never thought I'd say that, ever, but... That's what I don't want to lose."

"Why do you think you'll lose it?"

I kept my face in his chest, not looking at him.

"You'll tire of me one day," I said, adding a chuckle to lighten the moment. "I'm not experienced enough for you."

He didn't answer immediately. Eventually, I looked up at him. His eyebrows were raised.

"Excuse me for my moment of fucking stunned silence there. What utter bullshit. I have a whole stream of swear words I could use right now, but I'll just say this... Strike two!"

"Wait. What? Where was strike one? You can't jump a step."

"I can do whatever the fuck I want. Now, rest and don't talk shit again. I'm going to make us dinner, I'll call when it's ready."

"Do you clean as well?"

"And iron and make the bed. And pick up your fucking clothes you leave lying around." He gave me a wink as he slid from the bed. "Which are washed and dried and over there," he said, pointing.

I giggled as I wrapped myself tighter in the duvet.

"You're a right domestic queen, aren't you?" I said to his retreating back.

"Strike two and a half."

Sebastian called me a half hour later. I dressed in the T-shirt and sweatpants and padded barefoot down to the kitchen. I walked over to him, he was facing away from me and plating up a meal. I wrapped my arms around his waist and rested my cheek on his back.

"What are we having?" I asked.

"Steak, again. I guessed you needed some iron, and I need some meat."

"Do you want me to help?"

"No, just sit. Or maybe grab a bottle of wine? In the pantry."

I headed to the pantry and through another door to a wine cellar. I had no idea what wine he had, but I studied the labels. There was a bottle that was half empty so grabbed one of those assuming he'd drunk the rest.

"I don't know if this is any good," I said, waving it around.

"It's perfect. Now, sit"

He placed both plates on the breakfast bar and took the bottle from me. He opened it and poured it into a jug through a mesh funnel. "Let it breath for a little bit," he said, placing it on the bar.

He sat beside me and smiled. "Let me guess, you're starving?" he said, watching me ready tuck in.

"Always. I was born starving," I replied.

We ate and we chatted. Some of what we talked about was the funeral arrangements and he confirmed again he would attend with me. We made a small mental list of 'guests' and I realised it didn't amount to many.

"It doesn't matter how many are there, Ruby. Only that those who are there, want to be."

Again, I finished before him and placed my cutlery on my plate. He ate his steak extremely rare, and I'd been grateful mine was a little more cooked. He hadn't asked me how I liked it, and whatever stage it was at, was lovely.

He placed a piece of steak in his mouth, and I watched as he sucked the blood from it before he chewed.

"You're not a shifter, are you?" I asked, pouring us both a wine, assuming it was ready.

"A what?"

"A shifter, shape shifter. You know people that are also animals and switch between the two."

He paused, placed his cutlery on his plate and turned to me.

"What on earth are you talking about? Why the fuck would you think I was some mythical creature that doesn't exist. Pretty sure, I've proven I'm the real thing."

I laughed. "You are very... Wolfish?"

He laughed. "Wolfish?"

"Yeah, like, you run your tongue over your teeth, like a dog. You just sucked the blood from the meat before you ate it."

"So that makes you think I'm something that's not real?"

"No, it was just a thought, a fleeting one. But you are very... I don't know what the word is. Alpha maybe?"

"Good. Alpha is good. I'm a man, one that has looked after himself from a very early age. Too fucking right, I'm alpha, and I have no intention of giving up that title any time soon."

He lifted his glass of wine and sniffed it. He took a sip and swirled the liquid around his mouth. He then swallowed and nodded.

"I've never met anyone like you before," I said, quietly.

He turned to face me. "And I you, Ruby. Perhaps that's why we work. We're very similar in a lot of ways. We've both had to fight to get where we are. We've confessed our sins, or rather, my sin. One of them," he said, winking. "You need someone like me, and I need someone like you."

"Need is a strong word," I replied.

"No, it isn't. We want and we need. Nothing wrong in that."

"So, since we're pretend married, do you believe in divorce?"

"I don't believe in letting go of anything that is mine, Ruby. Not without a fight, and I've never lost a fight yet."

He'd closed the gap slightly between us.

"What if I ever wanted to leave?" I shivered at the thought, knowing it wasn't something I wanted at all.

He shook his head. "You don't, so the point is moot. End of, Ruby."

He sat back and picked up his wine again. He raised his glass to me in a salute and sipped again.

"Are we a couple? Like, for real?" I asked, and I held my breath waiting for his answer.

It was slow to come. "What do you think a *couple* is? Isn't it what we do?"

"Erm, well yes, but couples also make love."

"Is that what you want from me?"

"I wasn't saying it for that reason."

"You confuse me, Ruby. Tell me, what's the difference between fucking and making love in your opinion?"

"Well, men can fuck without emotion, can't they? Women know the difference between being fucked and being made love to."

He reached out and stroked my hair. "Has anyone made love to you?"

"No, I don't believe they have." I squared my shoulders. I'd started this conversation; I could hardly duck out when it became awkward.

"I have, Ruby. I don't just fuck you. If I did, I wouldn't kiss you. I wouldn't have any *intimacy* with you. I wouldn't hold you after. Life isn't like your books. I'm not one of your hero's. When I'm with you. Inside you. I'm giving you me, all of me. Maybe my version of making love to you is different to what you need. If that's the case, tell me. Instigate it. Teach me."

"Have you ever been in love before?" I asked.

"Never."

I didn't want to ask if he was in love now.

"Can we take a walk around your garden? I need some fresh air."

I didn't. I needed to halt the conversation in its tracks.

"Good diversion. Yes, come on."

I chuckled and shrugged my shoulders. "I have no shoes on."

"So? Neither have I."

He slid from the stool and held out his hand to me.

We linked our fingers, and it reminded me that was a fairly intimate thing to do. We weren't just *holding hands*.

"Who looks after all this?" I said, as we walked through the French doors and out onto a large patio. There was a large lawn and beyond that, the woods.

"I have a gardener. An old guy and his grandson come every week. This is beyond my capabilities."

"Finally, something you can't do," I said, laughing.

"I know. It kills me, of course, but I can't be perfect at everything."

We walked down some steps to the lawn. It was perfectly mown with stripes, very regimental. There were trees lining both sides.

"How far does it go?" I asked, looking down to the wooded area.

"I have something like twelve acres. I rent some of it to a girl for her horses. They're over there." He pointed to his right. "Tomorrow, I'm going to take you into the woods."

I shuddered. "Me and woods don't get on," I said, laughing.

"So you've said. All the more reason to walk through it with me."

"I've always been a little afraid of the dark," I said, as we came to a standstill.

"Sit," he said. He sat on the grass first and pulled me

to his lap. "There is nothing to be afraid of once you know what's there."

"When you were a child, what about the monsters?"

"My monsters were all real, Ruby. No one under my bed. No one in my closet. They lived in the same house. They presented themselves as honest men who loved the children they cared for." The spite in his voice chilled me.

"I'm sorry, I shouldn't have asked. I don't want you to remember the past."

"I like to remember the past. It keeps me focussed on what I want from life. I still have sins to perform, Ruby."

He fell silent and I felt his breath on the back of my neck. I should have been scared. I wasn't. I should have run from him a long time ago. I didn't want to. There wasn't anything he could tell me that would make me want to leave him. When he left me, he'd break me, I knew that. But I was willing to stay put until that day happened. I just hoped I'd cope with the pain.

"There is one more, Ruby. One more who must pay. I've been searching for him for a long time, but now I know where he is. How will you feel about me, then?"

His words were quiet, but I heard every word. They chilled me to the bone.

"Are you telling me you intend to do what you did before?"

"Yes."

I swallowed hard. His arms around me tightened.

"I guess I'll have to figure that out when the time comes."

It was the most honest I could be with him. His arms loosened just a fraction and he rested his chin on my shoulder.

"Thank you. That's an honest answer, and I appreciate it."

"Do you have to...?"

"Yes. Not just for me this time, but for all the boys. The ones who took their own lives. The ones who still want to take their lives. The ones that are so broken they are unlovable, their souls damaged, beyond repair. The ones who can't rest until every single man in that home is dead. For them, yes, I do."

"Where do you fit in there?" I asked.

He didn't answer. He just sat holding me, getting wet from the damp grass with me on his lap, and facing the woods.

"No, Ruby, there is nothing scary out there. I've been to hell, nothing on earth could match that."

———

We lay beside each other in his bed. We hadn't fucked, just climbed in, and held each other until he fell asleep.

"Which one are you?" I whispered, stroking the hair from his forehead.

Sebastian was a complex character. I wasn't sure where I stood in his life. It was still early days and there was a serious age gap. I didn't care about the age, but I knew other people would comment. I was then reminded of the man who came to visit me, the driver who spoke about him as if he was a friend. I hadn't seen him since. Sebastian had driven his own car the past week or so.

I watched his eyes move under his closed eyelids and knew he was dreaming. I wondered what about. He didn't seem to be frightened of anything, unlike me. I had lists of fears. Some irrational, some not. A man like Sebastian would have been on page one, for sure. I couldn't understand why I didn't fear him. He exuded danger. Yet, I was deeply attracted to him.

I watched him for ages. He shifted to his back and threw one arm over the top of his head. His chest was exposed. I placed my hand over his heart and felt it beat steadily. His body was imperfectly perfect. His scars were deep inside. I wondered what had happened to him, not that it took a magician to work it out. He'd been in a home and abused. He'd killed one abuser and was about to do the same to another. Even when I said the words in my head, I still didn't *feel* anything about it. I should have, I knew that. I wondered what that said about me.

Was I so screwed up that murder didn't affect me? Or was it because it was justifiable? I imagined I'd do the same if I were in his shoes.

He mumbled, something incoherent and his brow frowned. I gently kissed his lips and he responded. He wrapped his arms around me, pulling me close. He hadn't opened his eyes, but I caught one word, *need*. He had said that he needed me, I wasn't sure why. He wasn't the kind of person that *needed* anyone, I thought.

I was happiest, I guessed, when I was needed. Grandma had needed me for so many years, I'd willingly given whatever she required. I knew I'd do the same for him. This time, however, I was getting something back.

I needed him. I needed the calm and space to breath without thinking that he gave, whether it was intentional or not.

Feeling his breath on my skin was reassuring. It was also worrying. We'd got very close in a short space of time. He didn't *mess around* he'd told me. When he wanted something, he took it. It was our ages, I supposed, that had us think differently about that.

I watched the sun rise, and with it, his eyelids.

"Morning," I said.

"You haven't slept," he replied, stretching, and moving away from me.

"How would you know?"

"Because I felt you."

"You felt me?"

"Yeah. I felt you looking at me, your hand on my chest. I'm never *fully* asleep. My brain doesn't shut my hearing completely off. A defence mechanism, I suppose."

I shuffled over so I was lying on top of him. I rested my chin on my hand that I'd placed over his heart.

"I'm glad you felt me. And no, I've dozed, but that's probably because I slept a lot yesterday. I need to meet Monica today, and then if Mike's okay, I'll go back into work tomorrow."

"You do what you need to do. I have a meeting later, but I don't want you on your own. I can't cancel this, so Tony will drive you home and then bring you back here."

"Who's Tony? And I can stay at home on my own for a while. It's okay. I have to go home at some point."

"He's the one who soaked you, remember?"

Ah, the mysterious driver that called him Seb.

"As for going home, you only go when you want to, when you're ready."

I smiled at him and nodded.

I felt his cock harden beneath me. I reached

between us and placed my hand over it, gently squeezing. I slid to the side, wanting to tease him and when he was rigid in my hand, I let go. I smirked and moved to the side of the bed, not for one minute expecting it to be a mistake. I laughed as I climbed off the bed. I highly doubt he'd ever felt denial.

As quick as a flash of lightning, he was off the bed and standing in front of me. His movement had been a blur, in fact.

"No. Oh, no, Ruby. You're not brave enough to do that to me."

I frowned, and for a fleeting second, my heart stopped with fright.

Then he winked as he pushed me back against the wall. He placed his hands either side of my head.

My heart raced and my pussy pulsed with wanton need. I wanted to touch him, to have him touch me, but he just stared. I parted my lips and took in a breath. I swallowed hard as he lowered his face close to mine. He inhaled loudly.

"You are so aroused, Ruby, I can smell you."

I nodded and blinked rapidly, not able to hold his stare.

"Am I intimidating you?" he asked.

I nodded, again. "A little."

"Do you like it?"

"Yes."

He kissed me then, hard. He crushed his body against mine and I wrapped my arms around him. He grabbed my thigh and lifted, I raised the other and he held me. I reached between us and held his cock. When I was ready, he slammed into me. My back scraped against the wall, and I winced.

He fucked me quick, it was short, sharp, and so sweet. I laughed as he came, not because I thought it funny, but it was a release, I guessed. When he was done, he rested his forehead against mine and chuckled.

"I need to hit the gym if this is going to be a regular occurrence."

"I don't know, I think you're pretty fit already," I replied, and bit his shoulder.

"Strike... Where are we up to?"

"Need to hit the mental gym as well. I mean, at your age, you don't want to be losing your memory. And I'm not telling you." I smirked as he gently let me down.

He slapped my arse, hard, as I walked to the bathroom. Then followed me. We showered together and as I stood with a towel wrapped around me watching him shave, I kissed his back.

"Thank you, Sebastian," I said, gently.

He looked at my reflection in the mirror. "For what, baby?"

"For taking my mind off Grandma. For lots of things, really."

He smiled, gently. I walked into the closet and selected an outfit to wear. I had new jeans and a jumper that looked like it had a shirt underneath. It was stylish, something I wasn't used to, and I loved the combination. I grabbed a pair of his trainer socks, not having any of my own, and slipped them on as he walked in. He chuckled as he saw what I was doing.

"You need underwear, Ruby."

"I need lots of things, and I'll sort it, when I can."

"We'll clear that whole side for you. Fill it when you want."

It was said casually, and I wondered if he understood exactly what that meant. It was a significant thing to a woman, for a man to share his closet or wardrobe, with her. So I thought, anyway. Or was that just something in magazines. It wasn't like I had any experience to fall back on.

He sat on the bench next to me. "I hate leaving you today, even for a short time. Here, I need you to have this," he said, and he handed me a key. "Just in case... you know... I'm not back before you."

I heard a slight stumble in his last words, as if he was unsure how to do this. How to give me access to his home.

"We can't be in each other's pockets all the time. And thank you. But you know I can stay in my own home if you want your space back. I need to talk to my landlord about my house, at some point."

"What does he need to know?" he asked, pulling on his own socks.

"Well, I don't think I can afford it now I won't have the top up from Grandma's benefits. I know I'm getting paid well, but... Well, I still have some debts to clear."

I shrugged my shoulders.

"How about we talk about that later? Whatever you want to do, Ruby, we can work out." I smiled at him. "Now, let me guess? You're hungry."

I laughed and nodded.

I made the bed while he walked downstairs to start breakfast. He wore his suit trousers and a shirt. He carried his jacket and tie. I picked up his cufflinks and watch since he'd left them on the counter in the closet.

He was busy making omelettes and carving fresh bread when I arrived. I made coffee and then he dished up.

We ate, drank, and he asked me what my plans for the day were.

"I don't know, really. I'll get to the house, and Monica said she'd help me get Grandma's clothes and whatever together. Is it too soon?"

Sebastian rolled down his sleeves and fitted his cufflink. He dropped one, and I scooped it up. He held out his arm so I could attach it for him myself.

"I don't know, baby. Is there ever a good time? I'm going to cancel my meeting. I want to be with you today."

"No, I don't want you to do that. Whatever it is, it's important. I'm a big girl, I'll be fine."

Before he could reply, we heard the front door open and close. He didn't even look up, but I worried at who it could be.

"Ruby, this is Tony. He'll drive you today."

It was the 'friend' who had visited me. "I'm sorry for your loss, Ruby," he said. He patted Sebastian on the shoulder as he passed. "Coffee on?"

"No, but I'm sure you'll learn one day how to turn it on yourself."

"I can make it," I said, jumping up. If he was going to drive me, I could at least make him a coffee.

Tony raised his eyebrows and smiled.

"Sit, Ruby." Sebastian said. "He's a lazy fucker. Let me introduce my *brother*. We don't share birth parents, but we went through the system together. We've known each other mostly all our lives. He knows how to work a fucking coffee machine, and if he doesn't, it's about time he learned."

Tony laughed and rolled his eyes. "We've met, actually. And I'm not talking about when I *drowned her*."

"You've met?" Sebastian said.

"Erm, yes, well. He came and told me to call you, or

something, I can't remember. Said you were a miserable person because of me."

Tony held up his hand when Sebastian looked at him. "Hold on. I did *not* say that."

I was about to interject when Tony added, "I recall saying you were a miserable fucker."

Sebastian laughed, and then stood. He cupped my face and leaned down. "I'll be home early afternoon. Will you be here where you're done?"

I nodded, and he gave me a brief kiss. Then he turned to Tony. "Make sure to bring her home here, won't you?"

Tony saluted. "Yes, boss."

Sebastian left the room, and I heard a jangle of keys as he filled his pockets with what he needed.

Then I felt awkward. Tony came and sat next to me.

"Thank you," he said, smiling. "He's much nicer when you're around."

"I'm not sure what you have to thank me for. But... well, thanks."

"This is my number, programme it in your phone, please. I'll drop you back to your house, then, when you're ready to be collected, call me. If you need me in the meantime, you must call. Got it?"

"You always as bossy as him?" I asked.

"Not *always*, mostly... yes. It's not worth the headache if I don't do what he asks."

I thought it a strange thing to say, and I wasn't sure if it was a joke or not, but I didn't press.

"I'll grab my phone, and then I'm ready. Well, I'm not, but you know what I mean."

"I don't, sorry. Haven't had anyone die that I didn't hate. It must be really strange." It was a genuine response, I believed. I paused from heading out of the kitchen.

"Did you not know your parents, either?"

He shook his head. "No, I was put in a home as a baby. Seb was about three years old, I think, when he was given up. Not that he'd remember his mother."

"Have either of you ever tried to find them?"

"I did, once. Back when I was in my teens. My case is fairly straightforward, single teenage Catholic mother. No choice but to give me up. It was a Catholic home we were put in, so that suggests his mother was Catholic as well." He chuckled, not that I thought anything was funny. "Catholic, huh? Worst bastards in the world when it comes to being Christian."

His voice changed so rapidly, from jolly to utter hatred, it gave me shivers. I nodded, not knowing what to say, and left the room.

I took a moment to sit on the bed after I'd picked up my phone and put on my boots. Tony reminded me of a psychopath. Not that I'd met many, or any for that matter. But him going from laughing to an almost immediate switch of anger? I think I'd have hated to have gotten on the wrong side of him.

I made my way back down and Tony was waiting by the front door. I smiled as I passed him and walked to the car. He held the rear door open.

"Can I sit up front? And what type of car is this?" I asked.

"Sure. And it's a Bentley," He closed the door and opened the front one.

He drove in a more sedate manner than Sebastian, and it was nice to actually see what we drove passed.

"How are you managing Seb?" Tony asked, as he concentrated on pulling out of a junction.

"Managing him?" I had no idea what he meant.

"He's a difficult person. I know he'll tell you his story in time, but he was the most abused of us all. It affected him badly, still does."

"I imagine it affects you all, and for life," I replied.

"Some of us cope differently. Most of us work for him, did you know that?"

I remembered the ex-cons and the homeless Mike talked about. "I think there was a reference to that when I started. I didn't understand, though."

I wondered how Sebastian would feel with Tony telling me things perhaps he didn't want me to know.

"It must be nice for him to have you as a friend,

someone who understands what he went through," I said.

"And sometimes it's a curse. We remind each other of our trauma. Every day he walks in that office, and when he sees us all he really sees are the children he tried to shield from the monsters."

I found it interesting that he'd used the same words as Sebastian when referring to the perpetrators.

"How did he try to shield them?"

The words that followed chilled me to my very core.

"He offered himself, so they'd leave the little ones alone."

I caught the sob that threatened to leave my throat. I swallowed it back down and closed my eyes tight.

There weren't words in my vocabulary that could articulate how that must have felt.

"He walked into the devils' dens so other kids didn't have to," he added, and then we fell silent.

I blinked back tears the rest of the way.

When we arrived at my house, I saw Monica's car already parked. We sat for a moment. "I'm guessing he would be upset by you telling me all of that?"

"Furious."

"Then why did you?"

"Because you need to know. He's besotted with you, he also feels it's wrong. Sometimes, I don't think he can reconcile those feelings. He walked to men twice his age, willingly. He sees that age gap with you."

"He hasn't displayed any conflict," I said. "Well, nothing of substance, anyway."

"He won't. He internalises. And then he explodes. You're so good for him, Ruby. Whatever happens, keep in mind, he needs you. He's never been in love, and I think he's falling for you. Not that he will admit it."

"Ever?"

Tony shrugged his shoulders. "Who knows."

I looked at my house, and yet again, I wondered, why me. I was just a tenant, he had loads. I was just a kid in comparison to the women he'd dated. I was inexperienced in all things relationship and sex. I had an old soul, though. Maybe that's what attracted him.

"I need to go. Thank you for driving me. I'll call when I'm ready."

I left the car and took a slow walk to the front door. I paused, processing what he'd said. Did our age gap remind him of his past? I wasn't so sure. I hoped Tony was just assuming, and Sebastian hadn't actually told him anything about us. He seemed too loose lipped for my liking.

"Is that you, Ruby?" Monica called when I opened the door.

"It is."

"I have the kettle on," Monica replied as I walked

into the kitchen. "You look tired," she said, frowning at me.

"I feel tired. I didn't sleep much last night, but then I'd slept on and off most of the day before. Turning nocturnal, I think."

"Let's have a cup of tea and then decided what you want to achieve today?"

I nodded.

Once the tea was made, we took our mugs to the living room. "The hospital agency will collect the bed, wheelchair, commode, and stuff. They'll be here this afternoon."

"Okay, I guess we start in this room then."

We stripped the bed and I piled everything into the washing machine. Monica dismantled what she could, and we placed it in the hall ready for collection. I folded up clean clothes of Grandma's that were lying around and piled up the dirty ready to wash.

Monica had called the local charity shop and they'd come around with a van to look at any furniture they wanted. I'd decided, when I downsized, the furniture we had would be too old fashioned and probably, too large. We stuck stickers on the furniture that was to go and then I cleaned while she moved on to Grandma's old bedroom.

Once all her clothes were bagged up, and it didn't amount to much, I carried them downstairs. Monica loaded the boot of her car. I then walked from room to room and boxed up ornaments that had no monetary or sentimental value, items I'd collected from charity shops myself just to fill shelves.

We worked solidly until mid-afternoon, and it was the grumble of my stomach that alerted me to the time.

There was nothing in the fridge that was in date, so Monica and I decided to walk down the road to the local café.

"Thank you for doing this for me," I said, as we grabbed a table.

"I wouldn't let you do this alone, Ruby." She reached for the two menus propped up between the salt and pepper grinders.

I chose a good old fashioned English breakfast, despite the time, and she chose a sandwich.

"The funeral is going to be strange. There is literally like, five people going," I said, listing off those who had been invited. "They'll be more pall bearers than guests."

I chuckled at the thought. "She isn't here to know otherwise, is she?" Monica replied.

"Can I talk to you about Sebastian? I don't have anyone else I can talk to."

While we waited for our food, I spoke.

"He's a lot older than me, as you know. His friend, the guy that dropped me off today, said something interesting and I'm not sure that I should have been told it."

I then preceded to tell her about Sebastian offering himself to save the younger kids and how the abusers were so much older.

"I just don't know what it is we have. It's early days, but so intense already."

"Does that bother you?" she asked.

"No, nor does the age gap. I said to him, being with him allows me space to breathe. I know that sounds strange, but for years I've had so much on my mind. You know, like, how to pay bills, what to feed Grandma, how to ask for help. I don't have to do any of that. I don't have to ask for anything, either. It's odd, but I think he understands it." I chuckled as I recalled a memory. "I even asked him if he was a shapeshifter because he's so... out of this world?"

"*Out of this world?*" Monica laughed.

"No, not out of this world... intuitive to my needs. That's the right term."

"It's a good thing, isn't it?" she asked.

"Yeah. But strange."

"Only strange because you've never had anyone in your life who wanted to care for you."

We fell silent while our food was delivered, and I opened the can of cold Coke that was handed over.

"What about the abuse stuff? How do I deal with that?"

"What is there for you to deal with?"

I thought for a moment. "Nothing really, but I need to be supportive."

"Ruby, you are *the* most caring and selfless person I know. Have ever known. You couldn't not be supportive. When the time comes, and you'll know when it does, you'll also, instinctively, know what to do."

"Also, he's very... alpha, if you know what I mean." I felt my cheeks redden.

"I imagine he is. He's controlling every aspect of his life, not allowing anyone else to. He had no control over his childhood, even if he willingly gave himself to others. I would also expect that to follow into the bedroom. You need to be careful you don't fall into a relationship where he is over controlling, to the point of being an abuser himself."

"I hadn't thought of it that way. I don't think he'd ever abuse me. I feel safe, even when I'm apprehensive about things." I didn't want to detail what *things* I was talking about.

Monica nodded as if she understood. "The only advice I can give you is this. You're taking on a man who has lived a terrifying life, one we could never fully understand. It will affect him all the way through his life, no matter what he says. You need to be prepared. If you take on someone like Sebastian, you going to get all his insecurities, his fears, his *alpha* as you call it, because that's the only way he knows how to survive. For you, having met him, he's giving you respite from yourself, from your brain. Maybe, you'll get to a point where you can do the same for him."

I stared at her. I'd known Monica for a few years, firstly just as Grandma's carer supplied by the local council, but then as a friend. Those were the wisest words she'd ever said. I placed my hand over hers and squeezed. Then went back to eating, I was starving.

Back at the house, we filled Monica's boot and back seat with stuff. She left to drop off the items at the local charity shop, promising to call me the following day. I wandered from room-to-room cleaning and inspecting. The washing was done, and I placed all the bedding in the tumble and some, I hung over the banister. It gave the house and a nice smell.

I moved to my bedroom after.

I'd only just cleaned the room prior to spending the weekend with Sebastian. I fluffed up the pillows and placed a couple of read books I'd read back on the shelf. I opened my wardrobe; another sparse area, but I'd never needed much. I picked up my red hoodie and held it to my face. That jumper had been a staple in my life, as silly as it sounded. It had been a shield, I could put the hood up, lower my head and no one knew if I was female or male. It kept me warm. It was threadbare slightly on the elbows and the string that threaded through the hood had long been lost.

I slipped off the jumper/shirt and put it on. I flicked up the hood. Jeans and the hoodie were what I was wearing when I'd first met Sebastian. It felt like a long time had passed.

I grabbed my red military coat and placed it on the bed. I had my new clothes, most of which were at Sebastian's, and once I took out my newest charity shop purchases. What was left could really just go as rags.

I threw my horrid underwear and old tights. With my first pay packet, I vowed to get some new underwear.

I carried a black sack of old clothes downstairs and was startled by a knock.

It was the charity shop that had come to take furniture. They only left one item, a heavily scratched old coffee table. I hauled it outside hoping one of the neighbours would have it.

I sat and waited for the agency to collect the disabled items.

————

The house was way too quiet, so I turned on the radio. I wasn't listening, it was just a welcome background noise. I had no idea what channel it was set to, but thanked it wasn't a modern one. I couldn't deal with screaming or sad songs.

The house needed a repaint. Before Sebastian, I

decorated myself, only because it was too much hassle to get the landlords to do it. I chuckled at the number of shitty emails and phone calls his office would have taken from me. I remember having a conversation with the only sympathetic person I'd spoken to. She'd told me, when my name flashed up on their screen, the call handlers would groan.

I picked at a corner of wallpaper that had come lose, before I knew it, a whole strip had peeled away in my hand.

"Oh, shit," I said, and then laughed. It would have to be redecorated now.

There was a second knock on the door and expecting the hospital agency, I opened it. Instead, a man stood there. One I recognised.

"Hello, Ruby," he said, his accent pronounced.

I slammed the door in his face. He had the gall to chuckle. I wrenched it open again.

"She's dead."

"I know."

"How? How do you know?"

He sighed. "I have visited her, only through the window. I don't come in."

I frowned, shaking my head. "You're dead according to the police."

He chuckled again and I wanted to punch him in the face.

"And I'd prefer if it stayed that way."

"Do you have my money?"

He shook his head. "No, I needed it more than you did."

"Then fuck off, and don't you ever knock on this door again. In fact, I'll be moving out soon."

"She was my mother, Ruby," he said.

"*Was* being the important part there. Fuck off, don't ever come back. Do you hear?" I screamed the words and slammed the front door again.

I slumped against the door. I couldn't get my breath and started to hyperventilate. My vision blurred, and my fingertips tingled. I shook, my legs wouldn't hold me up. I stumbled to the living room and fell into a chair. All I could do was hold my throat. I felt like I was choking, my cheeks burned. My heart stopped when I heard another knock. I spun on my heel and wrenched the door open.

"I said—"

"What happened?" Tony asked. I guessed he'd come to check on me.

"My... he... I can't breathe."

"Lean over, Ruby. Deep breath in, okay?"

Tony pushed gently at my back, so I folded at the waist. I rested my head on my knees and tried hard to get my breath. All it did was to make me feel worse. I really panicked then. My diaphragm was restricted. I stood up, as much as I could, and started to scream. I was aware the sound was coming from me, but unaware that also meant I had air in my lungs.

"My father just showed up," I said, wheezing out the words. I then started to cry.

"Hey, come on. It's okay," he said, and he wrapped his arms around me. It wasn't him I wanted, though. It was Sebastian.

"Call... call..." I just couldn't get my words out.

"I have. He's on his way, Ruby. Let's sit, come on. I'm here, no one is going to get to you, I promise."

I tried my hardest to get my breathing under control. It had been so many years since I'd had a panic attack, I had to dig deep to recall my coping techniques. I focussed on one spot on the carpet and emptied my mind. I counted my breaths until I'd found an even rhythm, if still a little too fast. My head swam and I closed my eyes.

I heard Sebastian crash through the front door.

"Where is he?" I kept my eyes closed and counted. My heart rate had increased.

"Gone."

They whispered, I didn't hear, and then I felt him beside me. He wrapped his arm around my shoulders and pulled me to his chest.

"I'm here, baby," he said.

I cried, then. Big whacking sobs left my chest. Sobs

of fear and anger at my father showing up. The tears and sobs that I'd held in since Grandma had passed joined them.

By the time the sobs had subsided, I was only able to partially open my eyes. They were so swollen.

"I'm here, baby," he repeated.

I gripped his shirt, clutching the material as tight as I could. I needed to hold on to him, to something that smelled of him, to ground me.

I inhaled deeply and it calmed me.

Eventually, I looked up at him. "I'm sorry," I said, my voice croaky with emotion.

"You have nothing to apologise for." He kissed my forehead. "I want to get you home."

Home. The thought that my father had been spying through our window gave me shudders. He'd been on the missing persons list for years. Fucking years! And yet, he obviously lived close enough to spy on us. Anger and bile rose quickly. I leaned forwards and threw up. Sebastian rubbed my back and I started to cry again.

"Come on," he said, standing and pulling me to my feet.

"I need to..." I wasn't sure what I needed. I could smell vomit, but I wasn't sure if it was over me or just the floor.

"You don't need to do anything. Let's get you home. Your new home."

His voice was harsh, but I knew he was containing his anger. I assumed Tony had told him who had knocked on my door.

He held me to his side as we left the house. I saw the flash of a red car in front of me and then the door was opened, and I was helped inside.

I closed my eyes again. The light hurt them. I curled up on the seat and waited for Sebastian. He leaned over me to plug in the seatbelt and then I felt a breeze as he opened the driver's door. The roar of the engine was a comfort, the speed was welcomed. He was whisking me away as quick as possible, and I was thankful for that.

"After all these years, why now?" I whispered.

"I don't know, but I'm going to fucking find out."

"He said he knew she'd died. How?"

He reached over to take my hand. "I *will* find out."

I stayed silent the rest of the way.

CHAPTER FIFTEEN

I zoned out so much, I hadn't even realised we'd arrived home. It had been a huge shock to see my father standing on the doorstep. I'd gone to sleep one night; we had hidden in a woods and it was cold. When I woke, he was gone. I was alone in the dark, in the cold. That was ten years ago.

I'd cried fucking tears for him.

I'd called out his name, wanting him to come get me.

I'd walked for hours until I came to some services and called Grandma. She'd come for me when he didn't. She smuggled me home on a fake passport, so I didn't get caught.

I'd sobbed at night into my pillow with my grandma comforting me.

I'd begged him to come home, knowing he couldn't hear me.

And then, I'd struggled. Financially, emotionally, physically.

I detested him. I hated the thought he'd been close and ignored us. I loathed that he knew Grandma had died.

If he thought he was attending the funeral, he had another think coming, for sure.

"Come on, baby," I heard.

I turned in my seat to see Sebastian crouching down beside me. He reached in to take my hand. "Let's get you inside."

I took a deep breath in and then smiled softly at him. I slid my legs out, and then held out both hands. He took them and gently helped me up. When he let go of my hands, he cupped my cheeks.

"You okay? Can you walk in?" he asked.

I nodded. "Thank you for coming to get me," I said.

He kissed my lips. "I was local," he said. "But I would have travelled from anywhere to get to you."

He led me into the house, and I turned when I heard another car draw up. Tony pulled the Bentley beside the Ferrari. When he jogged to the front door, there was just a nod between the two men. I followed Sebastian through to the kitchen and pulled out a stool. I sat while he made coffee for us all.

"So, what happened?" he asked.

I sighed. "I was cleaning, or whatever I was doing. There was a knock at the door. I thought it was the people coming to take Grandma's disability things, so I opened it and he was standing there. I think I went into shock. I told him she was dead, and he said he knew. He said he'd visited, looked through the window."

"That's fucking creepy," Tony said.

"Do we know where he is now?" Sebastian asked, and Tony nodded.

"I don't want to see him, and he isn't coming to the funeral," I said, panic lacing my voice.

I wasn't sure what I was so panicked about. I hadn't seen him in ten years. Sure, he hadn't shown me any real love, and he'd beaten me when my mother died, but I wasn't frightened of him.

"He isn't coming anywhere near you," Sebastian said.

I sipped on my coffee, using the warmth of the mug to heat up my hands.

"What do you think he wanted?" I asked.

"No idea, but I'll find out."

Sebastian looked again at Tony.

"What aren't you telling me?" I asked, looking between them both.

"Nothing I want to divulge just yet," Sebastian said, then glared at Tony.

"So there is something?"

"Yes, there is something. And you'll know when the time is right."

I stared at him. His face was *closed*, there wasn't even the usual challenge to push him I'd seen there before. Nothing. Conversation was ended.

I looked back into my mug. "I need a shower. I stink of cleaning fluid," I said, gently smiling.

Sebastian insisted on walking upstairs with me. He took my mug and placed it beside the bed. He then grabbed the front of my hoodie and pulled me forward.

"This look on your face, these clothes, this is how you were when I first met you. Sad, and hurt, and tired." He spoke softly.

"I like this hoodie," I replied.

"I know. I like you in his hoodie. It's just, the past few days, you've laughed a lot, and now he's made you fucking sad and that angers me."

I shook my head. "I've made myself sad by letting him affect me. He means nothing, but he was all I focussed on for a long time. I used his disappearance to fuel my anger, in turn, that kept me going."

Something came to my mind. The looks between Sebastian and Tony. The whispered conversation. The confirmation that Tony knew where my father was when Sebastian asked him. It was all of that, but something more. It was the anger that had radiated from

Sebastian when he'd learned it was my father who had upset me. It was more than I would have expected.

I placed my hands on his chest. "Can I ask you one thing?"

"You can, whether I answer is another matter."

"Did you know my father before me."

He sighed and closed his eyes. He raised his head as if in thought. Then he lowered it. "Yes."

"Is that why you sought me out? Is what we have... *engineered*." I lowered my hands and took a step back.

"No!" He shouted the word and I blinked rapidly. "No, Ruby. I don't ever want you to think that. I drove past your house because I was checking out the street. We didn't even notice you standing there. I was looking across the road. Meeting you was coincidence."

"Did you know I was his daughter, though?"

"No. Not at first."

"Is he the man you've been looking for?" I swallowed hard and closed my eyes, waiting. I heard him take a step closer.

His breath brushed my lips, and when I opened my eyes, his were full of pain. I cupped his cheeks.

"Is he?"

He nodded. I broke down. I clung to him crying into his chest and he wrapped his arms around me. He held me so tight I felt like I couldn't breathe properly. My legs gave way, and he held me up. My father had to be the same age as Sebastian, or thereabouts. He couldn't have been one of the staff at the home, so he'd been searching for him for another reason. However, I also knew that the one person left had done him harm. So much harm that Sebastian wanted to kill him.

I couldn't deal with that.

"I need to be alone, please?" I asked, begged. "Please?"

He nodded and stepped back again. I reached for the bed and collapsed on top. "Just give me an hour."

He didn't speak but he did leave the room. The door gently clicked shut and I covered my ears as I buried my face into the duvet. I screamed. I screamed so hard my throat was raw.

The man I loved, and I did love Sebastian, was going to kill my father.

How the fuck did I process that?

———

An hour passed. I hadn't slept but just laid on the bed, doing everything I could to empty my mind of thought. That, of course, was impossible.

I believed Sebastian when he'd said he hadn't known I was his daughter initially. However, I carried my father's name, and it wasn't a usual name in Spain, let alone in the UK. It was a discussion I needed to have with him. And the word, *initially,* bothered me. At what point did he know I was his daughter? Why didn't he say something?

I felt like utter shit. My cheeks felt chapped and sore from crying so much. My nose was red, my eyes swollen. My lips were dry, and my throat was sore. My body ached.

Just a couple of days ago I'd felt so happy. Now I was a wreck. I had to go back to work in the morning, but I had no idea how I'd function. Another thought hit me.

Mike had said some of the guys were ex-cons. Tony had said some of the guys were from the home. Had my father hurt them as well? How had no one there connected me to him?

I sat up. There was no way I could keep mulling over these questions. I needed some answers.

I walked downstairs and found Sebastian sitting in the living room. He held a book in his hands, and he lowered it when he saw me.

"Come here, baby," he said, patting the sofa beside him.

I sat and curled into his side. "I have some questions and I really need answers to them."

"I imagine so. Ask away, Ruby."

"What did he do to you?"

Sebastian sighed. "He did nothing to me, personally.

It's what he did to others that is unforgiveable. I met your dad when I was in juvenile prison. Did you know he had been convicted of child abuse?"

I sat back and stared up at him. "In prison? He was born in Spain."

"Yes, he was. He came to the UK with your grand-mother, Ruby. He was convicted of child abuse, physical abuse. He befriended kids on the streets, in homes, and trafficked them."

I shook my head. "Are you sure you have the right person?"

He gently stood. "Come with me."

We headed to a small room that he used as a home office. He took a key from a cabinet and opened a drawer. Sebastian pulled out a folder and laid it down. He then looked at me.

"Are you ready to see this? This," he said, tapping the folder, "will throw what you think you know about your family in the air. I would rather you didn't do this. But, on this occasion, I'm going to step aside and let you choose."

I walked to the desk and stared at the folder. In the corner was a photograph. It certainly was my father, and one taken many years ago, probably before he met my mother.

"Did he meet my mother in Spain?"

"No."

"They went to Spain together, though, yes?"

"Yes. After he got out of prison."

"Is that why you couldn't find him?"

"Yes. Although I did look in Spain."

I stilled and stared. I didn't open it. "Were they my parents?" I asked, quietly.

"I don't know."

"I wasn't abused, not sexually."

"I didn't say he *sexually* abused children." He sighed deeply. "He sold children, abandoned children, to wealthy couples without any checks or care for the kid. He kidnapped them from the home. That is what he went to prison for."

"Why isn't he still locked up?"

"Because he was a teen himself. He didn't kill anyone. It was thought he was working for a larger gang, and he was thrown to the wolves to save arses higher up."

Thrown to the wolves.

"And now he has been thrown to the Wolfe?"

"And now he had to pay for what he did."

"Wouldn't some say he already has?"

"Prison didn't stop him, Ruby."

I turned and walked from the office. I didn't want to know what was in that file. I heard him lock the file away and then he followed me to the kitchen.

"Can I make a tea?" I asked.

He wrapped his arms around me, pulling me into his chest. "I'll do it. I wish it was different, Ruby. I really do. I didn't know you were his daughter at first. I hope you believe that. I don't believe he is your biological father. You don't bear his surname, you bear your grandmothers."

I frowned and looked up at him. I'd always assumed I had his name.

"He has his father's name. Your grandparents never married."

"I can't process that you know all this, and I don't. At what point did you connect me to him?"

"Only recently. Through research, one of my team connected his father to your grandmother."

"Were you going to tell me?"

"Yes. I just had no idea how or when if you want my honest answer." He sighed.

He released me and I sat at the breakfast bar. I rested my elbows on the cool marble and cupped my head. I was starting to get a headache. I rubbed at my temples and closed my eyes. I didn't want to go home in case he returned. I wasn't sure I wanted to be where I was, either. It wasn't that I needed away from Sebastian. I needed to be somewhere where I couldn't ask him more. I had hoped he wouldn't have told me, but now that can of worms had opened, there were things I was entitled to know, things I *needed* to know.

"Is this all why we moved around all the time, do you think?" I asked as he slid a mug in front of me.

"I imagine so. He knew I was looking for him. And I suspect he might have known we are together. If he's been watching the house, he could have seen me come and go."

"Why didn't he run?"

"Being on the run requires a lot of money. Who knows? Maybe he thought there would be some after your grandmother's death."

"Did the kids he... you know, did they have a nice life?"

He gently shook his head. "No, not many of them did. Maybe one or two, but mostly, no. And I don't want to tell you what happened to those that didn't."

I nodded and sighed. I didn't want to know, either. It wasn't that I didn't care about what had happened, but I had to protect my mind. Way too much was whirling around in it, as it was.

"What do I do?" I asked, not looking at him.

"What do you want to do? I know what I want, but this is your call now."

"I don't want to go home. I don't want to stay here. It's not because I don't love you, Sebastian, and I do... love you. It's because I don't want to know any more and I can't be here when... you know. If I'm here, I'm going to pester you for information and we'll end up unhappy, or at least I will."

He sucked in his lower lip and looked up to the ceiling.

"I was going to move out of the house. It's too big for me, and I can't afford the rent on my own. So maybe I should look for a flat. Know of any?" I asked, adding a quick chuckle, a bitter one.

"I do, actually. You can have it rent free for a short term let if you want."

"I can pay you."

"I don't want your money. I want you to be safe and comfortable, and I know you will be there. It was mine before I moved here."

I nodded. I'd take him up on the offer. I thought it was important we had some space.

"I need to return to work tomorrow, as well. I don't want to dwell and I don't want to know anything more. I think I just need some time to work through what I do know and reconcile that."

He stepped towards me, but I couldn't look at him. I'd crumble if I did.

"Can you take me now?" I asked, my voice so quiet and full of emotion.

He reached out and placed his hand on my head. He gently let it fall, stroking my hair. He then leaned down and kissed the top of my head.

"Okay."

I left my tea and slid from the stool. He held out his hand and I took it. "How about I take you now and then I'll drop off some clothes and things later?"

I nodded. "I'd appreciate that. I need some work clothes for tomorrow."

I knew I was leaving it all to him and I should have been packing myself, but I didn't have the energy or the space in my mind to even think straight.

We left the house as Tony was walking towards it. I gave him a small smile and carried on walking while Sebastian stopped to talk to him. I didn't want to hear. I waited beside the car, my head bowed.

When I heard the click of the locks being released, I opened the door myself and climbed in. I waited. Sebastian soon joined me in the driver's seat. He looked at me and I stared back at him. I couldn't work out what he was feeling, but his brow was furrowed.

"Are you mad at me?" I asked.

"Huh? God, no. Why would you think that?"

"I don't know. It's hard to read you sometimes."

"I'm gutted, Ruby. I wanted you to move in here with me, but I'm happy you're going to the flat. It's not far, you could probably walk here if you wanted to. I've given you a key, I want you to keep it and come and go as you want... for now."

He started to say something else but paused. He then turned on the car and we drove from the house.

He was right, it was a five-minute car drive to a small mews. When he'd said *flat*, I'd expected a block of them. But the building he pulled up outside was a terraced house. I waited until he helped me from the car, and he pulled a key from his pocket. He handed it to me.

"It's basement and ground, so you get the garden."

"Come in with me?"

"Of course."

He took the key from me, and we walked to a small metal gate that opened to a set of steps leading down below pavement level. There, I found a front door. It opened into a square hall with a tiled floor. The walls were painted white, but it wasn't stark, it was cool.

"Straight through is the kitchen and lounge. It's all open plan. Here's a toilet," he said, touching the handle of another door. "This side is a snug, or whatever you want to use it for."

We walked through to the kitchen. I expected a kitchen, what I got was a huge room that extended out to a lovely garden. At the end were bi-fold doors that, when opened, would expose the whole back of the house to the elements. Against one wall was an open tread staircase with wooden treads and a glass balustrade. I looked up.

"Two bedrooms, both en-suit," he said. It was then I noticed the sadness in his voice. "I'll bring your laptop, some clothes for the next couple of days. There are toiletries here, I stayed here a month or so ago when I had the builders in at home. I can grab some food; they'll be coffee I imagine."

"I can order that. I have my phone here," I said, tapping my pocket.

"Okay." He sighed and stood with his hands in his trouser pockets. "I'll go now. Let you settle in."

I walked towards him and wrapped my arms around his waist. "It's just temporary, Sebastian. Just until I can get my head around what I've learned. You do understand, don't you?" I looked up at him.

"I think, maybe, it might be hard for you to reconcile the man you thought I was with the man I really am."

"I've always known who you are," I whispered. "You're the man in the woods, in my dreams. I thought I feared you, but I understand, it wasn't fear. I wasn't running from you, Sebastian. I was trying to find you."

His eyes searched mine. He nodded very gently but I wasn't sure he was convinced. He kissed my lips and then walked away. I waited until I heard the front door close and then I wandered around.

It was a beautiful property, secluded and quiet. Perfect for me to regroup and decompress. The furniture and décor were muted tones. I opened a couple of cupboards in the kitchen and found some teabags, coffee, biscuits, the usual dry goods I'd expect to see. Mugs and plates were stacked in another cupboard. There were two bottles of wine, bottled water, and juice in the fridge. In the living area, there were two sofa's and two large cuddle chairs, a television, and a bookcase. Sebastian liked to read, and I walked over to take a look. He had a diverse range of books, ranging from comedy to thrillers. I picked up a book, one that looked well read, and turned it over. I placed it on the arm of a sofa. Perhaps I'd order some groceries, a takeaway, and then just sit and read. Perhaps the words on the pages would quell the screams in my mind, my reality needed to be replaced by fiction. Whether it would work, or not, was another matter.

I walked upstairs to the bedrooms. As Sebastian had said, both were en-suit. One was a shower room, the other had a bath. In the larger of the two bedrooms, was a super king-sized bed with an ornate frame. I opened a wardrobe to see some of Sebastian's clothes. I pulled out a pair of sweatpants and a sweatshirt. I'd wear those after I'd had a bath, I decided.

I held his clothes to my nose, there was a faint hint of him still on them. Tears pricked at my eyes.

"Only you," I said to myself.

Only I could fall in love with someone as complicated as Sebastian.

My phone vibrated in my pocket, and I pulled it out.

"Hi, Monica," I said, when I answered.

"Hi. Is everything okay? I had a call from the agency who said they couldn't get access to collect the bed and things."

"Oh, Jesus, yes."

I told her what had happened. I didn't tell her about Sebastian wanting to kill him, of course.

"He just showed up?"

"Yeah. Totally out of the blue. I sent him packing but I didn't want to stay there in case her came back."

"Where are you now?"

"I'm in Sebastian's flat at the moment."

"Is he with you? I'd hate you being on your own," she said.

"No, he's at his house. Monica, there's a little more. I can't tell you everything, but Sebastian knows him. They met when Sebastian was in prison, a juvenile place. He was involved in kidnapping children and *selling* them on."

"Who? Sebastian?"

"No. My... him." I wouldn't use the word, *father*.

"What? Bloody hell, Ruby. Are you sure?"

I sighed. "Yes. I saw a folder on him, and his photograph was on the front. I... I don't know how to process this right now, which is why I came here."

"Do you want company?" she asked.

"I'm fine. I'm going to have a bath, and just chill out. I'll order in a takeaway."

"I can't believe this."

"Neither can I. I don't know if my parents were even my parents," I said, quietly.

"Oh, Ruby. Oh, baby girl. Please let me come over."

"Honestly, I think I need to be on my own and process this," I said. "What if I was one of the kidnapped kids?"

"I don't know, Ruby. I mean, we can do DNA testing, I guess. You'd need something from your grandmother, I'd assume."

I hadn't thought about that, and it was a good idea. Or was it? Did I want to open that can of worms?

We said goodbye and I promised I'd call her if anything happened overnight, and that we'd speak the following day.

I pulled up a food delivery app and then realised, I had no idea of the postcode. I texted Sebastian.

Hi, I'm sorry to bother you. I need the full address here; I want to order some food in for tonight. I'm going to take a bath. I found some of your clothes that I'm going to wear. They still smell of you, and I'm glad. I miss you already. I've also had a thought. I don't know how to go about this, but I need to get something from Grandma to see if

I'm a DNA match. Will you help me? Ruby xxx

His reply was quick.

Have your bath, baby, I'll order some food to arrive in about an hour for you. I've also arranged to have some groceries delivered. They'll be there by nine, if that's not too late. I miss you, too. And yes, I'm sure I can organise a DNA test, but is that a route you want to go down? I'm here for you, baby. I understand your need to be alone, I don't like it, but... well, I'm here. I can be there in ten minutes if you need me. Sleep well, baby. Seb xxx

I placed my phone down and walked to the bath. I turned it on and found some bubbles to add. The room started to smell of lavender which I found very calming. I stripped and slipped under the water.

I lay thinking. Did I want to get a DNA test? What if it turned out she wasn't my grandma? I shook my head. She'd always be my grandma, regardless of whether we were related or not. I then started to think about my mother. She hadn't wanted me to call her mother, I'd assumed that was just her hippy shit. I'd called her by her real name. I tried to think about conversations, anything that had been said that would give me an idea of who she really was. Then I remembered. I sat up abruptly and reached for my phone. I dialled.

"I'm sorry. God, I just remembered something. When my mum was dying, she said she was so sorry for what she'd done. I thought she meant about being a shit mum, drunk all the time, that kind of thing. She said she'd pay in hell, and so would he. I didn't really understand what she meant at the time. What if she was part of what he did? It would be easier for a woman to steal a child than a man, wouldn't it? She never let me call her mum."

"Ruby, slow down," Sebastian said.

"What if they kidnapped me, Sebastian?"

I'd wanted a DNA test to see if I was related to him, until I thought about that conversation.

"I guess, if you want to know if that's the case, there must be a way. But I repeat, baby, is that a route you want to go down?"

"I don't know." I sighed. "I'm sorry, I just thought of it and wanted to talk to you."

I heard his sigh as well. "I can be there, if you want me to." His voice had quietened.

I closed my eyes. "I'm fine. I chose a book and I'll read. I'm going to sleep in your bed, and I'll call you in the morning." He sighed again. I guessed it wasn't what he wanted to hear. "Just give me tonight, please?"

"Of course, baby," he replied.

"I love you, Sebastian. I don't expect you to say it back, not yet. And it's still early days and all. But I just wanted you to know."

"I wish I were with you," he whispered.

"I know you do. And I'm grateful that you've given me this time here."

"I'll have my phone by my side, okay?"

"Okay. Good night, Sebastian."

I settled back in the water and closed my eyes. Had my whole life been a lie?

When I couldn't sit any longer, I climbed out and wrapped a large towel around myself and padded to the bedroom. I desperately wanted to change my mind, to call him and have him come and sit with me, but I didn't think it was wise. I'd push for information, something I didn't want. He possibly wouldn't give me that information, I'd get shitty about it. I knew how I was, which was why I hoped he understood my need for distance.

Once dressed, I walked down and grabbed a bottle of water. I checked the time and then waited. The first knock on the door was groceries. I was grateful because I really wanted a cup of tea. I unpacked milk, bread, jam, butter, croissants, and eggs. It was a breakfast bag, I assumed. The second knock was a delivery driver with a Japanese takeaway. I plated up what I wanted and took it into the living room. I turned on some lamps and settled down to eat. I enjoyed my own company; I'd been in it for years. I also enjoyed the silence. The television had been on constantly at home for Grandma. Just to sit and hear nothing was calming.

I ate, I drank my water, and then made a cup of tea. Only then did I settled back to read.

The book only *just* held my attention. It had nothing to do with the plot or style of writing, it was the battle in my mind between the fiction and the fact.

I placed the book on the side and took my mug up to bed. I peeled off the joggers and sweatshirt, and naked, climbed under the duvet.

I didn't remember being there for long before I drifted off to sleep.

At some point I felt a dip in the bed. Arms wrapped around me. I wasn't fully awake but knew Sebastian was there. I snuggled into his side, placed my hand on his chest and inhaled his scent. He kissed my forehead.

When I woke, I was alone. I frowned as I sat up. Then I smiled. As before, his shirt was over a chair in the corner. He had been with me. He'd held me, and I silently thanked him for that. In addition, he'd brought me some clothes for work the following day.

CHAPTER SIXTEEN

"Morning, you don't need to be here, you know that?" Mike said, as I walked into the office.

"I know, but I don't know what else to do. I need to stay busy."

"Okay, but if you feel overwhelmed or just want to leave, do so. No need to ask."

I smiled my thanks and went to make coffee. I asked people in the office if anyone wanted one and made a list.

"Sorry to hear about your loss," I heard. I had been standing at the coffee machine.

When I turned, I came face to face with a man I'd seen, but not spoken to. "Thank you. It was coming, but still a shock."

"Bloody horrible when someone close dies."

Another man joined us. He held his mug, and I took it from him.

I smiled at him. I appreciated their thoughts. I made us all coffee and delivered mugs to those at their desks.

Amelia wasn't in the office, so I continued with the redesign of the club. I'd made the storyboard, now I needed to gather swatches of material and paint colour. I asked Mike how we did that.

"We have some suppliers, I'll grab a list. You call them, explain what want and ask them to send swatches. If you're not sure, you can visit them."

I nodded my thanks and went back to my desk. I didn't have any emails to deal with, so I sent a text to Sebastian instead.

Thank you for staying with me last night. I know what I asked, but I didn't realise what I needed until you were there. Can we go out for dinner later? Or I can cook? I'm at work now. Ruby xxx

He didn't reply immediately so I assumed he was busy. I placed my phone on the desk and decided to get some course work done. I'd been sent some pre-course work to do, and had decided to use the project I was working on as part of that. I opened up the course website and started.

I tried my hardest to focus, but my mind kept drifting off. I minimised the page and brought up a search engine. I wanted to know how easy it was to get a DNA test. I found a company that offered the service and called them. I was told I'd need to visit my GP for my test and Grandma would need to provide hair, with the follicle attached, and finger nail clippings. I wanted to laugh when they reminded me I'd need permission. I then called the funeral company to ask if that was possible. According to them, they'd done this before a few times, all I needed were the sample pots.

I booked it all and then sat back in my chair and pondered. I'd decide if I was going through with it once the kit arrived.

Mike sent over the details for the paint and material suppliers, and I called both. I arranged for them to send swatches and paint charts to us. It seemed silly that we didn't have current ones anyway.

"Mike, can I have a word?" I asked as I approached his office.

"Sure, what's up, Ruby?"

"Can I go home? I know you said just to go when I wanted to, but I like to ask. I've ordered swatches and paint samples. I'm sort of kicking my heels at the moment. I've been online and done what I need to pre-course."

He nodded his head. "Ruby, I don't want to see you until after the funeral, unless you have an absolute desire to be here. How's that?"

"I feel bad, I've been here less than a week and now I'm off!"

"Go, before I change my mind. Work from home if you want to."

I smiled my thanks and gathered up my bag, laptop, and phone. As I walked to the stairs, I saw Sebastian had replied.

Hey, baby, I'm at home at the moment. I'd love to take you for dinner. Shall I collect you? Do you have enough clothes? I'll book a table for seven. Seb xx

I waited until I was down in reception to reply.

That sounds great. I can walk over to you, save you the journey. I'll need to get a change of clothes anyway. I'll be over about five. Ruby xx

I had a couple of hours to kill so decided to head back to the flat. I wanted to go to the house, it was within walking distances as well, but I worried *he'd* return. I'd have to ask Monica if she would meet the agency to collect Grandma's things.

When I returned to the flat, I made a coffee and opened my laptop. I needed to choose hymns. I scrolled through some *funeral arranging* sites and picked out a couple I liked and was sure that Grandma would, too. I wasn't religious in any way, and Grandma hadn't been to church all the time I'd been living with her, so I just chose some familiar ones that I might be able to mumble along to.

I refused the offer of an Order of Service; I thought it a waste of money. There would be the hearse, one car, and one display of flowers, that's all. Minimalistic, and cheap, was what she'd wanted.

I hadn't heard back from Sebastian so decided to just walk over to him. It shouldn't take me more than ten minutes, I thought. I walked everywhere prior to him. Sometimes my journey would take an hour, but it was the cheapest way of getting around.

I changed out of my work clothes and threw on some jeans and a T-shirt, I then put my hoodie on and grabbed my backpack. With Converse on my feet, I set off.

It was actually a pleasant walk, the maps app on my phone directed me through some lovely back streets and across a park. I arrived at his half an hour later. I let myself in and called out his name.

He didn't answer. His car was on the drive, and he'd said he was home. I noticed the French doors were open, and assumed he was on the patio. I left my backpack in the kitchen and wandered out.

Although only four o'clock, the evening was already drawing in. I shivered slightly, there was a chill I hadn't noticed when I'd been walking. I chuckled. I was turning into a softy, I thought. I'd walk all through the winter in just a T-shirt and hoodie, unless it was raining, of course.

I walked down the steps to the lawned area and called out again. I heard something in the distance, I wasn't sure if it was Sebastian or not, but it was a man's voice, for sure.

I headed towards the edge of the woods and waited. He'd heard me, I thought, so I imagined he'd come and find me. He had said he wanted to stock his log store up for winter. I smiled, I bet he looked sexy chopping wood!

I debated about whether to follow the path or not. I gave myself a mental kick up the arse and started to walk. I could always use the torch on my phone if I needed to and I wasn't deviating from a straight path. If he wasn't there, I'd simply turn around and head back the way I'd come. He'd know I was there; my backpack was on the counter.

I came to a clearing and a stone building. Sebastian had told me there was a building, but I couldn't remember what he used it for. Someone was in, however, there was a slight shining through a very grubby window. I laughed.

So, Mr. Wolfe did have a stone cottage in the woods, after all.

I pushed open the door and froze.

Sebastian stood in black jeans and a black T-shirt

with his back to me. Tony lounged against the wall. My father sat, tied to a chair in the middle of the room. His face was bloody, one eye already shut.

He laughed when he saw me, spitting on the floor at Sebastian's feet. "And here's the bastard," he said.

"What?" I replied.

"Ruby, I need you to go back to the house." Sebastian's tone was harsh.

"Let her stay, see what an animal you are," my father said. Sebastian punched him square in the face and blood spurted over his arm. My father's chair went backwards, taking him with it.

"Back to the house!" Sebastian shouted.

I wanted to turn and run; I really did. But my feet were glued to the spot. "I can't," I said, stammering a little.

"GO!" His voice rocked me on my feet.

I watched Tony pick my father up and wondered how many times he'd done that. Sebastian turned to face me. He had blood splattered over his forehead and cheek. His hands were bloodied, his fists tightly clenched.

I swallowed hard as he walked towards me. When he stood in front of me, I closed my eyes tightly. I shook.

"Go, Ruby, please," he said, gentler than before.

"I..." I didn't know what to say, it seemed ridiculous to tell him my body had frozen in shock. It was just a metaphor, however, in that instance, I really was unable to move.

"You should tell her the truth," I heard. My father coughed and spluttered. "Look what your boyfriend did to your father, Ruby."

"You're not her father," Sebastian spat back, not looking at him.

"She thought I was." He laughed and I looked around Sebastian to see him.

"Are you my father?" I asked.

He laughed again. "No."

"Was she my mother?"

His laughter was maniacal. "No. She was just the dumb bitch who wanted to keep you."

I launched for him. I was screaming with my arms outreached. I wanted to scratch his eyes out, cut out his vile tongue so he couldn't say any more words. Sebastian caught me around the waist and lifted me off my feet. I kicked at him, punched, and slapped him to get free. I dug my nails into his hands as he walked me outside the cottage.

"Let me go," I screamed.

"Tony!" Sebastian shouted. He came running. "Take her home."

"NO! Let me go, fucking let me go," I shouted.

He handed me over to Tony who got the same treatment as Sebastian had. I was crying hard, and I couldn't catch my breath.

"Don't leave me," I said, calling out to Sebastian. He paused as he entered the building, cocking his head as if deliberating what to do. "Come with me, please," I said, sobbing.

He walked through the door and closed it behind him.

I was thrown over Tony's shoulder and he marched back to the house.

"If I put you down, you have to stay put, okay?" he said.

"Fucking let go of me. This is assault."

"There's a phone there, if you want to call the police."

"This isn't fucking funny," I screamed.

He placed me on my feet but stood close.

"I know, Ruby. But what that man has done... He deserves everything coming to him."

"I don't care about that. I have questions! I need answers! You could have...You could have done whatever you wanted after."

I paced but he blocked the doors. When he could, he closed and locked them, then he pocketed the key. I paced some more. There had to be a way out. The house stood, detached from any other, in the middle of the grounds. If I could get out, all I had to do was run around the side. I highly doubted I'd get far, though.

"Hey, I get it. I honestly do, but you'll be glad you're not related to that piece of scum out there."

"Who am I related to? Who the fuck am I, then?"

Tony shook his head and walked towards me. "You're Sebastian's, that makes you mine and a hundred other people who have formed a family. You don't need to be a blood relative, Ruby. You don't need to share DNA to be a member of a family. This one wants you, appreciates you."

"You don't know me," I said, quietly.

"My brother loves you, that's good enough for me."

I shook my head. Platitudes, that's all it was. I slumped into a chair. "What is he going to do?"

"Beat the fuck out of him, then hand him over to the police."

"Really? Because last time I asked, he was going to kill him!" Sarcasm dripped from my lips. "I can't sit here while he does that."

Tony walked over and crouched down in front of me. "Let me tell you about that man out there. The one you're desperate to get answers you won't like from. As a teenager he befriended kids, bought them sweets, toys, then kidnapped them. Sold them to adults. Do you want to know what for, Ruby?"

I shook my head and covered my ears. Tony pulled my hands away.

"He was part of a gang. Some of that gang are now dead, some in prison. Sebastian, *our* family, have spent over twenty years disbanding them, rescuing those kids still alive. You want answers from him? He's kidnapped so many, he wouldn't remember where the fuck he picked you up from, Ruby. Is that the man you want to speak to?"

I stared at him with tears running down my cheeks, snot leaking from my nose; my body shaking.

"What can he tell you that Sebastian can't?"

"Who my parents are?"

"Do you think he would remember? And who knows, he might still be your father!"

The thought he could made me feel sick. I clutched my stomach and heaved. I vomited all over the tiled floor.

"It's okay," Tony said, gently. He rubbed my back until my heaving stopped.

"I'm sorry," I said, looking at the floor. It was mostly water.

"Up you get." He took my hands and helped me stand. My legs shook, and he led me to the stools at the breakfast bar.

While I sat, he grabbed me a bottle of water. He

then pulled off reams of kitchen towel from the roll and mopped up.

When he was done, he washed his hands and came and sat beside me.

"Why not just give the file to the police?" I asked.

"We will. The police have been looking for him for years as well. But do you think we're just going to hand him over to sit in a nice little cell, or in solitary until he's convicted?" He shook his head as he spoke. "Not a fucking chance, Ruby."

I nodded then and closed my eyes.

We sat in silence then until I saw a light approaching. Someone was walking across the lawn and carrying a torch. Sebastian paused at the door and Tony unlocked them. I slid my stool and rushed over to him.

He was covered in blood, and he had a metallic smell about him. I wrapped my arms around his waist and rested my cheek to his chest. I could feel wetness and wasn't sure if it was blood or sweat.

Tony passed us and patted Sebastian on the back. "I'll finish up," he said.

Sebastian gently pushed me back. "I'm sorry you saw that," he said.

"Is he dead?" I asked.

Sebastian shook his head. "No, but he wishes he was."

"What happens now?"

"Tony will dump him at a police station and leave the file we have on him."

"Won't they arrest Tony?"

"No, he's not going to walk in the front door and announce himself. We've done this plenty of times before."

I picked up his hands. "Was it worth it?" I whispered, looking at the cuts and blood.

"Yes," he whispered back. "It's always worth it, Ruby."

I nodded, there wasn't much we could say. I took his hand and led him upstairs and to the bathroom. I ran the bath as he had done for me. While he undressed, I sat on the edge and ruffled up bubbles. He climbed in and lowered. He sighed, and then closed his eyes. I picked up a sponge and dipped it in the water. I placed the sponge to his forehead and squeezed. The water washed the blood from his face. I did the same to his neck, and then I gently washed his hands and arms. He sunk under the water for a moment and when he emerged, he swept the water from his head. He looked at me.

"Get in, Ruby," he said.

I stripped off my clothes and slid in, my back to his chest. All I did was rest back and let the hot water soothe us both until Sebastian shuffled behind me. I leaned forwards to allow him to stand. He stepped from the bath and wrapped a towel around his waist.

"I can't sit still for too long," he said, holding out a towel for me.

He wrapped it around me, and we walked into the bedroom. While I sat on the edge of the bed, he dried himself.

"Is that it now?" I asked. "Is he the last?"

"For now."

He sat beside me. "I never wanted you to see that. It's why I said I'd collect you."

"I did text back. I thought I was doing you a favour by walking over."

"Well, it's done now. He isn't your father, Ruby, I'm sure of that."

"I'm glad. I can't imagine having him as a father. Do you think he was telling the truth about my mother?"

"I do, sadly. We know she would snatch new-borns from hospital. She had gotten caught once but had pleaded some mental health issue and hadn't been charged. They fled to Spain when the police were getting close to them."

"Why you, Sebastian? Why did you take on this role of ridding the planet of them?"

He sighed and looked up at the ceiling. "I had a sister; she was taken from the home in the middle of the night. I did what I could to protect her, but I wasn't old enough. I lost her. I don't want another child to go through that."

"But you can't stop them all," I said, holding his hand.

"No, but I can make it known that there is a group, over two hundred strong, Ruby, who will hunt them down and serve our own brand of justice."

"A vigilante group?"

"If that's what you want to call us."

"Where are you all?"

He chuckled gently. "You work with some. We're scattered all over the country. We only come together occasionally."

"Were they all kids from the same home."

"No. Some have joined us at different times in their life from different places. We have a common goal and that is to stop what happened to us, Ruby."

"Can you talk about it?"

He shook his head. "No, not now. You have too much to process. All I can tell you is that I was given up, I don't know why, to a Catholic children's home. *All* of us suffered some form of abuse, whether that be physical or sexual... emotional. Some are dead, some are not. Some will die long before they should, some will live in utter hell. That's all I want to say right now."

I nodded, then raised his hand to my lips. I kissed his bruised knuckles gently. "I love you, Sebastian, do you believe me?"

He looked down at me. "Not yet, but I'm sure I will. You need to give me time."

"I can do that. We are pretend married after all."

He chuckled. "I promised you dinner."

"You still want to go out?"

"Of course. What happened out there? Parked, done, filed away." He'd pointed to his head as he spoke. "Get dressed, I'm hungry this time."

I was a little surprised he could just switch off as quick as that. I couldn't, for sure. However, I dressed and applied a small amount of makeup. I was sure there were more clothes in the closet than I'd remembered.

"Did you buy me new clothes?" I asked as he stood dressing on one side, while I was the other.

"Yeah, is that okay? You said you needed some things and I wanted to choose them for you."

I ran my hand over a couple of lovely fitted dressed and paused on a black one. It was sophisticated, the kind I'd see in a magazine and lust after but believe it wouldn't suit me.

"Of course it's okay. Don't suppose you bought me some underwear, did you?"

"In the drawer."

He chuckled as I looked. It was full of everyday knickers and some super sexy ones. The next drawer was full of bras and a couple of basques. Underneath those, socks, and tights.

"Blimey, Sebastian." I pulled out a pair of knickers. Well, I say knickers, they were more like dental floss!

"I can't wait for the day I undress you and find those."

I turned back to the rails. Beside them was a row of shelves that contained casual and smart tops, jeans, and hoodies.

"Look in the next cupboard," he said.

"Oh my fucking God!" There were three different pairs of Converse, some Vans, trainers, two pairs of boots, and some shoes.

"I wasn't sure on the boots. You can exchange anything you don't like. Tony thought you might be annoyed I'd chosen them, since women love shopping so much."

"I hate shopping, and these are all perfect. You can shop for me any day!"

I picked a blue dress from the rail, some cotton knickers, and a matching bra. I dressed and then tried on various pairs of shoes to see which ones suited the outfit. "I need some handbags," I said.

"Those, I thought you might like to choose yourself."

We were ready at the same time. Before we left the closet, he placed his hands on my cheeks. He gave me a brief kiss on the forehead, and then one to my cheek.

"Thank you, Ruby, for being here. I understand

your need for some space, and I will honour that, but I hate it."

"I hate it, too. I don't know what to do right now. I don't know who I am."

"You're you. You're tough and courageous. You're beautiful and sassy. You care and love passionately, and despite our age gap, I'm grateful to have you by my side."

I stared at him. His intensity was comforting, it instilled his words in my brain. I meant something to him, really meant something. My chest swelled.

"What's the time, Mr. Wolfe?" I asked.

"Time for dinner, Ruby," he replied and chuckled. He took my hand and led me downstairs.

The Bentley and Ferrari were lined up outside. "Don't you garage them?" I asked.

"Normally, but only if I know I'm not going out again."

"What did Tony drive?"

"A van, unmarked, unregistered, then it'll be burnt."

"That's a waste of money, isn't it?"

"If it had been bought in the first place, yes, I guess so."

"Car theft as well as assault and battery. Mmm, Mr. Wolfe, you have quite the reputation."

"Vigilante leader, don't forget that."

He winked and for a moment I felt proud of him.

Not for the battery and assault or the car theft, but for his morals being so strong that he felt the absolute need for action.

"What?" he asked, as he held the passenger door open.

"I'm proud of you, Sebastian." He stilled. "I really am. All those things you said about me, the same applies to you."

I climbed into the car, and he gently closed the door.

Sebastian drove us to a restaurant in Kent. It was small and tucked away in a village high street. It was wonderful. We ate, and we talked. We held hands, and we drank a glass of wine each. We talked about the funeral arrangements, and I mentioned the black dress he'd bought would be perfect. We purposely didn't talk about what had happened at the house.

"Do you need hair and nails, or whatever, done? I can arrange for someone to come to the house," he said.

"I guess so. I haven't had a decent hair cut in years. As for nails..." I held up my hands and showed him my bitten down fingertips.

"You need jewellery," he said. I folded my hands back in my lap.

"No, I don't. I need to stop biting my nails, though. I might get some fake ones."

"So you don't want this?"

He reached into his pocket and pulled out a square

black box. I held my breath as he opened it. Inside sat a beautiful diamond bracelet. I'd seen similar in magazines; a tennis bracelet I think they'd been called at one point.

He took it from the case and opened the clasp. "Yes, or no?" He smirked at me.

"Yes! Bloody hell, Sebastian!" I held out my arm and he fixed the bracelet around my wrist.

He twisted it so the clasp was underneath, and I angled my wrist in all directions to look at the beautiful piece. I'd never worn much jewellery. I had my ears pierced and I'd occasionally wear a selection of silver rings. But with the work I'd done in the past, I was always removing them.

"Shit," I said. "Diego."

"Who?"

"My old boss. He was a friend of my grandma, and I haven't told him about her yet."

"I'm sure you can do that tomorrow. For now, do you want to come home, or back to the flat."

I loved the way he said *home*. He was my *home*. It didn't matter where he was, what property I was in, as long as he was with me.

"Home, with you."

He smiled and paid the bill. "What about dessert?" I asked.

"You are my dessert, and if you want ice cream, I have a freezer full."

He led me back to the car.

It felt surreal in one way. We arrived home and only then did I feel the urge to talk about what I'd witnessed.

"Can we talk for a moment?" I asked.

"I don't know if I like the sound of that. Do I need wine?"

"I do, if you want to pour."

He grabbed an opened bottle of wine from the fridge and poured two glasses. We sat in the living room.

"How does it feel to beat a man?"

Sebastian frowned at me. "Any old man, or that man?"

"That man."

"Satisfying, Ruby. Cleansing. Every punch I deliver, every inch of skin I open, every drop of blood I help spill, cleanses me. It removes some of the hatred and dirtiness inside. I'm not sorry for what I've done in my lifetime. I've taken a man's life, maybe others haven't survived my justice, but I don't care. Once I've dealt with them, they're ticked off a list and that's it. I don't think about them."

"No nightmares?"

"I lived a nightmare while awake, Ruby. I don't dream when I sleep, and night is when I get respite from the *monsters in the closets*."

329

"And now I'm making you talk about it," I said, gently.

"This will be the only time I do, and only because you deserve to know this about me. I was sexually abused from the age of three until about twelve when I could fight back. I was physically and physiologically abused as well. I have spent many hours with therapists and none of them helped. The only thing that calms me is knowing I am removing the scum from the streets. That brand of therapy is all I need. And you, Ruby. I need you. You ground me. You remind me there is a life that isn't all about a desire to kill. I know how I feel about you, although I can't articulate it. I can't say those words because I was made to say them to men who fucked me. All I can do is show you how I feel."

I swallowed back sobs that built in my chest.

"All I can do is carry on doing the same thing. I can't change. I don't want to. I can't stop being the man I am because I spent too long a time becoming him. I have walls, thick walls. But maybe there are a few gaps, and you have managed to get in one."

He leaned towards me and smoothed hair from my forehead.

"You have gotten to me in ways no one else ever has. At first, I didn't like it because of your age. Now, I understand. You are way older and wiser than your years and I want you in my life. I want you to live here with me. I want our *pretend marriage.*" He chuckled at his words. "Soon, I want that to be for real."

I sat wide-eyed. "If that was a proposal, Mr. Wolfe, you're going to have to do a lot better than that!"

"And I will. For now, we will settle down. There is a gap in the list, I have time to concentrate on us. Now tell me how you feel by what you saw and what you know."

I sighed. "If I'm honest, I never felt a connection to him. I focussed my attention on getting my money from him, the fact I was owed it. Now, it doesn't matter. I'm glad Grandma is dead; I'd have hated for her to have learnt any of this. But I do wonder what she did know. When he went to prison, she would have known what for. Maybe her mind shutting down was her way of coping with that. She can't be held accountable for his sins, I guess. Now I'm left with that one question...Who am I?"

It occurred to me suddenly, he hadn't known his parents either.

"We're the same, aren't we? Orphans, I guess. I have an urge to find out the truth, where am I from, but at the same time, I know I need to slow down and process all this."

I then told him about the DNA test kits I was waiting for.

"Why would Grandma take me in if I wasn't her grandchild?" I asked.

"Did she know you weren't?"

I shrugged my shoulders. There were answers I would never get, I knew that. It didn't make it any less frustrating.

"There is an organisation that might help if you really want to start down that journey. I help fund it. It's for abandoned people to help find relatives through DNA profiling and research. We've been able to reunite some. For others, just getting a medical background is enough to satisfy them."

I nodded. "I'd like to at least know a medical background and then decide from there."

Sebastian stood and held out his hand to me. "Time for dessert, Ruby," he said, and immediately, his eyes darkened.

We walked up the stairs and into the bedroom. He stood in the middle of the room and looked at me.

"Come here," he said.

When I walked towards him, he turned me around. He moved my hair to the side of my neck and slowly unzipped my dress. While he held my hair, he kissed the back of my neck, slowing licking his way over my skin and I shivered. He slid the dress off my shoulders, and it pooled at my feet. I stepped out of it.

When he stepped back, I slowly turned to face him. I stood wearing just my underwear and high heeled shoes.

"Beautiful," he whispered, appraising me.

"As are you," I replied.

He closed the gap again and picked me up. I wrapped my arms around his neck as he walked me to the bed where he gently laid me down. I then watched him remove his clothes.

Sebastian stood at the end of the bed naked with his cock rigid. I wished I had a camera to capture the moment. He was a stunning looking man, raw and brutal, damaged, and broken, yet there was a small gap forming in his armour allowing a kind soul to filter out. I could see that.

He crawled onto the end of the bed and lifted my foot. After he'd slid my shoe off, he kissed my instep and then up the inside of my leg. I parted my legs when he got to my upper thigh. He then kissed down the other leg and removed the shoe.

"Touch yourself, Ruby," he whispered.

I slid my hand under my panties and stroked. I had only ever managed to bring myself to an orgasm once before. Having him watch me was causing my stomach to flip and my arousal to heighten. I was wet and hot. He reached up and pulled my knickers down, I lifted one leg and then the other so he could remove them.

He watched me, licking his lips as he did. He was waiting for the right time. The time when he'd get his dessert.

CHAPTER SEVENTEEN

The following day I headed out to meet with Diego. When I told him about Grandma, he slumped into a chair and wept. He'd known her for years; his father had known her.

"I can't believe it, Ruby. But it's a good thing, I guess," he said.

He made us both a coffee and we sat at one of the restaurant tables. It was empty, not open, and I found I missed the place.

"Do you remember when I arrived at Grandma's? Can you tell me anything about that?"

He frowned and I decided to tell him the basics of what I'd learned. "He wasn't my father; she might not have been my mother. I've discovered a lot the past week. I might have been a stolen baby. The police were after them, which is why they fled to Spain, it seems."

Diego stared at me. "But you're the spit of your grandmother," he said.

I shrugged my shoulders. Was I? Sure, I looked Spanish with my long curly hair but if my mother wanted to pass me off as their child, wouldn't she have been selective when choosing me?

"Oh, Ruby. I don't know what to say. It sounds so unbelievable. She loved you, I do know that much."

"I know. I'm struggling with it myself. My... he came here, to the house a few days ago. He confirmed I wasn't his child, so I know it to be true."

"He came here!"

"Yep. Now he's gone again. I can only assume he was after money. Maybe he thought Grandma might have some."

Diego shook his head and sighed. "I hope you sent him on his way."

"Oh, I did, don't worry. Anyway, these are the funeral arrangements," I said, handing him a card with the details printed on.

"I'll be there, and if there is anything I can do, you call me."

I smiled at patted his hand.

"This man of yours, he's doing you good. You've changed, Ruby. Not so..."

"Bolshy? Annoying? Late?" I chuckled.

"All of those, but you're smiling. I haven't seen you do that in years."

"I know, and I feel like I shouldn't be. Grandma has only just died and I'm laughing and smiling. I'm dining in restaurants. I'm living a life as if she didn't exist, or she'd died a long time ago."

"She did die a long time ago, Ruby," he said. "We all grieve in very different ways. You lost her body suddenly, but maybe you already grieved when she lost her mind, and you lost your grandma for real."

I stood and he followed. He held my shoulders and kissed my forehead.

"We will always be family, don't you forget it," he added as I left the restaurant.

I walked back to the house I shared with Grandma knowing I'd be safe. When I opened the door, the hallway was clear of the disability items. I walked around making a note of what I wanted collected to take to Sebastian's. It wasn't much, just some personal items, some childhood things, and the trunk of clothes in the loft. I wouldn't climb up there, though. I chuckled at the thought of how cross Sebastian had been. My safety was obviously very important to him, but he was prone to overreacting. I'd have to watch out for that.

I called him.

"Hey, baby, how did it go?" he asked when he answered.

"Good. I'm at the house and I'm going to box up some things I want. Other than that, the house can be handed back to the landlord," I said.

"Good, maybe the landlord will come along and help you."

"I'd like a lift home."

"I'll be there in five."

He cut off the call and I smiled. When he arrived, I had everything, except the trunk, piled in the hall.

"I'm not going to get all that in my car," he said, staring at it.

"I wasn't expecting you to. I'll get a man and a van, or whatever. I want the trunk from the loft, oh, and there is a record player up there I want as well."

"Tony can sort it. Make a list."

I waved a piece of paper in the air, he took it. "Where now, my princess?" he said.

"Princess? Is that a step up from baby?"

"Absolutely. A promotion now you live with me."

I raised my eyebrows. "Mmm, I like that. But I'm not going to have sex with you in return for rent, you know that, right?"

"You're going to have sex with me whenever I want it," he replied, taking a step towards me.

"What if I refuse?"

He smirked, raised his middle finger to the side of his eye and rubbed.

I giggled.

"Strike one, Ruby."

My stomach fluttered.

"You're mine now," he whispered, and it wasn't said in jest or with menace. He meant it. I belonged to him, and I wanted to. "And I will cherish you."

"Forever?"

"Yep."

"You know what happened to Mr. Wolfe in the fairy tale, don't you?"

He stepped closer to me, and I backed to the wall.

"Yep."

"She killed him."

"I know," he said, placing his hands either side of my head. "I've said this before, Little Red Riding Hood, you will be the death of me."

———

Grandma's funeral came and went in a flash, so it felt. We were just a handful of people and a couple of random strangers. There was no wake, once it was done, we congregated outside as another funeral arrived and just chatted.

"Let's get together for coffee soon," Monica said, and

I nodded. She'd sat one side of me while Sebastian sat the other. Both had held my hands.

Tony stood by the Bentley, and Sebastian and I climbed in. I hadn't cried, I'd shed all my tears already, but I pulled a tissue from my bag and wiped my nose. That morning, Sebastian had arranged for a hairdresser to come to the house. My hair was beautiful, and the stylist had also applied a little makeup for me. We had decided to head straight home even though Sebastian had offered to pay for a meal somewhere for us all. I just wanted to shower off the makeup and change into some sloppy clothes. I wanted to curl up on the sofa and watch Hallmark movies. Christmas would be upon us in another month, and I wanted to plan for it.

Grandma had loved Christmas; it was her favourite time of the year. We'd attend Midnight Mass, put a goose on to cook overnight, and wake up early to open gifts. We only had one gift each, she wasn't big on the commercial side of the festivities, but it was always something thoughtful.

"What are you thinking?" Sebastian asked as we drove home.

"Christmas. What do you want to do?"

"Stay in bed all day and unwrap you," he whispered.

I saw Tony chuckle. "Cheesy, mate. Super cheesy."

"I might like the idea, if you please," I replied.

My relationship with Tony was growing. I was still

wary of him, still a little anxious if I was on my own with him, but I understood how important he was to Sebastian.

"What did you do before me?" I asked.

"Ate, drank, watched a movie, the usual," Sebastian replied.

"Moaned like a bitch, got drunk, went to bed, more like," Tony added.

I laughed. "How about this year, I cook for us all."

Tony looked in the rear-view mirror at me. "*All* of us?"

I got his meaning. There was the group, his *vigilantes* as I called them. Would they all be alone at Christmas?

"Maybe not *all* unless you can hire in tables and chairs... Why not? You said you all meet occasionally, so why not Christmas?" I looked between Tony and Sebastian.

"I don't know. I mean... we could, I guess," Sebastian said.

"There, sorted. You get numbers, I'll get planning."

I was sure we could have a heated marquee on the patio. I smiled and it widened.

"I want to go to church at midnight, though. Anyone volunteer to come with me?"

"Fuck that," Tony said. "We'd burst into flames if we ever set foot in a church."

I laughed and it was the first time in a little while that I felt happy. Which was strange considering I'd just buried my grandma.

When we arrived back home, I washed the makeup off my face, tied my hair in a ponytail, and changed into some sloppy clothes. I loved the outfits Sebastian had bought me, the shoes, and underwear. I also loved to just throw on some joggers, flipflops or slippers, and a sweatshirt.

With a cup of tea and a book in hand, I curled up in the corner of the sofa. Sebastian left to head to the office and catch up on some work and I had the house to myself. It was peaceful and I felt content. I read a little, I dozed a little. I opened my laptop and worked a little as well.

I was keen to get back to work, my course was due to start in the New Year and I wanted to be ahead of the game. I also wanted to open the email I'd been ignoring.

I wasn't shocked to learn I wasn't related to Grandma. I think I'd prepared myself for that over the past few days. I was sad, of course, but there was also a part of me that was glad. The thought of being related to *him* appalled me. I was still to learn the full extent of what he'd done, Sebastian wasn't about to tell me, but I knew it would hit the news at some point. Then people might come forward, parents of missing kids, kids looking for their parents. I knew I'd find it hard to cope with. The last thing Sebastian had said about him was that he'd been charged with multiple counts of kidnap and trafficking. Word among the police was they were about to blow one of the largest cases London had ever seen. I wondered if I ought to get some therapy in advance of that. Maybe have someone teach me some coping methods. I knew I'd have to speak to the police at some point and Sebastian had hinted that I'd sit with his legal team before it happened.

There was just too much going through my mind. I wanted some fresh air and decided to take a walk. Maybe it was time to face the woods in the light of the day and lay some ghosts to rest.

I pulled on some walking boots and a slid my arms into my red coat. I chuckled as I caught a glimpse of myself in the mirror. The coat didn't exactly go well with the rest of my outfit, but I didn't care. No one was going to see me.

I left a note on the kitchen table just in case Sebastian returned and headed down the lawn towards the entrance.

I stopped to admire the trees. Large oaks, having already shed their nuts, stood tall and I realised, they were a natural barrier. When the clouds decided in that moment to lose some weight, I walked under them and onto the path.

I breathed in deep, and the smell of rain, damp

earth, and foliage was a comfort. It was nice to walk along the path, hear the crunch of leaves and twigs beneath my feet. I heard the odd winter bird, and a scuttle as a rabbit shot across the path in front of me. It was a beautiful place, perfect for walking a dog. I doubted Sebastian was the pet kind of person, but I might ask. I chuckled to myself.

I came to the clearing with the stone cottage and paused. I didn't want to go inside, but I did admire it. The architect in me surfaced. It would make a wonderful place to come and stay, to picnic in the summer, or curl up in front of the open fire in the winter. I wondered if Sebastian had thought about doing it up. It needed a lot of work; I could see holes in the roof. I decided to circumnavigate it.

The stonework above the door and windows was beautiful, the placement of the flint perfect. I imagined it had been an estate workers cottage back in the day when the area had been one large fancy property with land.

A little further behind the cottage was a lake, it looked as if it should have been larger, but the sides had collapsed in and there were a lot of fallen trees and bushes in it. I skirted around to a jetty. I imagined kids jumping into the water in the height of the summer or a small rowing boat moored up. The lake wouldn't have been large enough for anything bigger. Perhaps the owner fished.

A strange feeling came over me. I turned and looked around me. I wasn't wary of the woods; it didn't scare me anymore. I felt at peace among the trees with their swaying branches and gentle rustle.

A thought hit me, and I sat on a log to process it.

All those years I'd drawn a stone cottage in some woods.

Had that image been leading me here?

My cottage wasn't the same as the one standing near me, of course, but similar. All those years I'd had a feeling that I would never get to the cottage and yet, there I was facing it. I'd been as far as the door just a week or so prior. I'd reached the point I'd been trying to get to for years.

"Ruby?" I heard.

"Over here, by the lake," I shouted back.

Sebastian came through the clearing and walked over to me. "What are you doing here?"

"Just investigating. Isn't this beautiful? What do you know about this?"

"Not much to be honest. It was a large estate at one point. Lord someone or the other owned it. Then it got sold off into smaller parcels and people built houses. I bought the house, and then when the land came up for sale, I bought it so no one could build on it, to be honest. Why?"

"My dreams were always me trying to get to the cottage in the woods and not making it. Here I am now, in real life, by a cottage in some woods."

He sat beside and placed his arm around me. "We'll do this place up, make it a *holiday home* in the back garden," he said, chuckling.

"I'd like that."

I leaned into him and sighed. I felt happy and content. I didn't care who my parents were, where I came from, as long as I had him. I told him that.

"Also, I want to be real married sooner rather than later. Or at least I want a ring to show we are pretend married."

"You want something that binds you to me?" he asked, smirking.

"Yep. I want people to know I'm yours and you are mine."

He laughed. "Leave it to me."

We sat for little while just watching the trees sway in the breeze.

"You know, maybe you've found your way home, finally, Ruby. This, me, is your home."

He was right. I was home. I was in the place I'd longed to be. A place of comfort and safety, of wanting and needing. Of being wanted and being needed.

I shuffled around until I'd straddled his lap. He held my hips and looked at me.

"Yep, I'm home, finally."

I lowered my head and kissed the man that made it all happen for me.

My Mr. Wolfe.

My wolf in sheep's clothing.

The leader of his pack.

"What's the time, Mr. Wolfe?" I mumbled.

"Time for dinner, Ruby."

The End

ACKNOWLEDGMENTS

Thank you to Francessca Wingfield from Francessca Wingfield PR & Design for yet another wonderful cover.

I'd also like to give a huge thank you to my editor, Anna Bloom. I promise to cut out the 'for sure'!

A big hug goes to the ladies in my team. These ladies give up their time to support and promote my books. Alison 'Awesome' Parkins, Karen Atkinson-Lingham, Ann Batty, Elaine Turner, Kerry-Ann Bell – otherwise known as the Twisted Angels.

My amazing PA, Alison Parkins keeps me on the straight and narrow, she's the boss! So amazing, I call her Awesome Alison. You can contact her on AlisonParkinsPA@gmail.com

To all the wonderful bloggers that have been involved in promoting my books and joining tours, thank you and I appreciate your support. There are too many to name individually – you know who you are.

ABOUT THE AUTHOR

Tracie Podger currently lives in Kent, UK with her husband and a rather obnoxious cat called George. She's a Padi Scuba Diving Instructor with a passion for writing. Tracie has been fortunate to have dived some of the wonderful oceans of the world where she can indulge in another hobby, underwater photography. She likes getting up close and personal with sharks.

Tracie likes to write in different genres. Her Fallen Angel series and its accompanying books are mafia romance and full of suspense. A Virtual Affair, Letters to Lincoln and Jackson are angsty, contemporary romance, and Gabriel, A Deadly Sin and Harlot are thriller/suspense. The Facilitator books are erotic romance. Just for a change, Tracie also decided to write a couple of romcoms and a paranormal suspense! All can be found at: author.to/TraciePodger

facebook.com/TraciePodgerAuthor

ALSO BY TRACIE PODGER

Written under the name T J Stone

Written under the name T J Podger

The Second Witch of North Berwick House

The Last Witch of North Berwick House

Printed in Great Britain
by Amazon

24462282R00198